CASTLE
DEADLY,
CASTLE
DEEP

Veronica Bond

BERKLEY PRIME CRIME
New York

BERKLEY PRIME CRIME
Published by Berkley
An imprint of Penguin Random House LLC
penguinrandomhouse.com

Copyright © 2022 by Julia Buckley

ISBN: 9780593335901

First Edition: July 2022

Printed in the United States of America
1   3   5   7   9   10   8   6   4   2

Book design by Alison Cnockaert

For Graham,
who helped so much with this book.

And for Linda,
who sorted through the nonsense.

While I nodded, nearly napping, suddenly there came
  a tapping,
As of something gently rapping, rapping on my
  chamber door.

—EDGAR ALLAN POE, *THE RAVEN*

Nora, Nora. How like a woman.

—HENRICK IBSEN, *A DOLL'S HOUSE*

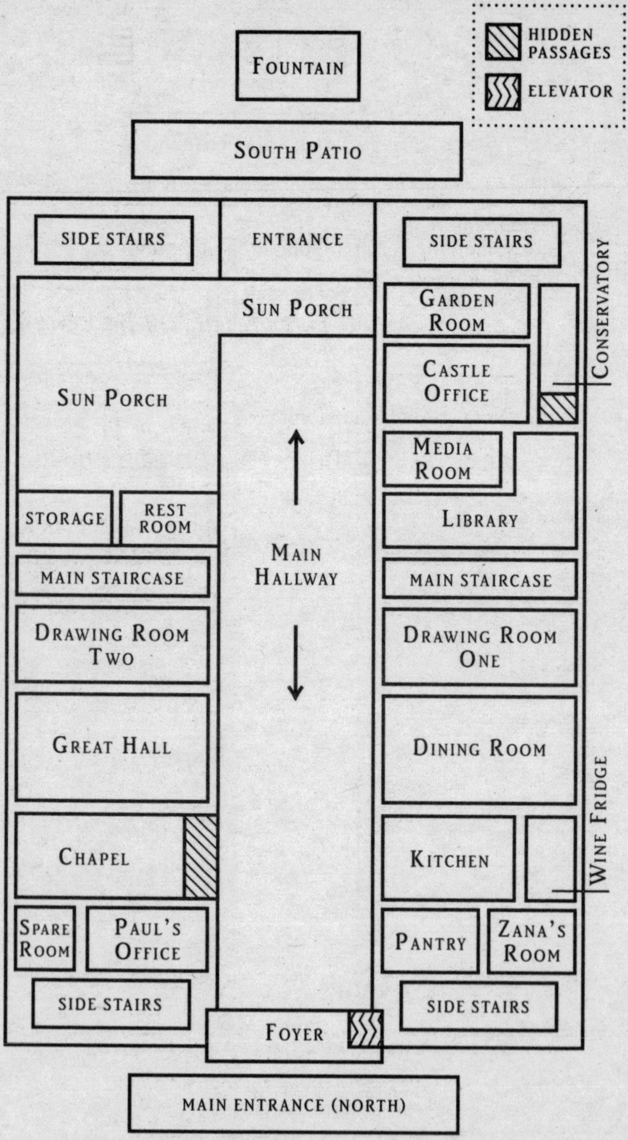

CASTLE DARK FIRST FLOOR

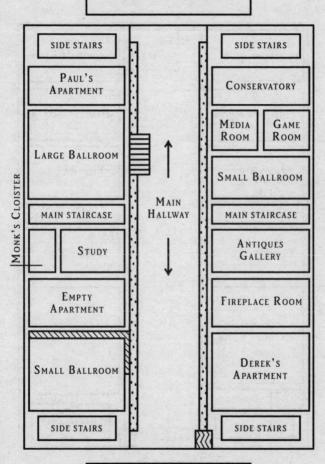

CASTLE DARK SECOND FLOOR

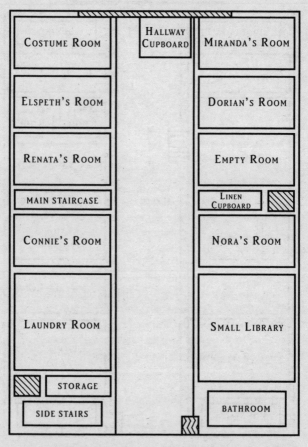

COSTUME ROOM

HALLWAY CUPBOARD

MIRANDA'S ROOM

ELSPETH'S ROOM

DORIAN'S ROOM

RENATA'S ROOM

EMPTY ROOM

MAIN STAIRCASE

LINEN CUPBOARD

CONNIE'S ROOM

NORA'S ROOM

LAUNDRY ROOM

SMALL LIBRARY

STORAGE

SIDE STAIRS

BATHROOM

CASTLE DARK THIRD FLOOR (THE DORMS)

1

The Catacombs

THE CANDLE IN my hand shook slightly, the flame
flickering in the drafty cavern. In the silence, my heels
scraped softly against the stone floor, accentuating the hol-
lowness of this space beneath the castle. I swept my light
over the crumbling wall to my right, where skeletal remains jutted from the ancient stone, and a skull suddenly
loomed into sight, jaws gaping, lurid in the darkness. I sti-
fled a scream and stepped away, bumping into a form next
to me—no skeleton, but a living being. I shouted in surprise. The form moved swiftly past me, and moments later,
a light went on, dispelling some of the gloom and revealing
these ghoulish catacombs for what they were: a carefully
constructed facade.

"How do you like my Halloween display?" asked Derek
Corby.

Derek was my employer at Castle Dark, and he had persuaded me to come down early, before we had to perform
here for the autumn show, to "familiarize" myself with the
space. In other words, to make sure I didn't have a panic

attack once the show began. He led me around now, pointing out that the bones were made of plaster, and the cobwebs hanging from the walls and ceiling were carefully
placed, meticulous as tinsel on a tree. At the end of the
cavern, he assured me, were a spacious and attractive wine
cellar and some neatly tended storage rooms.

"It's all for show, Nora. You have to get into the spirit of
the thing."

I agreed and thanked him for bringing me down for an
early look, but I longed for the main floor, with its blissful
sunlight. And I tried not to look at the mournful skull calling
to me in a silent scream. On our way to the stairs, I said, "Why
do people love being scared, anyway?"

Derek paused on the first step, turning to look at me.
"Because it's invigorating. Fear can be a blissful experience."

"Blech. Give me flowers and puppies and happy endings."

Derek laughed. "I think my brother would agree with
you, about the happy endings at least."

"Paul would?"

But of course he would, I thought. Paul was a romantic,
but Derek and I both knew he hadn't gotten the happy ending he had envisioned with Gen.

Reading my thoughts, Derek said, "He was hoping to
have more of a chance with your sister. He would have been
willing to try a long-distance relationship."

"Gen was being realistic," I said. "She's a practical
person."

I felt defensive on her behalf. She lived in New York, and
Paul was determined to stay here in the Chicago region,
living in the castle that he loved. He had finally retired from
his job in Indianapolis, and much to everyone's delight, he
was back in the castle full-time as CFO.

"They would have made a good couple, though," I admitted.

Derek turned back to the stairs and began to climb. "Yes, they would have," he said.

A light appeared at the top of the stairs, and Connie's golden head was visible, her hair floating like a halo around her. For a surreal moment, it seemed that she was Persephone, and Derek was Hades, climbing out of the darkness to be with the woman he loved.

"Where have you guys *been*?" Connie asked with her usual intensity. "I'm getting lonely."

Derek bounded the rest of the way and wrapped her in his arms. The two of them, recently a couple and paradoxically both beautiful to behold and annoying to be with, were my most frequent companions when I was not in the presence of my own new boyfriend.

I frowned at the thought of John Dashiell. I would think about him later.

Connie peered at me over Derek's broad shoulder. "Nora, you said we could run our lines this morning."

"Yes, that's fine. Should we go on the back patio? It's really nice outside, and I'm craving sunshine after being in the dungeon."

Derek laughed. "A perfectly nice wine cellar."

"Don't drag Nora to your dreary catacombs," Connie reproved. "She thrives in the light, like most living things."

Derek held up his hands. "Two against one. Okay, go practice. I have to talk with Paul." He kissed Connie's cheek and turned away, but not before I saw the worry in his eyes.

I followed Connie down the main hall and out the south entrance to the sunny patio. She looked at me, her face smug after her bout of kissing. "He's so perfect."

"For you, yes."

"And John is perfect for you."

"Yes." I changed the subject. "Derek seems kind of worried. Is it just because of the financial stuff?"

"Yeah, I guess he's brainstorming with Paul about some other income possibilities. I never thought about it before, but the castle is so huge—just the basic maintenance is outrageously expensive."

"That makes sense. I wonder if there's anything we can do to help."

"Derek is proud. He probably wouldn't accept it."

"Hmmm."

Connie fluffed her hair and said, "Anyway. I brought the script, but I guess we can try it without first."

"You never understood our father," I said coldly. "It was never about the money for him. It was about his children—all five of us—and the life he wanted to provide for us."

Connie sneered. "You always thought you had some sort of special bond with Dad, but you weren't his favorite, and you weren't special. You weren't even legitimate. Don't pretend you're like the rest of us."

"I was his favorite," said Dorian Pierce, our newest actor, striding toward us with a slight smirk on his handsome face.

Our friend Tim had left the castle a month earlier to get married and move to Seattle. Derek had hired Dorian at the end of August, and I hadn't yet determined what I thought of him. He always wore a slightly condescending expression, but Connie told me that I was judging him too harshly.

"Are we running lines?" Dorian asked, joining us at the table without waiting for an invitation.

I shrugged and continued with my dramatis persona. "You weren't his favorite, Dorian. I heard the two of you fighting last night. You were screaming at him. And two hours later Mara found him with a knife in his chest."

Dorian's eyes sparkled with malice; he really got into character, I had to admit to myself.

"You know what they say about the person who finds the body. They are often the perpetrators."

"You say that about your own sister?" Connie shouted.

"Aren't you saying the same about me?" Dorian said.

His eyes had darted away from us and begun watching something in the northwest corner of the castle, near the parking area. I followed his gaze and saw Derek and Paul gesticulating, their heads close together. From this distance, they looked sinister.

Dorian stood up suddenly. "We'll have to continue this later," he said as though Connie and I were expected to stop rehearsing, as well. "I have to speak to Derek."

Everything Dorian said was weighted with faux gravitas. Connie rolled her eyes at me and I smothered a laugh.

Connie watched him stride away. "I'll say this for him, he's got a really handsome face."

I shook my head. "His expression is always sarcastic. That ruins it."

"I think that's just his face."

"Your boyfriend is much more handsome," I said.

Connie's smug smile returned. "Like I said, he's perfect. But that doesn't keep me from appreciating the attractiveness of a certain detective who hangs around here."

I looked away. "True. We're surrounded by handsome men."

She heard my tone and leaned forward to touch my arm. "Is something wrong? Is everything okay between you and Dash?"

"Yes, of course. I mean, we've only been dating a couple of months. We're still getting to know each other." I turned back to see that Connie's eyes had widened.

"That's not what you said last month," she objected. "You were practically ready to walk down the aisle. What's changed?"

I sighed, fiddling with the edge of the script that sat in front of Connie. "Back in July, I told him he had to make time for me if this was going to work. He did, and August was amazing, and then Derek talked me into joining the cast of his other play, and now I can't seem to make time for Dash." My eyes met her blue ones. "It's not going over well."

"You have a chance to make things right," she said.

"What? How?"

"He's here," she said.

I looked toward the west wall and saw that four men were now talking. One of them was Detective John Dashiell.

He did not look happy.

2

Dark and Brooding Men

"LOOK AT THEM," Connie said, her face wry. "I miss Tim and his blond hair. Every guy at this castle has dark hair. It looks like the casting call for a Gothic soap opera."

"Or auditions for Mr. Darcy."

Connie laughed. "I mean, how seriously do they take themselves?" She put her chin on her chest and spoke in a low voice. "I'm a guy, and I'm super important and I make decisions that affect the fate of the world."

Now it was my turn to laugh. "I'm so glad you're here, Connie. Life at the castle would be so boring without you. I don't think I would have taken the job if I hadn't met you that first day."

"You fell in love with my energetic personality," she said, batting her eyelashes.

"Your effervescence, more like. Uh-oh—he's coming. I'd better meet him halfway."

She patted my arm and said, "He's crazy about you. Just work it out."

I nodded. My stomach was suddenly full of butterflies. I forced my legs into motion and moved toward John Dashiell, whose eyes were on me. He had a sort of hungry look, which I always found flattering, but today I found it burdensome.

We reached each other and I put my arms around his neck; his wrapped automatically around my waist, pulling me against him.

"Hi," I said, and I kissed him. It was a nice kiss, and I relaxed against him. "I've missed you."

"Me, too." His hazel eyes studied my face. "I suppose you have both practices today?"

"Yeah. We have castle practice after lunch, and then rehearsal at the BC." This was what all the actors called the Blue Curtain community theater.

"Ah." He sighed and let go of me. "Are we still together?"

A blend of fear and anger rose in me. To prevent what seemed an inevitable conflict, I took his hand and led him back to the patio table, where we sat down and faced each other.

"You know we are! Unless you've had a change of heart?"

His eyes narrowed. "You know I haven't."

"Then what are we upset about?"

I tried to smile, but I was on the verge of tears. I turned to see that Connie had disappeared from the table.

"Let's sit down over here," I said.

"I can't stay long," he murmured in a distant voice. "I thought maybe I could have breakfast with you or something, but I interrupted your meeting with Pierce."

"Dorian? I was practicing lines with Connie, and Dorian barged in. And if you had texted me that you wanted to have breakfast, I could have made that happen." I was angry again, but I reached out to touch his arm.

He brooded over that for a while, and I fumed. What was this, high school? This was nothing like the Dashiell I knew. I had always admired him for his quiet maturity. Today he seemed aggrieved for no reason.

I made a mighty effort to change the subject. "What were you guys talking about over there, anyway?"

His eyes flicked away from me. "Nothing much."

I stared at him. "You all looked pretty grim about nothing much."

He shrugged.

A heavy silence fell between us, during which he offered nothing.

"Dash?" I said, feeling helpless.

He rubbed his eyes and said, "I'm sorry. I didn't sleep much, and I didn't have coffee. I'm afraid I'm treating you to a foul mood."

"Not really a treat," I said, my voice light.

"How can I make it up to you?" he asked.

"Tell me about what's bothering you."

He stretched his long legs and studied the tips of his shoes. "I don't see enough of my girlfriend."

"We'll work on that. What else?"

He sighed. "My job is—unsatisfying."

I had wondered about this. Two months earlier Dash had solved two high-profile crimes, catching a stalker and a murderer within days of each other. Life had been exciting in the days before those arrests, and the excitement had lingered for some time afterward.

"Nothing much going on in Wood Glen?"

His lip curled on one side. "Not unless you count a stolen Deer Crossing sign and a string of burglaries."

"The burglaries sound mildly interesting."

He nodded. "Not my case, though."

"Okay. That's a little harder to fix, but we can brainstorm."

He laughed and looked more like himself.

"What else is going on?"

He hesitated, then shook his head. "Nothing. And I have to get going. Work awaits, boring or not." He stood up, and I felt a brief burst of desolation.

"Derek says you're welcome at practice anytime. You know where the Blue Curtain theater is located?"

"Yes. I saw a terrible version of *Our Town* there about five years ago."

"That was before Derek was a director. He's really quite good."

"Hmm." My hair blew in my eyes, and he leaned forward to brush it away with gentle fingers. "I suppose I'll come when I can. I don't know if tonight will work."

"There are lots of little nooks and corners backstage where a person could sneak off to kiss his girlfriend," I said, sending him a significant glance.

"That is the first appealing detail you have offered about this theater."

I giggled, and he hugged me goodbye, kissing my mouth and then my hair. "I'll call you later," he said. "Or text more likely."

"Okay."

I let go of his hand reluctantly and watched him walk away. Moments later Connie materialized beside me.

"Spying on us, were you?" I asked.

"Absolutely. Out the window in the south door. The same window you used to spy on Derek and me when he first kissed me."

"Pretty good view, right?"

She nodded. "Are you okay? That didn't look super positive."

"I've never seen him like this. He was so irritable and short-tempered. He said he hadn't slept well."

"Just a bad day," Connie assured me. "Come on, we'll run our lines again."

We sat at our table once more, but I was still brooding.

"I feel like there's something else, something he's not telling me."

"Probably better not to open that door," Connie said. "Just try to move on."

I wasn't sure I agreed with this solution, but I settled down to practice lines and scenarios for our new Castle murder mystery. Perhaps twenty minutes later, Derek approached our table and began to stroke Connie's hair.

"Hey, ladies. Paul and I have to run some errands, but we'll start practice right after lunch, and it will probably run long. We'll only have time for a quick dinner and then we'll head over to the BC. Make the most of your morning," he said.

He strode off, and Connie sighed.

"Yes, I know. He's perfect," I said, feeling grumpy.

Connie didn't bother to hide her dreamy expression. "I think you need some kitten therapy," she suggested.

"I think you're right."

I had adopted three sweet gray kittens back in June—three females that I had named after the Brontës because of their moody gray color. They weren't tiny anymore, but were still small and kittenish, and they were beloved companions. They lived in my room on the third floor.

I stood up. "I think we're both ready for rehearsal. I'm going to chill in my room for a while."

"See you at lunch," Connie said.

I waved and let myself in the south entrance with a key I had brought down for the purpose. I hadn't walked more than a few steps when I saw a woman gliding out of the sunroom, along the veranda on the west side of the first floor. It was Miranda Pratt, another new cast member. I recalled that her shock of white hair had surprised me when I had seen her in the parking lot lifting a box out of her car on the day she moved in. When she turned, I had been surprised to see a young, lineless face—she was perhaps thirty. That night at dinner Derek had introduced her and we learned that her hair had been white since she was twenty years old. Something about her white hair combined with her gliding walk seemed absolutely appropriate, and I felt it enhanced her beauty. She reminded me of some serene water bird.

Today she was wearing a pair of blue jean shorts and a sweatshirt with the Art Institute of Chicago logo, complete with stone lions.

"Hi, Miranda," I said.

She lived on the third floor with me, but I had barely talked to her since she had started. In my defense, I rarely saw her.

"Hi," she said in her quiet voice. "Have you seen Derek? I wanted to ask him something."

"He and Paul are running errands."

"Oh." Clearly this was putting a wrench in her plans, but she shrugged. "Oh, well."

"Derek says practice will start right after lunch and will run long."

"Thanks for the info," she said with a brief smile. "See you later."

She moved swiftly to the south staircase and disappeared up the narrow stairs. I kept walking. I was feeling lazy and the elevator, which let out near my room on the third floor, was at the other end of the main hall. So I decided to take the leisurely route. I didn't see anyone on the way to the north entrance except for Hamlet, Derek's giant Labrador, who walked toward me wagging his giant head from side to side in a behavior I had learned was a friendly greeting.

"Hey, boy," I said. "Do you want to ride the elevator?"

Apparently, he did, because he followed me to that conveyance and climbed aboard. Hamlet knew the castle better than I did, and he was utterly at ease on the elevator.

We rode to the third floor and emerged in front of our little third-floor laundry room. I saw my door, complete with its Green Crown label, as a soothing and beckoning reality, but I paused in front of the room on my right—the small library.

I wasn't sure why there were two libraries in the castle: the large library on the main floor, and this attractive little book-lined room located conveniently next to my own. I loved it, and I had unjustly come to think of it as my own because of its proximity to my living space. I visited the room regularly, poring over the eclectic selection within. So far, I had managed to find a number of good books.

I opened the door now, enjoying the waxy scent from the polished floor and the lavender scent that emanated from the carpet after cleaning day. Below these aromas was the slightly musty smell of old books. I breathed in both the scents and the sights of the beloved room, lined with shelves on three walls and made more lovely still by the large window on the wall facing the door, beneath which was a padded window seat. I moved to a familiar bookcase, which I knew contained many fiction titles, and scanned for mystery and suspense authors. I found a Mary Stewart novel called *Madam, Will You Talk?* and had a vague memory of my mother recommending this author. I pulled it down and had just begun to read the jacket copy when a shadow loomed over me and I looked up to see Dorian Pierce smiling at me in his sardonic way. He made me think of those stories in which the devil took the guise of a handsome, charming man.

"I've been meaning to investigate this room," he said, wandering in and sitting at the wooden table in the center of the rug.

"Oh?" I said coolly. Dorian didn't seem like the type who read books.

"Yeah. Can you recommend some good bedtime reading?" He made his words sound suggestive somehow, and it irritated me.

"I doubt we like the same sorts of books."

He feigned indignation. "How would you know what I like to read? You've barely said five sentences to me since I moved in."

This was true, and it made me feel mean. I relented. "Most of this wall is fiction. Over there is more nonfiction—biography, true adventures, political stuff."

"Not my thing," he said.

"Lots of history on the wall behind you. At some point someone tried to organize these books. Someday I'll continue the job."

"Very ambitious," he said. "Commendable."

"Anyway, I'll leave you to your hunting."

"No, wait—I need you to help me find the perfect thing."

This could have simply been an appeal for friendship, but he made it sound like a come-on, and I felt uncomfortable. Still, I realized that he knew no one well, and he might simply have been looking for someone to talk to.

I went to the history wall. "There's an interesting book about the brave women of World War Two."

"Hmm . . . getting closer."

"There's another one by an explorer who crossed the Atlantic in a homemade boat."

He clapped. "Sold! We're all adventurers at heart, aren't we, Nora?"

"Yes, I suppose so. Well, I want to read some of this before we have lunch. After that, we'll be rehearsing all day."

"Yeah. But rehearsing is what we all love, right? It's our calling, the acting profession."

I nodded. "Yes. And my room is also calling, so I'll see you later."

I waved vaguely and left the room with my book, aware that he was still grinning behind me, and his smile stayed with me, lingering unpleasantly like that of the Cheshire cat.

In my room at last, I flopped on my bed and endured the Brontës' curious sniffing of my hair, hands, and face. "Stop it," I said, giggling.

They eventually nestled against me, purring. I looked listlessly at the book, realizing that I wasn't in the reading mood, after all. I set it on my side table and stared at the ceiling, indulging in daydreams about my favorite person: John Dashiell.

We had started dating in July, and for more than a month I had felt head over heels in love with him, which my rational mind had assured me was infatuation. But Dash was like no one I had ever met before: calm, measured, smart, brave, professional, yet also sexy and dangerous and mysterious. He had taken a week of vacation at the beginning of August and we'd gone to the city, where he had grown up, to see the sights. We spent a day at North Avenue Beach, swimming and playing in the water, stealing kisses when our slippery bodies floated close to each other's. We explored bookshops and the art museum and the aquarium. At night Dash would find romantic, uncrowded restaurants where we could share life stories and touch each other's hands across the table. Then we would walk through the city, enjoying the lights and holding hands with an easy connection that I never questioned. Unlike other men I had dated, Dash never made me worry over my appearance, or whether what I said was clever, or if I was eating too much or being interesting enough. I never had to do anything but enjoy myself, which I did. I remembered with a shiver of delight a particular night when we walked back to his car, and before we even reached it, he swung me around and pulled me into a warm, deep, and delicious kiss—something with a hint of darkness, but also with a promise of future delights. I had lost myself in that kiss, and a tiny voice in my pleasure center had asked even then if this was the man for me. The forever man.

He pulled away and I stared at him dumbly, my mouth slightly open, and he whispered, "I have never had such a good time with anyone, ever."

Despite the fact that Dash and I had met under strange circumstances (he had been investigating a murder), our relationship had felt as perfect and natural as the kind in books.

Nothing had changed, really. I felt the same. Dash felt the same. So why were we both unhappy?

I sighed and closed my eyes, listening to the purring of the cats around me.

I would solve this problem the way I solved problems in my teens: I would take a nap.

3

Players in Place

WHEN DEREK HAD asked me to be in a play he was directing at the Wood Glen community theater, the Blue Curtain, I was reluctant. Then he told me it was Ibsen's *A Doll's House* and he wanted me to play the role of Kristine Linde. I had always loved the play, and I'd long felt that Kristine was an undersung character—a catalyst for action over the three days of the drama. I had agreed then, excited to work with Derek in another context and thrilled to be able to collaborate with him about my vision of Kristine.

Connie, of course, was cast as Nora Helmer, the oppressed and beautiful main character. Dorian was the seemingly villainous Krogstad, and all of the main cast had understudies. Mine was Miranda, the white-haired beauty from the castle; Connie's was a woman named Priscilla; and Dorian's was Paul.

We had gone through two weeks of rehearsals, and as I could have predicted, Derek had turned out to be an excellent director: patient, meticulous, visionary. We had worked out all of the staging and cues, and now we were working on the nuances of our lines. Several people from Wood Glen were in the cast; apparently most of them had a whole résumé of shows they'd done at the Blue Curtain. Only Dorian and I were absolutely new to the stage.

After we finished the castle rehearsal, I had time to freshen up briefly and don a sweater (it was a cold evening) and then join the others for the quick dinner Derek had promised. Then we piled into two cars. Derek, Connie, Renata, and Miranda rode in Derek's SUV, while Dorian, Paul, Elspeth, and I piled into Paul's Volvo. It was fun bundling up together this way, like a big family, although I wished I hadn't ended up in a car with Dorian, who managed to smirk at me several times during our drive.

When we got to the theater, Derek told Nora and Torvald Helmer, the main characters, to take their places for Act I. Jack Yardley strode onstage with a confident air. He was tall and ostentatiously handsome and, I guessed, in his late thirties. He waited importantly while Derek switched on the houselights and made sure the whole cast was present, with the understudies sitting in the front row.

Connie had told me Jack was the most eligible and sought-after bachelor in Wood Glen, and I sensed that he relished this role. Like many actors I had met in my career, he was incurably vain, although he earned some points for knowing it about himself and occasionally making self-deprecating jokes about his narcissism. Jack obviously had a good relationship with the local tanning salon, because it was almost October but he still looked tanned and fit. Derek had cast him—brilliantly, I thought—as Torvald, Nora's husband and a tyrant disguised as a loving spouse. To give Jack his due, he played the part quite well, finding little nuances of character that humanized Torvald. Jack viewed us all as would a benevolent king.

"Torvald reporting for duty," he said. "Where are my lovely Noras?"

Jack must have been in heaven when he learned not only that Connie was to play his wife, but that Priscilla Atwood would be her understudy. If Jack was the most sought-after man in Wood Glen, Connie assured me, Priscilla was the most desired woman. I watched Priscilla now as she pulled her long blond hair into a ponytail and settled into her seat in the front row. She wore snug faded jeans and a rose-colored sweater. A quick glance around the room told me that every man there was looking at her, except for Derek, who was looking at his watch.

"Let's go, everyone. Connie, come up here with Jack. Ben, our beloved delivery boy, I need you in the wings. Dorian and Nora, you, too. Let's get in place, people."

Ben Boyle leapt to his feet. He was about twenty or so, a local interested in theater; I knew him from his job at Balfour Bakery, a place I frequented too often, sometimes just to visit my friend Jade, a precocious teen who had not been allowed to try out for this show because her mother felt her grades were suffering.

I followed Ben into the wings, and I felt Dorian breathing down my neck. My character was to enter early in Act I and Ben's character entered soon after. I ignored Dorian and pointed at Andrew Portnoy, who was chatting amiably with his wife, Millie.

"Come on, Dr. Rank, you need to be up here, too, along with sweet Helene."

Andrew played the part of Torvald's longtime friend Dr. Rank, and Millie had the very small role of Helene, the maid.

Elspeth, who was Millie's understudy, sat knitting something in her chair and chatting with Renata, who was also knitting. They had told Millie earlier in the day that it was the time of year to begin knitting Christmas presents, and they both had a long list of recipients.

We marched onstage, we thespians, and Derek paced around, speaking in low tones to Jack and Connie, who were both onstage early in the scene. Connie was the first face that people saw when the curtains opened; Nora Helmer was a fresh-faced young wife and mother, convinced that her life was perfect and that this Christmas would be the best ever. In the play, it was Christmas Eve. Elspeth and the rest of the stage and costuming crew had already started on a beautiful set, and a still-undecorated Christmas tree, huge and real-looking, sat at the back of the stage.

"Let's begin," Derek said.

Jack disappeared behind a prop door that was supposed to lead to his office. Connie waited behind an entrance door. Derek gave the cue, and Connie swept into the room, looking rosy as if she really had just been out in the snow. She was followed by a delivery boy (Ben), who informed her that the tree would cost half a crown. Derek had to alter this part, since the boy was supposed to carry the tree, freshly chopped at some Norwegian tree farm, into the house. Instead, Connie (as Nora Helmer) said, "Thank you for delivering the tree. How much do I owe you?"

The delivery boy disappeared after thanking Mrs. Helmer. This was his only line in the play, so Derek had given him an additional role as prop master, and Ben had proudly taken his place at the prop table in the wings, treating each prop like a sacred relic as he handed it to the actor.

Soon Jack had joined Connie onstage, and the couple began to argue gently about money and what Torvald perceived as Nora's extravagance. Jack was so good at capturing Torvald's condescension that I began to feel uncomfortable. Eventually Torvald treated her to a long-winded sermon and then told her not to disturb him, essentially because he was an important new bank president. Jack puffed himself out with pride, and Connie looked at him worshipfully.

Then the maid told her that someone was there to see her, and I took my place onstage, waiting tentatively in Connie/Nora's sitting room. She came in and said, "I'm sorry. I don't— Kristine? Is it really you?"

I moved toward her, smiling, remembering the friend I had not seen in ten years. "Yes, it's me."

"Kristine, how you've changed!" Connie cried, all innocence and unaware of the potential rudeness of her words.

"Yes—I suppose I've changed a lot in—what is it— nine, ten long years?"

Elspeth had put strands of silver in my hair; I was not that much older than Nora, but I'd had a hard life, and it was meant to show in my weathered appearance.

Connie led me to the stove and sat me down, saying she wanted to hear everything about my life. Soon we fell into our dialogue, becoming our characters and forgetting the stage and the chairs filled with people. This was my favorite part of acting—letting the role gradually consume me until I felt quite comfortable

By the end of Act I, Connie (as Nora) had suffered a reversal; she was being blackmailed by Krogstad (Dorian), and she feared her husband would find out a secret she had kept for seven years. Torvald had sermonized her again, making her feel as though she was somehow terrible and morally infectious, and she was afraid to go near her children. Connie played the scene with remarkable subtlety, looking vaguely sick as she came to the realization that her life had changed in the space of a few hours.

Derek clapped for us and came forward, congratulating us on Act I and giving us his performance notes. "Take a quick break," he said. "Understudies, come on up and we'll go through the staging and some of the lines."

I marched down the stairs at stage right and did a quick

scan of the darkened theater, looking for Dash. Apparently, he had not made it out tonight; I told myself I didn't care even as my stomach twisted with disappointment.

I was standing next to Renata; I heard the gentle clicking of her knitting needles, but it stopped, and her warm hand touched my arm. "What's wrong, dear?"

I looked at her soft brown eyes. "Oh, nothing. I was hoping Dash would come by tonight. I don't— We haven't had much time to see each other."

Renata, whom Elspeth assured me had a secret boyfriend in Wood Glen, pursed her lips and shook her head. "Just a temporary state of affairs. Sit down here."

I sat beside her. Renata had a motherly aura, and she had acted as sort of an aunt to my twin brothers since she met them back in July. Luke and Jay tended to make a strong impression on people—not always in the favorable sense, as their school dean would attest—but Renata had loved them instantly. Since I had seen her genuine tenderness for my brothers, I had felt closer to her as well and often strolled down to her room for tea, sometimes to confide and other times just to chat, to hear about her childhood visits to Germany or about her early days as an actor. I sat beside her now, feeling dejected and near tears. Dash's absence felt like a rebuke.

"What's going on?" Renata said, resuming her knitting.

"He— I don't know. He seems to be distancing himself from me. He's cold somehow, and he finds reasons not to see me. But a month ago we were inseparable, just so happy and—attracted to each other. I can't believe he feels so differently now."

Renata looked amused. "He doesn't, Nora. He feels exactly the same."

I shook my head. "He came to the castle this morning. He had this miserable expression, and he and the Corby brothers were talking very seriously—Dorian, too. I don't know what that was about, but then he came to me and he wasn't smiling. He said we didn't spend time together, so I suggested he come by tonight. As you can see, that was not an idea he liked."

"He might have had to work. Doesn't he sometimes have evening shifts?"

"Yeah." I slouched in my seat like a moody teen. "I don't think that's it, though."

"Nora, young love is painful sometimes, but it also makes people blind. Dash is devoted to you, absolutely. I see it in his eyes whenever he comes to the castle."

"Yeah, well. It doesn't feel that way."

"Give it time. Don't do anything rash or assume what you don't know."

"What do you mean, something rash?"

"Don't break up with him."

My eyes felt warm and wet. "I don't want to break up with him."

"Good," she said calmly. "Just give it a bit of time." She sent me a secretive look. "Do you see my understudy over there?"

She discreetly pointed at Barbara Wendly, who was Renata's understudy in the role of Ann-Marie, the nursemaid to Nora's children.

"Yes."

"Apparently, she once dated the man I am currently dating. I did not know this until I noticed that she was glaring at me and asked the gentleman in question, who admitted it was so. Now I'm in the middle of what young people call 'drama.' And not the good drama that you and I love."

"Really?" I looked at Barbara, who stared steadily at the stage. I turned back to Renata. "I mean—is your boyfriend encouraging this?"

She shook her head. "No. But he's a shy person. He wants to pretend the problem isn't there. So even for old people, love can be confounding."

"Love?" I said, studying her face.

"Well, I should say 'dating.'"

"You said love," I insisted, and Renata laughed.

"I also said *old*," she said. "Oh, I think it's my turn. Derek is beckoning."

She stood up and moved regally toward the stage, her brown bun sitting on her head like a crown.

WHEN WE HAD finished for the night, it was almost ten o'clock. Jack approached Derek and spoke in his loud voice so everyone could hear.

"Derek, our thespian society is thinking of making your new castle show our fall event. Normally we go out for dinner or something, but members are interested in doing the full castle experience."

"Wonderful," Derek said. "We can talk dates."

"There's just one problem," Jack said, looking rueful. "Some of the ladies think it might be too scary, and they're reluctant. Can you tell them a little about it?"

Derek turned to look at some of the Wood Glen players. "I assume some of those ladies are in the room?"

Jack laughed. "Yes, three of them."

Derek turned on his charm as his gaze swept over Millie, Priscilla, and Barbara. "The first thing I can tell you is this isn't a haunted house. Nothing to jump out at you or drown you with some horrible noise or visual. Think of the catacombs as a stage set, which is what it is. Yes, you're in a darkened space, which is Halloween appropriate, but you're also watching a performance. And many of your friends from this show are in the castle show, as well. Come on by the castle anytime, and I'll show you the space."

Jack looked eager. "Can we see it now? I'd like them to see it in the dark so they get a real sense of it, and we were hoping to do the event next week if you have any openings."

Despite this rude request, Derek remained pleasant. "Of course. Bring the gang. We'll run you through the space; but we have to be finished by eleven, as I promised my beautiful Connie a walk in the moonlight."

"Great!" Jack yelled, and he turned to chat with the town contingent: Ben, Andrew, Millie, Priscilla, and Barbara.

Derek mobilized the rest of us to do a check to make sure everything was neatly put away, and he turned off the houselights.

People bundled out into the dark night; it was cold now, and I wrapped my sweater around myself, wishing I'd brought a coat.

I managed to get in the same car as Connie, and we chatted quietly on the short ride back to the castle. When we arrived—in four cars this time—Derek bustled his visitors into the castle, with Paul bringing up the rear. Connie and I started toward the castle door, but I said, "Come here. I want to show you something."

I took her hand and we ran to the west lawn, which I could normally see from my third-floor window. I had left the light on in my room, and opened the window so that sounds could be heard through the screen.

"Look up there," I said. Then I called, "Brontës! Charlotte, Emily, Annie! Come say hi to us!"

Moments later we could see three little figures on the windowsill, six curious ears twitching.

"That's adorable," Connie said. "Let's go play with them."

I laughed and said, "See you in a minute, girls," and we ran back to the front door.

"I think I'll cancel the walk in the moonlight and request cuddling in front of Derek's fireplace instead. It's chilly out here."

I sighed. "That sounds nice."

We turned the corner, heading back to the entrance, and were surprised to see Miranda coming out. She had changed her clothes and donned a warmer coat, and now she was walking away from the castle, headed not toward the parking lot, but toward the woods. Soon she blended in with the dark, and all I saw was the shimmer of her white hair.

"Weird," Connie said.

"I guess she's a night owl," I said. "Maybe she's meeting up with friends."

"Hmm." Connie took my arm. "Meanwhile we little homebodies can get into our warm pajamas."

"Yes. Do I live like a grandmother?"

Connie laughed. "Everyone wants to snuggle in cold weather."

For some reason we were lingering in the cold, though, and suddenly we heard the loud, cacophonous voices of the catacombs group, back from their venture into the deeper dark. The high-pitched voices of the women could be heard interspersed with the booming laughter of the men.

The noises came closer, and suddenly the whole crowd of them was rounding the castle, heading toward the main entrance, where we stood.

"How did it go?" Connie asked.

Priscilla emerged from the general throng, looking ethereal in the moonlight and the muted castle security light. She shrugged. "It was fine. It doesn't feel real, so it's not that scary."

"Exactly," Derek confirmed, sidling past her. "Let me run in and get those brochures for the rest of your group."

He jogged lightly up the steps, touching Connie's arm affectionately as he went past.

Even in the dark, I could tell her color had risen; she was in a constant state of desire for him. The realization made me feel lonely. I thought of John Dashiell's eyes, his August eyes, when he had said that he had never met anyone like me. . . .

"I don't know," said Millie's voice in the darkness. "It seemed pretty real to me."

Dorian loomed over her. Had I seen him go down with them? But of course, he would have wanted to be part of the impromptu performance. He seemed continually bent on impressing Derek.

"It's a theater, Millie. Think of it that way. A theater dressed up for Halloween."

Millie shivered a little. The group started separating and emerging as individuals. Andrew had Ben in a light headlock, and both of them were laughing. Andrew was murmuring something about how Ben should ask out the girl if he was interested in her. I had noted in previous rehearsals that Andrew and Ben had a special father-son dynamic that was rather sweet.

Jack strode forward, projecting handsomeness and self-importance even in the dark. He was dragging Barbara by the hand. She was pale and reluctant.

"Barb, it's fun! A way for our group to celebrate fall and do an activity together that isn't rehearsing."

"I'm fine with our traditional pasta dinner," she said with a weak smile.

"Boring!" Ben called. "This will be way more fun. I'll stand by you for protection, Barb."

Derek emerged from the castle, holding brochures and his appointment book.

"Okay, here we go. Jack, you can pass these around to the rest of the group. Ben, make sure Jade gets one when you do your bakery shift tomorrow."

"Sure," Ben said.

"So what's the best day for our outing?" Jack boomed.

Derek looked chagrined. "Well, that's the bad news. This was a last-minute idea, and my schedule is pretty much booked until early December."

"Oh, no!" Ben shouted.

Derek held up a hand. "So I'm thinking we'll have to do an extra performance at a nonstandard time. Maybe after one of our rehearsals."

"That would work," Priscilla said with a bright smile.

Jack sent her a look of approval.

Derek nodded, flipping through his calendar. "Thursday, we have an early rehearsal at three. We'll need at least three or four hours, but then we could head over to the castle at about seven. Dinner and a show," he said.

"Perfect!" Andrew shouted. He seemed to be mimicking Jack's dominating manner. "We can do that, can't we, everyone?"

The group nodded with varying levels of enthusiasm. It struck me that this moment itself looked like a performance: the group at the foot of the steps serving as a chorus while handsome Derek stood on the steps alone—a classic man-versus-society script.

Paul appeared suddenly next to Connie and me. Where had he been? Hamlet sidled up next to me; he had obviously been Paul's companion in whatever nighttime task he had done. A perimeter check? I wondered vaguely. Back in the days of Detective Dashiell, when Dash haunted the castle with his wary presence, perimeter checks had become the norm. But now that the threat was over, there was nothing more to fear.

I studied Paul's face and saw nothing but geniality. He slung a casual arm around me as we listened to Derek finalizing things with the group.

"Good night, then," Derek said at last, and the assembled cast went straggling off to their cars.

Derek turned to us. "Alone at last," he said with a grin.

I had never known Derek to be anything but energetic. He wouldn't have been able to do all of his jobs without that boundless life-force throbbing within him. Tonight, he looked tired; perhaps it was a trick of the dim light.

Connie went to him and they shared an embrace.

"I believe I owe you a moonlit walk," he said, his voice soft.

Connie shook her head. "It's going to be cuddling by the fire instead. But first I have to say good night to Nora's kittens."

Derek chuckled. "That works out fine; I have to talk to Paul and Hamlet here."

I patted Hamlet's head and said good night to the Corby brothers, then followed Connie into the castle.

The main hall was dim and drafty, and I shivered as we walked to the main staircase and began our ascent. "You and Derek are sweet together. I really don't know how you went more than a year without each other."

"I don't, either," Connie agreed.

Dorian was suddenly on the stairs behind us. "Ladies," he said as he reached us on the first landing.

"Where were you?" Connie asked.

"Midnight snack. Zana is staying tonight, getting stuff ready for the first castle show. She gives me food when I act charming."

"Blech," I said.

Dorian sent me a wounded look. "Why are you always so disapproving of me, Nora?"

I sniffed. "Right now I disapprove because you just said you were *acting* charming, which means you were being false and manipulative just to wheedle food out of Zana. Taking advantage of her generosity, probably expecting her to serve you when she just wants to go to bed."

"I don't think I'm the first man who put on an act to get something out of a woman." He raised his eyebrows suggestively as though he were exposing some secret about me.

"Probably not," I said. "I disapprove of them all."

"Me, too," said Connie.

We sent him some frosty glances that made him laugh. We had all reached the third floor, and Connie and I headed for my room, where the little Brontës waited, their warm gray fur a constant source of consolation.

Dorian paused, his hand on the doorknob of the Small Library.

"What do you want in there?" I asked suddenly.

The question was inappropriate; he had as much right to the room as I did, but I felt nervous about having Dorian stomping around in there.

He gave me an innocent look that held something beneath it—mischief? Mockery? "Just looking for some nighttime reading. I couldn't get into the book you gave me."

"Ah," I said. "Well, good night."

We kept walking, and Dorian slipped softly into the book-lined room.

The Brontës were indeed waiting by the door with indignant fuzzy faces. I scooped up Emily and Annie, and Connie grabbed Charlotte

"Hello, my little sweeties," Connie intoned, pressing her nose against Charlotte's in an affectionate gesture.

"They look sleepy. I wonder what they've been doing up here to use up their energy." I look sternly at Emily, who was sometimes a ringleader, and then cast a glance around the room, looking for broken things.

"They just need a lot of sleep because they're still little babies," Connie said. "Let's put them on the bed and sing a lullaby."

We had done this before; the Brontës were quite starved for attention.

We set the cats down. Emily hid her paws beneath her body, transforming into a little gray boat. Charlotte remained upright, her white paws arranged neatly before her. Annie, who was fond of second helpings, stretched out on her back, her round belly pointing up at the ceiling.

Connie started singing "When You Wish upon a Star," and I joined in with a harmony. We sang softly, barely above a whisper, and the kittens blinked in appreciation. I petted Annie's soft belly with one finger.

"So cute," said Connie. "But I have to run now to cuddle a larger animal."

I laughed, and Connie waved and whisked out of my door.

I sat with my kittens, my small gray muses, and took out my phone. There was no text from Dash. I sighed, and sent him one:

Just back from rehearsal and thinking of you. Good night.

I heard nothing back; he was probably already asleep.

I realized suddenly that I hadn't heard any sounds from the room next door. Dorian was awfully quiet in there. Perhaps he had left? I felt mildly curious, but I had no interest in talking to him again tonight.

I shrugged and stood up to get ready for bed. Dorian Pierce could keep his little mysteries to himself. I had experienced my share of castle drama. Now I just wanted the happy-ever-after.

4

Rising Action

THE FOLLOWING MORNING, I woke to the sight of frost on my window. It was October first, and with the change of months had come a greeting etched in ice. The previous October had been unusually warm. I had been an actress in Chicago then, doing nightly performances of a play that had lasted for two months. The theater had not been air-conditioned, and the hot stage lights had made my makeup run, creating a clownish effect by the end of the evening.

And now, a year later, frost on the window of a castle. A very different October indeed.

My phone rang; I picked it up to examine the screen. *Dash*. Butterflies fluttered around in my abdomen while I swiped the phone on.

"Hello?"

"Hi." His voice caused an intensifying of the butterflies.

"Hi. How are you?"

He cleared his throat. It sounded as though he had just awakened. "I'm sorry I missed your text. I fell asleep on the couch watching some stupid movie."

"That's okay. I just wanted you to know I was thinking of you."

"I appreciate that."

We were both friendly and polite, but a bit too stiff for my liking. "Do you work today?"

"Yeah. In fact I'd better get moving. I've got an early meeting. I was thinking I'd be getting your voice mail." So he hadn't wanted to talk to me.

"Oh, well, it's lucky I picked up, huh?"

A pause. "Nora," he said, and my phone buzzed in my hand.

"I'm getting another call. Looks like it's from my brothers."

Dash's voice lost some of its formality. "The twins! Tell them I say hey."

"I will. Have a good day. Do you think you'll—"

"Oh, shoot. Gotta go—work call."

He said goodbye and ended the call.

With a weary sigh, I answered Jay's call and got both brothers on speakerphone.

"Hey, Nor," said Luke and Jay in unison.

"Hey, guys. How's school going? Does it feel great to be seniors?"

I could practically hear them shrugging. "It's okay," Luke said.

"It's already boring," Jay said.

It sounded like he was eating cereal. I had a sudden image of them as toddlers, eating their Cheerios with tiny spoons.

"But we're not calling about school."

"Oh?" I got out of bed, depositing a clinging kitten on the floor. "What can I do for you at"—I consulted my clock—"seven ten in the morning?"

"We have great news," Luke said. "All of our weekends are free in October."

"How nice for you," I murmured, heading toward my little bathroom.

Jay slurped some milk in my ear. "He means that we are free to come out to the castle for a visit. Sample the charms of a castle in autumn, chat with the locals, get into some kind of awesome trouble. Stuff like that."

"We're pretty busy around here right now," I said. "I'm in two plays, remember? And Mom said you'll all be coming out to see the show in town."

"Boring," said Jay.

Luke was slightly more diplomatic. "We want to see your show and everything, but Derek said we could come out for some castle fun."

"When did he say that?" Derek was busier than anyone, and the last thing he needed was two extremely intrusive teens hanging around.

"Recently," Jay hedged.

"I don't know. I would like to see you guys again, but I don't want you to wear out your welcome."

I could picture Jay's indignant face. "We've only been there one other time, and that was months ago! We were texting Renata."

"What? You've been bothering Renata?"

Luke sighed patiently. "We were not bothering her. She likes us. We mostly just send her GIFs. They crack her up. And then she sends us these puzzles we have to solve. Sometimes they're in German; those are more challenging."

Renata really did love those two. "And why does she send you puzzles?"

Jay cleared his throat. "If we solve them, she sends us little gift certificates and stuff."

"Do not take money from my friends!" I said.

"She's our friend, too," Jay countered. "She loves to lavish us with gifts because we're so adorable."

I sighed.

"Anyway, Nor, back to the subject at hand."

"Stop crunching cereal in my ear."

The crunching became louder. "We can come as early as this weekend," Jay said.

"Say the word and we'll pencil you in," Luke said, riffling some papers.

"Don't make it sound like I'm requesting a visit," I said. But my lips were curling upward of their own volition.

"Just talk to King Derek," Luke wheedled. "Tell him we shall be his jesters."

"That's for sure," I said. "A couple of clowns. Or oafs, maybe."

Jay's voice was bland. "We know you miss us, Nor, so don't even pretend."

He was right. I did miss them, especially the way they made me laugh.

"Okay, I'll talk to Derek today. You persuaded me."

My brothers yelled, "Huzzah," over and over in my ear.

BY THE TIME I emerged from the shower and donned a black sweater and jeans, I had received a text from Derek, sent to all actors in the castle.

Check the costume room schedule. Elspeth is doing final fittings today and dress rehearsal is tomorrow.

"Ah," I told the cats, who were waiting for their food. "The busy day begins."

I fed my sweet kittens, locked them safely in my room, and walked swiftly down the hall to the south stairs, where the costume room sat across from Miranda's room.

A schedule was taped on the door, and I saw that I was second in line, after Connie. I wandered into the room and saw Elspeth assessing Connie's outfit as she turned around. We were supposed to be a sophisticated French-American family of the mid-twentieth century, and Elspeth had made Connie a white silk suit with palazzo pants. It looked amazing, especially with high-heeled gray-white shoes with rhinestone straps. Elspeth had tucked Connie's blond hair up in a sophisticated twist.

"Wow," I said. "That is absolutely perfect."

"Great timing, Nora," Elspeth said. "Connie, you can take that with you now; I'm finished with the hemming."

Connie spun around, admiring the suit in Elspeth's long mirror. "You really are a genius, El," she said. "Derek is going to love this."

"Nora's turn," Elspeth said.

Connie obediently stepped down from the little round platform, and Elspeth handed me my outfit. Connie was the dead patriarch's legitimate and favorite daughter, while I was a child of his mistress, never quite welcomed into the family. Elspeth had put me into a maxi dress with a black bodice and a black-and-white-checked skirt. My grandmother had worn a dress like it once; I had seen pictures.

I slipped into the gown and took my place on the platform while Elspeth's big marmalade cat, Ollie, watched from atop a nearby shelf.

"Yes," Elspeth murmured.

"Nora, you look so dramatic!" Connie said. "That black velvet with your dark hair . . ."

"I have a chignon for your hair," Elspeth said. "Used to be all the rage back in the day. Let's have a look."

She climbed on the platform with me, holding something that looked like a soft slinky. She made some deft movements with her hands, and then with a hair pick, and then she turned me to the mirror. I had a perfectly round bun on the top of my head, but two long dramatic strands of hair hung down on either side of my face.

"I like it," I said.

"I love costume day," Connie said. "The clothing always makes me feel so much more ready for the performance. Like girding for battle."

"Agreed," I said.

Miranda appeared in the doorway. "Knock, knock," she said in her soft voice. "Should I come back?"

"No, come on in. I just finished with your daughter," Elspeth said with a wink.

Despite the fact that Miranda wasn't much older than Connie and me, she had been cast as my mother, the patriarch's mistress. To her credit, Miranda did a great job with the role; she appropriately captured the weary patience of a long-neglected woman.

"Have fun." I waved at Miranda and Elspeth, and Connie and I floated out of the room in our fancy attire, holding our casual clothes.

"Let's change and grab some breakfast before rehearsal. Derek makes them last so long that I always end up starving if I miss my morning meal."

"Sounds good—meet you in the hall in five minutes."

ON SOME DAYS I still felt like a child on Christmas Day when I wandered around the castle, and I felt that magic now, too, as Connie and I descended the large staircase and saw the poetic etchings of frost on the landing window. How had I ended up in this place? How had this place ended up in the world? The castle was a carefully constructed illusion, neither historical nor relevant to anything else. It was one man's vision, and now I got to enjoy it.

I was still feeling dreamy when we entered the kitchen

and saw Zana filling the chafing dish on the sideboard with fluffy scrambled eggs. Suddenly I was very hungry.

"Thank you, Zana. You're an angel," I said. "My brothers are threatening to come and visit again, so I'm warning you in advance: they will try to consume your stores."

Zana brightened. "The twins? Oh, my gosh, they were so fun. Eriza friended them on Facebook and they joke around all the time. She wants to meet them."

"Yes, yes, everyone loves them," I said, pretending to be annoyed. "Meanwhile I've spent eighteen years trying to get them out of my hair."

Zana shook her head. "Girl, you can't even hide how much you dote on those boys."

Connie had already filled a plate and taken a bite of toast. "It's true, Nora. You're always talking about them with this soft look on your face. Clearly they are your little babies."

An unbidden memory: of my parents bringing the twins home in matching carriers. Even as infants Jay and Luke had looked calculating. My mother had set them down on the floor, and Luke immediately made a gigantic sound in his diaper. Jay actually turned and looked at him, and my mother swore that he was laughing.

LATER THAT MORNING, we found ourselves in the large drawing room, rehearsing our lines. The castle's first show would be the following evening. And then the busy fall season would be upon us.

Derek stood with his hands on his hips, ever the director, Hamlet sitting near him like a codirector. Derek made sure to point out to us that our paying guests were the actual detectives and that we had to be ready for their questions.

"Remember that depending on what the Inspectors say, our dialogue might start with different people. We have to be flexible. Let's start this one with Nora."

I stepped forward in my flowing dress, trying to project fury and hurt feelings. "Oh, what a surprise to find you all here together! I guess my invitation got lost in the mail. All talking about Dad's will, are we? Wondering who's going to get the lion's share? Well, guess what. He loved my mother and me far more than he loved that grasping woman who measures love by price tags—"

"I assume you are referring to me," Renata said grandly, emerging from one corner in an expensive-looking wool dress. "And I suppose you feel no shame about making such insulting comments in my house. But of course, neither you nor your mother has any shame. If she did, you wouldn't exist."

I moved forward, intent on slapping her, but Dorian caught my arm. "That's not going to happen, spitfire. You're right. We should have invited you, but you can't possibly think our dad would leave you anything. You or your mother. You can tell her that she has no right—"

"Tell her yourself," said Miranda, stepping out of the shadows behind me. Elspeth had made her up to look middle-aged, and she wore such a weary expression that I actually felt sorry for her.

Dorian was not embarrassed. "Hello, Miranda. Does the house look different since you were a kitchen maid here?"

Miranda's lips curled. "Not much has changed. You were a rude little boy, and you're a rude man."

Connie swirled wine in her glass. "That seems a bit hypocritical, Miranda, since you bore my father's illegitimate child and now have the gall to show up here to see if he left you money. I wouldn't be surprised if the Inspector here told me that you killed him."

Miranda was trembling with emotion. "I loved that man. Thank God he had someone in his life who loved him. His spoiled children and his mercenary wife brought him little joy. And where were all of you when he died? At least my daughter was willing to sit by his side, reading from the poetry books he loved."

Derek clapped his hands. "Oh, yes, the sainted Miranda. And I don't suppose that you used that time at his bedside to ingratiate yourself with him, right? You were too busy making sure he was happy."

"Yes. Like any decent human being, I wanted to bring him comfort and happiness."

"Enough of this," Renata said sharply. "The lawyer will be here soon to read the will, and then we will never see these two women again, and I will be quite glad."

Elspeth wandered in and joined her "siblings" Derek, Dorian, and Connie. "What did I miss? I was talking to the cook."

"Nothing worth repeating," said Renata coldly. "The will shall reveal everything."

I turned to an imaginary guest. "Inspector, you might want to know that there was another will."

"What?" yelled several voices together.

"My father told me that he'd been having second thoughts about the will and the disbursement of his money. He said he wished he had never been rich at all—that the money spoiled the natures of his wife and children, and he felt guilty about it."

"That's a lie!" shouted Dorian. His eyes sparked with fury.

"Is it?" I met Miranda's eyes. "My mother and I are here because we know where he put the new will. He said it's in the catacombs."

A gasp from everyone in the room,

I spoke again to the imaginary guest. "Inspector, if you'll lead us downstairs, I think I know just where he hid it."

"You wrote it yourself!" Derek cried.

Miranda smiled. "No one could possibly duplicate Pierre's handwriting. You know how eccentric it was."

"Besides," I said, "he told me it was witnessed by some-one he did not name."

Renata and her children looked frozen. Derek recovered first. "Well, then, to the catacombs it is!"

We all stood still, and Derek said, "Great job, everyone. Then we go down to the catacombs and I have my argument with Dorian, Miranda tries to break us up, and we accidentally stab her."

"Very Shakespearean," Renata said approvingly.

"Connie should be skulking around, looking nervous, so I assume by that time one of the Inspectors will accuse her, and we can go have wine and cheese."

"A good wine always helps to cleanse the palate after a murder," Renata said.

We laughed. Paul came in, smiling. "Sounded good," he said. "And I just booked two more events. You'll all be very busy actors."

PAUL WAS RIGHT. The first castle show happened the following day; it went quite well, even though Elspeth forgot to plant one of her clues, and Dorian almost laughed out loud when I tripped over a carpet flap in the main hallway. I glared at him, and we played it off as part of our general antagonism.

Even though the castle shows had begun, our rehearsals at Blue Curtain continued, and it was an exhausting time. On Thursday afternoon Derek reminded us that after rehearsals we would be doing a special castle show that evening for the Wood Glen Thespian Society. We all knew this, but it was a bit daunting to consider it, since we had hours of rehearsal left and most of us longed for a nap.

By five o'clock, Derek said, "All right, we want to try Act Three. Kristine and Krogstad, let's get you onstage. Nora and Torvald, be ready in the wings."

Dorian and I climbed onto the stage. No matter how tired I might be, I never ceased to feel a thrill when I stood in the footlights and looked out at an audience (though the audience in this case consisted of a couple of understudies and Derek). There was a magic in it, and in the connection between performer and audience, that was impossible to explain. It was energy generated by art, and it was real. I looked forward to opening night with low-grade excitement that was growing each day. It had been quite a while since I'd been on a stage, and the BC, though small, was a pretty little theater.

I walked across the stage and sat down at a table. Dorian came in, frowning in his role as Krogstad. He demanded to know why I had summoned him and curled his lip at the idea that we just had to meet in the Helmers' house.

I waited for him to vent his irritation, and then I said, "All right, Krogstad, let's talk." I loved the directness of the line, of Kristine's refusal to let Krogstad assume things when she could simply communicate with him directly.

And so, leaning forward with an earnest expression, my hands close to his, I told him why I had left him a decade ago. That I felt proud to have married a man who could provide for my mother and my two little brothers even though I had not loved him.

Krogstad continued to snap at me, hurling barely concealed accusations.

I continued to tell him the truth in plain language until he started to understand: I was alone. The husband I had not loved had died three years earlier. I had come back, at Christmastime, because I had heard he was also widowed, and I had thought we might find comfort in each other.

Dorian looked astonished. "Kristine, did you really have some thought of me?"

By the end of our simple scene, we had agreed to reunite, and Krogstad's bitterness had been transformed.

"I've never been so happy!" he called to me as he left the stage.

I said my final lines in a brief soliloquy, and Derek clapped. "Great job, Kristine and Krogstad. Nora and Torvald, get in place by the door."

I had a brief scene with the married couple before I left their house for good. I waited in the sitting room as Jack practically dragged Connie across the threshold. Torvald had had champagne, and he had sex on his mind. Nora, on the other hand, was planning to kill herself for Torvald's sake. The tension grew with each exchange.

Torvald made a point of "showing" me his wife, Nora, telling me how beautiful she was and that she was "Mine, all mine." I said I was glad to see Nora's costume, and then I exited the stage and spied John Dashiell in the audience.

"Dash!" I yelled. Derek turned and spied Dash and waved briefly. Then he was a director again. "Take it to the lobby, lovebirds."

I flew to Dash and kissed his cheek. He rose from his theater chair and the seat slapped up against the backrest. We looked guiltily toward Derek, and I led Dash into the lobby, which was shadowy and cool.

"Hello," I said, and I pulled his head down to mine. "It's so nice to see you."

"You, too. I saw you in that castle show when you played the piano, but I've never seen you onstage. You're very good."

"Well, thanks. To be honest, I don't think Dorian and I have very good chemistry. The scene should be more moving than it is when we perform it. I wish I could do it with Paul; he's Dorian's understudy and I think he has a more sensitive take on the role."

"Well, it looked good to me." His eyes looked away from mine. "And I think you have pretty good chemistry."

"Meh," I said. "So how long do I have you? I'm done in

this act. Should we be like teens and sit in the back row making out while the show finishes?"

He grinned. "Sounds good to me."

I gave him another kiss and a tight hug, then led him back to the theater. We found seats in the last row. Derek had turned on minimal houselights, so we were essentially in darkness.

"After this, we do a special performance of the castle show. Can you come? It would be so fun if you were there."

"I can come," he said.

"Yay," I whispered, pretending to clap my hands.

"I'll probably have to leave right after that," he murmured. "Wow. I don't know if you should do that, Nora." I was nibbling his earlobe and slipping my hands into his dark hair. "A guy could get carried away."

But he turned and kissed me in earnest. When he pulled away, he whispered, "Why is Connie crying? Dr. Rank is happy."

"He's dying," I said under my breath. "That's what he meant when he said that his tests had given him a final answer. Nora understands this, but Torvald doesn't, because he's kind of drunk. There's this great tension between the two who know and the one who doesn't. Torvald insults Nora, saying she knows nothing about science. But he's the one who looks like a buffoon."

Dash watched for a while with genuine interest.

"You shouldn't get spoilers," I said. "I want you to come to opening night."

He studied my face with his hazel eyes, which looked almost black in the shadows. "I'll probably come to every performance, Nora."

Something about his tone filled me with elation, but before I could comment, a shadow fell over us, and I looked up to see Dorian, who had slipped into the row in front of us and stood facing us, looking casual and comfortable as though we had called him over.

"Nora, Derek says he'll need you to run the scene with Paul tomorrow."

I stared blankly. "What scene?"

Dorian smiled at Dash as though to suggest that women were dense. "The one we just did. Paul is the understudy."

"Yes," I said patiently. "And Miranda is mine."

Dorian shook his head. "Miranda's out. She told Derek today. So you'll be doing all six performances."

A selfish little part of my heart was overjoyed to hear this, but I also felt concern. "What's wrong? Is Miranda okay?"

Dorian shrugged. "She has another job. It was hard to juggle all three projects."

"Oh, I see."

"Anyway, he also said that we need to change in about two minutes when we get back to the castle so we can be performance ready. So you'll need to slide into your sexy dress pronto."

Dash slid an arm around me but said nothing.

"Dorian, you've met my boyfriend, haven't you?"

Dorian grinned. "Yeah—it's Dutch, right?"

"Dash. Or John," said John Dashiell in a tone that would have made most men think twice about giving him a hard time.

Dorian grinned again, but there was something malicious behind it. "Coming to the evening performance?" he asked Dash.

"I wouldn't miss it."

They stared each other down for a moment, and I was the only one who seemed uncomfortable. "Anyway, Dorian, we were having a private conversation, so if you don't mind—"

"Sure, I get it. See you around, lovebirds."

He moved slowly out of the row and walked toward the stage with studied indifference to his surroundings.

"He's a piece of work," Dash said in a low voice.

"I don't pay him much attention," I said mildly. "Women don't like egotistical men."

Dash raised an eyebrow. "I disagree. But let's get back to us."

"Yes, let's." I looked at him meaningfully. "It's only a couple more weeks, you know. Then two weekends of performances, and then I'll never be in one of Derek's Blue Curtain plays again."

"Of course you will. You're talented, and you love to act. I get that. But the timing has been—unfortunate. This summer, we said—"

"I know."

On the stage, Torvald was saying, with a mixture of misery and surprise, "Then you must not love me anymore."

Connie as Nora said, "No, Torvald, I don't love you anymore."

The grimness of the scene seemed to permeate our conversation.

I looked helplessly at Dash, who shook his head. "We'll talk about this later. Let's just watch the play."

We sat holding hands and watched the ending. Connie's performance was powerful—in one sense she was still the light and airy Nora, but she was a sadder, wiser Nora, who had no idea what would become of her. She only knew she had to leave. I almost didn't recognize my friend in the somber woman who sat across from Jack.

Then the play was over, and Derek was giving his notes, and then he was waving his hands. "All right, everyone, it's castle time! Let's head back for the fall show and celebration! Performance starts at seven," he said.

Derek made quick work of cleaning up the stage and

turning off the houselights while everyone else drifted out to their cars. There was much murmuring and bustling as people prepared for a party. Someone opened the outside door, and a blast of cold air floated into the theater, scented with woodsmoke and leaves.

"Time to go," Dash said, standing up. He held out his hand. "Let's see what this fall show is all about."

I followed him, grateful for his willingness to work around my schedule but worried about that unhappy something that kept creeping into our conversations. I told myself that after the show, I would get him all to myself. Like the characters on the stage, we would have a direct talk and clear the air.

With that determined thought, I followed my tall, dark-haired boyfriend out of the theater and into the frigid night.

5

Darkness and Death

DASH DROVE ME back to the castle, along with Renata and Elspeth, who had asked for a ride. They chattered happily in Dash's backseat, excited about the additional castle show.

"I'll try not to mess up my clues tonight," Elspeth said wryly. "I was distracted the other day because Dorian's hem was coming down and I was wondering if I could sew it up while the Inspectors were in the sitting room. And then Renata's chignon looked like it was going to topple. My costume mistress role overcame my actress role. I hope Derek doesn't fire me."

Renata snorted. "He couldn't bear to lose you. You do the jobs of four people."

"Well," Elspeth said, happy to hear these words of affirmation, "I do think he appreciates me generally."

"We all do," Renata said, patting her hand.

Then she spoke in the regal voice that she was so good at. "Dash, I play Nora's nursemaid in the town play, but also her only mother figure. So I should ask you about your intentions."

Dash met her laughing gaze in the rearview mirror and said, "My intentions are honorable. For the most part."

Renata and Elspeth giggled, and the castle road appeared. Dash swung into the narrow opening and proceeded up the long driveway. Dark trees loomed on either side of our car, their branches occasionally tapping against our window like spectral gray fingers.

The castle rose before us, luminous in the muted landscaping lights, its turrets thrusting into the pale clouds. The stars twinkled brightly above the silent trees, and Renata intoned, "Stars, hide your fires/Let not light see my black and deep desires!"

"Quoth the woman who's been in two different productions of *Macbeth*," I said, recalling that Renata had been in a gender-blind *Macbeth* and played his nemesis, Macduff.

"It does stay with you," Renata said contentedly.

Elspeth perked up. "I would have loved to see your Macduff, Ren." Then, wanting to include my boyfriend, she said, "I think Dash should join the Castle Troupe. He has the look of an actor about him."

"But alas, not the talent," Dash said. He pulled up to the entrance. "I'll let you ladies off here and go park the car."

Renata and Elspeth thanked him and stepped out of the car.

I touched his hand. "I have to do a superfast costume change, but I'll see you in the drawing room."

"Sure," he agreed.

"I'm glad you're here."

"Me, too."

I leaned across to kiss him, then jumped out of the car and ran with Renata and Elspeth to the elevator, which we took to the third floor.

"Five minutes," Elspeth said. "Derek wants us there by seven."

I darted into my room and paused to kiss each kitten, then fed them and donned my glamorous dress. I lifted the matching heels but decided it would be easier to run to the main floor in stocking feet, and I did so, moving silently down the grand stairs like an ancestral ghost.

When we finally assembled, Derek stepped forward and spoke to the group from the local drama club. This included Jack, Priscilla, Andrew, Millie, Barbara, and Ben, as well as a few people who weren't in the main production. I noticed that my teenage friend, Jade, wasn't there; I assumed that was because it was a school night.

"Welcome, Inspector," Derek said. We always referred to all guests as one basic Inspector, a police officer who had come to investigate. Tonight's "Inspector" was the drama club.

"I'm glad you could be with us this evening. We need to get to the bottom of my father's murder, along with his stolen will. As you may have heard, we children have had trouble getting along since his death, which I'm sure you'll agree is understandable. . . ."

Derek continued, and we siblings stepped forward one by one, asserting our claims on our father and his money. Derek had kept the lighting muted so that the costumes seemed to glimmer, as did the jewelry Elspeth had picked out for us.

I caught sight of Dash at the edge of the crowd, but I kept my eyes off of him, fearful that I would lose concentration if I looked at his face.

When the time came, I stepped forward to assert that my father had made another will and that he had hidden it in the catacombs. And then the great migration began: Derek and Dorian led the way, arguing and complaining in their loud entitled voices, demanding respect as the sons of the fictional dead man. The Inspectors were close behind them, fascinated and obviously having fun.

Later I recalled the surreal nature of our descent; I heard the rustling of costumes as the voices grew quiet, perhaps because people were concentrating on the stairs, poetically lit and therefore slightly treacherous. I was close behind Connie in her white silk; Miranda was behind me, and she wore a scent that somehow evoked the past and sadness. The first people reached the stone floor, and their voices echoed strangely as they started up their lines again. When I reached the bottom, Millie said, "I want to take a picture!" And we posed beneath one of the torches jutting out of the brick wall: Jack in his blue button-down shirt and tight blue jeans, looking handsome and excited; Priscilla, also in jeans and an orange sweater, her arm around Barbara, whose expression was a cross between amusement and aggravation. I had heard her complaining about the dim lighting and the chill of the lower level.

"It's supposed to be cold," said Andrew jovially. He was wearing brown slacks and a beige sweater vest; this made him look avuncular and vaguely like a math teacher. "It's part of the scene."

Barbara shrugged, and Ben grinned at her. He wore a blue polo and black corduroys. "It will be fun, Barb. And we're all doing it together, which makes it more fun."

Some other voices agreed—people I did not know and had not met.

I also recalled that at one point Priscilla yawned and stretched, and her sweater rose slightly, revealing a thin band of skin. For an instant, everyone seemed to freeze—every man in the group seemed to have fixed his gaze on her, as did the women for different reasons—and Priscilla seemed genuinely unaware of anyone's attention.

"I'm bushed," she admitted. "Let's hope this wakes me up."

We shuffled forward. Dorian and Derek, who had stopped talking while we posed for pictures, began arguing again, leading us along the catacombs, which I had visited with Derek in advance. Here were the familiar crumbling brick walls, the faux skeletons jutting out of them.

I was about to say my line, at which point the lights would mysteriously go out (Dorian was to flip a hidden switch when Derek pushed him against the wall), and then we had about ten seconds to build suspense and scare people before the lights went back on and we found Miranda's "body" lying on the floor. Then the Inspectors were going to have to solve two murders right there in the catacombs.

I was behind Jack, who was blocking my view, and I was trying to get a glimpse around him, but the narrow hall was suddenly crowded with bodies. I waited for my cue and called, "Stop fighting, you two, or I won't tell you where the will is hidden!"

I heard scuffling as Derek and Dorian fought, and Dorian was pushed against the wall. The lights went out, and the crowd gasped.

"What's happening?" cried Renata's voice.

"Mother, tell Gustavo to put the lights back on," Connie demanded querulously.

I was still trapped behind a line of tall people, and then someone shoved me from behind, trying to see in the dark perhaps, and several of us fell at once, tripping over one another.

The lights flashed back on, and the crowd moved forward, drawn by a sight in the distance: Miranda's body lying in a graceful silken heap. I was still trying to scramble upright; I had scraped my hands on the cobbled floor, and I examined them to see how badly I had scratched them. They were both covered in blood, and I stared in confusion. Had I fallen that hard? Where was the blood coming from? I stared harder at my hands, until my eyes were distracted by motion—something running in a rivulet across the stones in front of me: blood.

I turned to the tall man who still lay on the floor. "Are you okay?" I said. "I know we all took a tumble, but I hope you didn't—"

I stopped, froze, then leaned in. Was it Jack? No, the shoulders were not quite as broad. It was Ben; his glasses had been knocked off in his fall, and his face looked young and vulnerable in the artificial light.

"Ben?" I whispered.

My gaze moved to his back, where his shirt was torn and stained a brownish red. If he had fallen forward, why was there blood on his back? Why was he not moving, not talking? These questions floated vaguely in my brain until my sluggish mind reached the inevitable conclusion.

"Dash," I croaked. "Dash!"

The second one was a scream, and Dash was beside me in an instant; the rest of the room went silent.

It took Dash far less time than it had taken me to determine what had happened.

"Derek, can we get a signal down here? We need an ambulance."

Derek was pale. "No. I'll run up and call now."

Derek ran back toward us, and Dash murmured something in his ear. Derek nodded, and then he ran.

Paul joined us and knelt beside Ben. "Is there a pulse?" he asked quietly.

"I—I—" Rational thought seemed to have left me.

The rest of the crowd edged closer. "What's going on?" Millie asked.

Barbara yelled, "Is that Ben?"

"Is it Ben?" Priscilla repeated. "What's happened to him? Did he fall?"

"Ben," said Andrew, looking sick. "What happened? Does he have a pulse?"

Paul looked up soberly and shook his head. "Dash, help me roll him over and I'll try chest compressions."

The two men rolled Ben over, and Paul began his ministrations.

Sick to my stomach, I could look only at Ben's face, which was devoid of all expression as it stared up at the ceiling of the catacombs, where a wisp of Derek's carefully placed cobweb drifted slowly down, like a descending spirit.

Minutes later the EMTs came charging down the stairs and took over for Paul. I stood up then, still staring at Ben, and my body began to tremble.

Dash came to stand beside me and his arm tightened around me. "Are you all right?"

"I—don't know," I whispered. "Dash, was he stabbed?" I asked so that only he could hear, and he nodded grimly.

"Then I was there. I was right there when it happened, but I didn't see— I have no idea what happened, but I felt someone push forward, charge forward, and then everyone was gone except for Ben and me, because we both fell. . . ."

I turned to look at the people who faced us from fifteen feet away, a whole group of them, pale faced and wide-eyed, as they watched the EMTs load Ben onto a stretcher and rush toward the stairs. Moments after they disappeared, some uniformed police officers appeared at the hallway entrance, accompanied by a very attractive Black woman in an impeccable brown pantsuit with a crisp white blouse and a lanyard that looked like the one Dash wore when he was on duty.

Dash saw her and let go of me to walk to her side. The two conferred in low tones, their faces close together.

Then Dash turned toward the people who waited in silence. "For those of you who don't know, I'm Detective John Dashiell of the Wood Glen Police. This is Detective Bradley, and these are Officers Gentry and Bettis. A crime has been committed here, and it was committed by someone in this room. We will be searching all of you for a weapon or for any other evidence that might link you to the crime. Paul, is there a place . . ."

Paul knew what he meant. "Yes. If everyone will keep moving down that hall, you'll see the winery to your left. There's a big room there where people can sit down and wait to be interviewed."

At least a couple of people looked hopeful that this might still be part of the show.

Dash saw this and said, "The dead body down here was supposed to be Miranda there."

Miranda waved; she had long since gotten off the floor and joined the crowd.

"That was the scripted story," Dash said. "This body was not planned, and we can only hope that he is not dead."

And then, as if of one accord, we walked in silence through the catacombs, our feet echoing hollowly on the stones, our bodies trembling in the chill and drafty hall. A skull screamed at me from the wall, its bony jaws wide, and I closed my eyes to the very real horror that had happened in the catacombs, far worse than I could ever have imagined.

6

Castle Legends

DEREK HAD FLIPPED on bright and glaring lights, dispelling all illusion about catacombs or simulated horror to reveal a truly terrifying scene.

We stood huddled in the airy open floor of the wine cellar, where high wooden tables were scattered about the space, under which nestled wooden stools. Some people, including Renata and Elspeth, had seized a stool and sat upon it, probably because they had a sense of just how long we would be here.

Dash had conferred with the police officers and the lovely Detective Bradley (had he had to put his face so close to hers? Had it my imagination that they seemed very comfortable together?), and then he spoke to the group.

"When your name is called, please go with the police officer who calls it and answer the questions that are asked. You may need to show your identification, and some questions may be deemed personal, but the answers will be a necessary component of our investigation."

"I should think you could let us all go home and interview us there," Millie said, aggrieved. "Derek knows who we all are and where we live.

Dash considered her with a grim expression. "I assume that Ben is a good friend of just about everyone in this room. He did not fall down in that hallway there." He pointed back to the catacombs. "He was stabbed."

A gasp came from someone in the crowd and a great deal of murmuring from the various clusters of people.

"Not only that," Dash said, "but he was stabbed by someone in this room. Obviously, we can't let you go until we have collected all the evidence we might require from you. I'm sure you all understand."

I barely heard what Dash said after that. I was looking at the people in the room—those from the little drama group with whom I had become familiar; my own Castle Troupe, who could not possibly have had anything to do with an attack on a kid like Ben; and some of the other drama club members I had not yet met. *It has to be one of them,* I thought.

I noted that other people were looking around, too—we all wore the same expression of disbelief.

I had stayed by myself in one corner, unwilling to speak to anyone, still in the midst of shock and horror. I watched the others as they attempted to comfort one another. Jack pulled a tearful Priscilla into his arms and kissed her hair; his own blue eyes were filled with tears. Andrew and Millie stood close together, their eyes wide and disbelieving. Andrew seemed to have crumpled in on himself, and I recalled his easy, fatherly affection with Ben. I did not think the Portnoys had children of their own. Barbara stood with some woman I did not recognize, but whom someone had called Stephanie. Both women looked resentfully at the police as though they had arranged the crime.

Dash appeared in front of me and pulled me into a brief hug. "Are you okay?" he asked.

"It's just—this happened to me not long ago, in the chapel, and I'm having flashbacks—"

"God, I'm sorry." He looked rueful but also urgent. "Listen, Nora, this is a time-sensitive situation, so I need to get back to my interview. Officer Bettis will talk to you in a minute, but I wanted to ask you: what exactly did you see when Ben fell?

I closed my eyes, trying to recall that moment, the rushing crowd, the darkness and chaos, and losing my balance. . . . "I was behind the Blue Curtain group or some of them, I think. It was hard to see even before the lights went off. I think I was behind Jack for a while, and then later I was behind Ben, obviously, because when the lights went out, people rushed forward, and I tripped, and so did Ben, I thought, because we both went down, but then the lights went back on and he didn't answer me or make a sound, and then I saw his face. . . ."

Dash touched my hand. "Who rushed forward?"

"I don't know. I thought it was a whole group, but I had also thought no one was behind me, except maybe Millie, because she had been taking pictures and had lagged behind a little, but I'm not sure. I didn't actually look back. I should have." I studied Dash as a new horror occurred to me. "Whoever rushed forward—they stabbed him, didn't they? They stabbed him right next to me, and I fell because I tripped, but he fell because he was horribly wounded."

Dash nodded. "Don't dwell on that. But if there's anything you can remember, anything that seemed out of place . . ."

I thought. There had been something, a little tiny something that had struck me at the time, but I couldn't bring it back now, chaotic as my thoughts were.

Dash nodded. "Okay, that's fine. I need to—" His phone rang; he swiped it on and said, "Dashiell." He listened for a moment, his face grim, and then said, "Right. Okay, yeah. Thanks." He swiped off again.

"Ben's dead," he said in a low voice.

"Oh, no!" I cried without thinking of being discreet.

Now many eyes were on us, and Priscilla cried, "Is it Ben? Is he okay?"

With a sigh, Dash moved toward the center of the room. "Your friend and colleague Ben Boyle was pronounced dead when he reached the hospital."

A collective cry rose from the crowd, something between a scream and a moan. I studied the miserable expressions of Ben's friends and fellow actors and could not see one face that looked inauthentic. And yet one of them was responsible for Ben's death. It had been no accident. We had all been frisked when we walked through the doorway of the wine cellar, so where had the murder weapon gone?

Murder. This was a murder investigation now. Detective Bradley joined Dash and put her hands on her hips. She spoke in a low and lovely voice that made me unaccountably angry.

"This is now a murder investigation. You are all expected to cooperate fully and to answer every question posed to you. It may take time, but we have a very specific protocol we need to follow. Derek has reminded us that there is a washroom to your left, behind the final shelf of wine. No one is to go toward the hallway we were in earlier; the CSI team is there now, and absolutely no one may go back to the scene of the crime."

She stationed herself at one of the wood tables and began calling people to her. Dash did the same at a different table, and so did one of the police officers.

The other, Officer Bettis, came to me and put a gentle hand on my arm. "Are you doing okay?" she asked. "It's hard, I know."

"He was just a nice kid," I said in a toneless voice. "He worked in a bakery."

Suddenly Barb cried out, "He had animals! Can someone text Jade and tell her to look in on Ben's dogs?"

"I'll do it," I said.

I texted Jade several times a week because we were friends. I wrote her a quick note now:

> Jade, I need you to look in on Ben Boyle's animals if possible. Ben will not be coming home tonight and someone needs to look after his pets. Can you do it?

I sent the text and began to answer Officer Bettis's questions. Then my phone buzzed.

> I'll do it. Is he okay?

I hesitated. Jade was only a teenager, but she was very matter-of-fact. She would not want me to lie.

No, I wrote.

A pause. Is he dead?

> I'm sorry. Yes. The police are investigating.

There was a longer pause. Thanks for thinking of the animals. I'll tell my mom and dad.

I called out to the group, "Jade will care for the animals."

"Thank you," Barbara said in a low voice.

I turned back to Bettis.

As she asked me questions, my mind was racing with questions of its own: who would have wanted to attack Ben? Why had the attack happened in the catacombs? And how could the attacker have known that the lights would go out at that particular moment? Did that mean that it was someone from our Castle Troupe?

It was two in the morning by the time the police let people go. Dash spoke sternly to the now grumbling group. "I will let you return to your homes, but none of you is allowed to leave Wood Glen. If you try to leave town, I will arrest you on suspicion of murder."

Sounds of outrage. Dash stared everyone down. "There is a murderer in this room," he said. "I don't know yet who it is, but I will know. Until I find out the truth, you will support your local police and your late friend, and you will remain in town. And now Derek will escort you out one by one via a very narrow fire exit."

I too had to leave via the fire exit and make my way back to the castle entrance in the cold darkness. Connie found me and held my hand, but we walked in silence. When we got into the castle, we stood irresolutely in the main hall.

"I'm so tired," I said. "But I'm so hungry. We never got to eat our dinner. I assume someone told Zana not to bring it down after all her work."

"Yeah, and I think Derek hired Eriza and her friend to help waitress. They were so excited."

I sighed. "Do you have any interest in a postmidnight snack?"

"I do," Connie said. "It looks like the light is on in the kitchen, so obviously someone else had this idea."

Connie and I made our way to the kitchen, only to find several people sitting around the wood table: Elspeth, Renata, Paul, and Dorian.

"Welcome," said Paul. "We're commiserating with some sustenance. Zana is feeding us because she insists that food is comfort."

"It's true," said Zana, walking in with a pan of appetizers that had obviously been meant for the dinner portion of the show. "And don't feel guilty about eating. You all need your strength, and I don't want all my work to go to waste."

"Did Eriza and her friend go home?" I asked.

"No, they're sleeping in my bed." She gestured with her head toward the little room that Derek had made hers for any nights that she worked late in the castle and didn't want to drive home.

"Where will you sleep?" Connie asked.

Zana shrugged. "On the floor."

"That's ridiculous." Connie sat up straight. "I want to keep an eye on Derek tonight, so I'll be in his room. You can stay in mine. I'll put clean sheets out for you."

Zana was too tired to argue. "Thank you," she said. "I'm pretty wiped out today."

"We appreciate all your hard work, Zana," Paul said. "I'm sorry—"

We sat in silence. It was understood that Paul was sorry not just that Zana's effort had been wasted, but that a much more terrible thing had been wasted pointlessly and violently.

"No one in that room could have done it," Elspeth said. Her expression was still stunned. "Someone must have gotten in. Some crazy person. I mean, who would have had a motive? Ben is like a teddy bear."

Everyone seemed to notice her use of the present tense, and this cast another pall over the table.

Eventually Renata said, "Zana, this is delicious. The pastry is so light, and the chicken is so tender."

Zana thanked her. "I've got some nice desserts back there, too."

Elspeth said, "Has anyone ever seen that Detective Bradley before?" She looked at me. "Nora, doesn't Dash usually work alone?"

Zana brightened. "Is Robin down there?"

We all turned to her, and she said, "She's my cousin. She works in the Morristown Station, but she had said something about them sending her over to help with a burglary investigation. Those are her specialty."

"Huh. And yet now she's on a murder," Paul said.

"Good looks run in your family," said Dorian, who had been wolfing down food in a shameless manner until this moment. "I can see the resemblance."

This seemed utterly inappropriate, but I looked at Zana and saw that she was smiling. "Thanks, Dor."

Dor? It was true, then. They had really struck up a friendship in the weeks since Dorian had arrived.

Renata sighed and pushed away her plate. "Will this be bad for the castle, Paul?"

"It won't be great. And Derek was already worried about finances. . . ."

Connie stood up. "Speaking of Derek, I need to see how he's doing. Zana, I'll get your room ready first. Do you know which one is mine? Nora can show you in any case."

I nodded, and Zana smiled at me. "Thanks again, Connie."

Connie stood up and took her plate to the sink; then she gave Zana a half hug and waved at the rest of us before she left the room.

Paul looked sober. "Two murders within a couple of months."

Dorian looked thoughtful. "Why would someone do it? I read an interview with P. D. James once—"

"You know P. D. James?" I asked, surprised.

Dorian raised a brow at me. "Yes, I do read, Nora, as I told you. I am a literate person."

"I just didn't think you read classic female crime writers."

"I read all sorts of things. Anyway, in this interview she said that the motives for murder were love, lust, and lucre. And it all comes down to lucre in the end, right? Follow the money, and you'll find the truth." He thought about this, then looked at Paul. "Could this have something to do with that castle legend? The one about the treasure?"

"What?" Zana asked, intrigued.

I recalled sitting with Zana in the library of the castle, searching through books for the "treasure" of photographs, dollar bills, or any other items that people had used as bookmarks and then forgotten. Zana had the heart of an adventurer.

"What legend?" she asked.

Paul rubbed his eyes, looking weary. "Oh, it's nothing. When Derek and I were first renovating the castle, we found this old box with some documents written by our distant uncle Philip. Various legal forms but also some of his creative ramblings. He had a remarkably innovative mind." Paul thought about this for a moment. "Anyway, there was this little poem about the castle and treasure. It seemed to suggest that one just had to follow the clues."

"Fantastic," Dorian said, his eyes shining.

Paul looked thoughtful. "Derek and I looked into it for a while, but we ultimately concluded that he had written it as part of the castle's debut. It was open to the public at first; he wanted to share his vision with the world, after seven years of construction. Derek figures that the poem was a metaphor for the creative spirit and that it encouraged people to look for it within themselves. We thought he might have included it in some sort of grand-opening program."

"Or maybe it was real. Maybe Ben knew something about it, and—"

"Probably best not to speculate," said Renata wisely. "The police know what they're doing. I'm sure they'll want us all to stay out of it. In any case, I must go to bed. Zana, can I help you wrap these things up?"

"We'll all help," Paul said, standing.

We followed him to the counter, where we made quick

work of wrapping food in plastic wrap and stowing it in the large refrigerator.

"Thanks, everyone," Zana said. "Nora, I'm ready whenever you are." She was practically asleep on her feet.

And so it was Zana, not Connie, who linked arms with me and ascended the dark staircase at my side.

"Do you and your cousin Robin see each other often?" I asked.

She nodded. "We've always been close. She just has brothers, so I was the one she came to for girl chats."

"Ah. Does she have a boyfriend?"

Zana didn't seem to find this question odd. "She's on-again, off-again with this guy named Tom. He's a park ranger who works up at Prescott National Forest. Robin met him while she was hiking there. Really romantic. And he is *gorgeous*. I mean, just gorgeous."

"Wow. Sounds amazing. So are they on again right now?"

She shrugged. "She's always making up some kind of drama, probably so they can have dramatic reunions. I think they're pretty—physical."

I thought Tom seemed like a wonderful man. "Well, I hope they work things out."

"Oh, they will. Even when they're on the outs, she doesn't date anyone else. She just bides her time and then goes prowling after him again."

We had reached the third floor, and I guided Zana to Connie's door, which stood ajar. The bed linens had been changed, and Connie had left the coverlet pulled back. I saw that Zana was looking longingly at the mattress. I touched her shoulder.

"Bathroom is over there"—I pointed—"and you can get a cup of water in there." I gestured to Connie's tiny kitchenette. "Good night, Zana."

"Night, hon," Zana said vaguely.

I walked out and closed the door behind me. I crossed

the hall, about to unlock my own door, but was arrested by a sound, not from my room, but from the one beside it. Curious, my fear deadened by exhaustion, I walked to the Small Library, opened the door, and flipped on the light. There was nothing there. The table was empty and the chairs were tucked neatly beneath it. Whatever the sound had been must have come from outside. Or I was hearing things, caused by a tortured imagination. I went back to the hall, unlocked my own door, and faced a barrage of indignation in the form of aggrieved meows.

"Sorry, girls," I said. "It's been a long night."

I fed my little gray cats, got quickly into pajamas, and dove into bed. The cats, forgiving now that their bellies were full, clustered around me, but I didn't even have a chance to pet them before I fell asleep.

7

Fair Genevieve

I WOKE IN A patch of sun, which warmed me and made me feel contented beneath my blue quilt. I had a blissful ten or twenty seconds in which I was still half in a dream, awake but not yet remembering who or where I was. Then it hit me, my eyes flew open, and misery found its way back in. Poor Ben. It didn't seem real.

I dove for my phone and checked texts. Nothing from Derek or Dash. I frowned. Derek would write sooner or later, letting us know the plan for the days going forward. Dash had not followed up to ask how I was. Granted, he had probably been up half the night and must have felt terrible, letting a murderer go free, but I was his girlfriend, and he should have confided that to me.

I sighed and climbed out of bed. The kittens had already risen and had apparently been playing with a toy mouse suspended from a scratching post, but they, too, had been lulled by the warmth, and they lay sleeping in a wide square of sunlight near my fireplace. Annie was once again on her back, her tummy rising and falling with cartoonish cuteness.

I checked the weather on my phone: it was expected to be twenty degrees warmer than yesterday and was already fifty-eight degrees.

"Well, that's a relief," I murmured.

I showered quickly and dressed in jeans and a red sweater.

I kissed the groggy cats and locked them in, then knocked tentatively at Connie's door.

"Zana?"

No answer. She had probably gotten up to make breakfast. I made my way down the staircase, my thoughts darting from Ben to the castle show to the Ibsen play to Dash to Detective Bradley to the catacombs. I made it to the kitchen without noticing anything about my surroundings.

A voice said, "Nora?"

"Hmmm?" I looked up to see Zana and Dorian.

"Would you like some coffee?" Zana asked. "Breakfast is just cold stuff today, but we've got sweet rolls, cereal, oatmeal, stuff like that."

"Thanks. I'll help myself."

I went to the sideboard and poured myself a cup of coffee, then selected a cheese Danish and went to the dining room table. Dorian sat down across from me.

"Any word from Derek?" I asked.

He shook his head. "I can't imagine that the shows won't both be canceled, which means we don't get paid, right?" He looked at me expectantly since I had been in the castle longer than he had.

"Uh—normally Derek keeps paying us. It isn't our fault he has to cancel. But I know that money is tight. . . ."

Suddenly the thought of no paycheck had me feeling truly afraid. I couldn't survive without that check, even with the generous addition of room and board that Derek provided. I was trying to create a nest egg so that if I ever had to leave the castle, I would have enough money to put a security deposit and a month's rent down on an apartment in Chicago. Or perhaps somewhere closer to Wood Glen, since my boyfriend lived there. . . .

"I'm sure Derek will call a meeting today, and we can ask him then," I said.

Dorian said nothing. I realized that for perhaps the first time since I had met him, he was subdued, even quiet. There were dark smudges under his eyes that suggested he had not slept well and something in his eyes that spoke of unhappiness.

"Are you okay?" I asked.

He looked up, surprised. "What?"

"You seem a bit down."

"I'm okay. Thanks for asking, though," he said. Then, just as I was about to consider that he was human after all, he summoned up his sarcastic smile and said, "Have I finally won over the elusive Nora Blake?"

I sighed. "I asked if you were all right, not if you would marry me."

Dorian laughed, displaying his attractive white teeth.

And a condescending smile.

I shook my head and sipped my coffee. The Danish was particularly good, and I was tempted to get another one, but I talked myself out of it.

I took my cup to the sideboard and left after a vague wave to Dorian. Zana had disappeared, and I could hear sounds of her doing dishes in the kitchen.

I wandered, suddenly at a loss, toward the chapel hallway and the front entrance. I saw no sign of the Corby brothers or of my friend Connie. As I tried to think of ways to spend the empty time, I thought of the Small Library, the room I thought of as mine. I could go there and lose myself in books until someone texted me with more information.

As I moved toward the chapel hall, I spied a torn piece of paper on the floor. I picked it up absently, prepared to throw it in the first wastebasket I saw. Then I glanced down at it and saw the word "Genevieve."

It was my sister's name, and it appeared in what seemed to be a poem.

Fair Genevieve,
You may be far away, but parts of you remain
    imprinted on my memory:
The softness of your hand in mine, the startling
    beauty of your smile,
The merry music of your laughter, the sweet garden
    scent of you,
The warmth of your lips when I stole a kiss.
Fair Genevieve, you said we could not be, but part
    of you
Is waiting here with me.

I stared at the words, stunned. I knew that Paul had felt an immediate chemistry with my sister when she'd visited the castle in July, but I had not realized she'd made an impact this large; she had inspired him to poetry.

And I was an intruder when I had not intended to be so. I turned into the chapel hallway, where Paul's office was located, and found his door slightly ajar.

"Paul?"

I went in and found the little room empty. I set the poem on his desk and moved automatically to his side table, on which sat a green bowl that he routinely filled with chocolate for all the sweet-tooth occupants of the castle. I found it full of Rolos today, and I scooped one out automatically. As I did so, I glanced to the side and saw a little framed poem on the wall near Paul's floor-to-ceiling bookshelves.

I moved to it, wondering if this was the verse Paul had referenced at our late-night meal in the kitchen.

The poem, on yellowed paper in a simple wood frame, read:

The source of knowledge, light, and lore
Is just behind a certain door.
And those who would enlightened be
Must find the door they cannot see.

"The door they cannot see," I murmured, intrigued.

Dizzy from the surreal nature of the moment—a series of poems encountered in an empty room inside a giant castle in which a murder had been committed—I left the room and espied Elspeth, Renata, and Miranda emerging from the chapel.

"Hello, Nora," Renata said. "We were looking for you earlier. We were going to invite you to join us in the chapel. We had an impromptu prayer service for Ben."

"Oh, that's good of you. I would have joined, but I'm afraid my growling stomach sent me to the kitchen. And I was just looking for Paul, but he's not there."

Elspeth said, "We were just telling Miranda some stories about Ben."

"From the community theater?" I asked, joining them as they walked back to the main hallway.

"No, more from the bakery." Elspeth looked at Renata. "Renata and I are both addicted to Balfour Bars—have you had one?"

"No. What are they?"

"It's these special brownie-like things they make at Balfour Bakery. Layers of cake and chocolate chips and caramel and more cake and frosting."

"I think there's marshmallow, as well," Renata said.

"Wow. I'll have to try one."

"Yes." Renata nodded. "A chocolate lover's delight. We would go there at least once a week for a bar and a coffee. We sat at one of those little tables in the window, and Ben was often our waiter. He would joke with us about chocolate and how much ladies loved it. It was rather adorable, since Ben clearly had no experience with ladies. He was an innocent," she said, wiping her eyes.

Miranda patted her shoulder and said, "It's just terrible."

I met her eyes and said, "I was sorry to hear you dropped out of the play, although who knows if it will even happen now."

Miranda shrugged. "I realized I had too many irons in the fire. Basically, I was working three jobs, and something had to give."

"Like the one you weren't being paid for?" I joked.

She nodded. "Sad to say, yes."

We paused when we reached the main hallway and Elspeth pulled out her phone. "We got a text from Derek. He says there will be a castle staff meeting at two p.m."

A burst of fear went through me, inexplicable and sudden. Somehow, I didn't want to know what information Derek had for us.

The women with me were murmuring about breakfast, and I said, "They don't have Balfour Bars, but there are some alluring sweet rolls down there."

"Sold," Renata joked. "Coming, Nora?"

I shook my head. "I had breakfast, so I'm going to head up to my room. See you all later."

I waved at them and walked swiftly to the elevator, which was conveniently located just at the end of the main hall, and climbed aboard. When I emerged on the third floor, I heard scrabbling sounds from the Small Library. There was no question about it now—someone, or something, was in there. Slowly, I opened the door and looked inside. Once again, not a living thing was visible, but a chair was pulled away from the table, and a large pile of books had been scattered across its surface.

"Weird," I murmured.

I shut the door and went to my room. I scooped up the Brontës and gave them all kisses on their little noses, then let them sniff my face for a curious moment. I sat on the bed and let them explore while I thought about the library. Yesterday all had been neat and untouched. Today I had heard another noise, but again I had found no one inside, although there was evidence that someone had visited. It was most likely Dorian, since he had expressed an interest in reading books from the shelves. Perhaps the sound was not at all related to the scattered books. It was always possible that we had a raccoon or some other wildlife intruder. Plenty of those animals could climb, and it was certainly possible that a raccoon might have scaled the building in hopes of finding somewhere to nest for the autumn.

The kittens began a fluffy and silent war on the bed, and I left them to their tumbling play. I wandered to the window and looked out, my thoughts troubled by the impossibility of events. Impossible that someone had killed poor Ben Boyle. An "innocent" Renata had called him. Impossible that I kept hearing noises in an empty room. Impossible, too, that Paul could have become so enamored with my sister after meeting her only one time? And impossible, infuriating, that a gulf had risen between Dash and me when I had marveled, mere weeks ago, at our closeness.

I cranked open one of the windows and felt a cool but not cold breeze. I studied the west lawn, so smooth and lovely as it sloped toward the forest, and I was treated to the sight of a fox jumping through the grass. He looked buoyant, bouncy, but I knew that he was being predatory. He was probably after a mouse.

The thought of predators made me feel sick. I lay on my

bed and grabbed the Mary Stewart novel. It was set in the post-WWII era and was blissfully old-fashioned. A young woman, staying with a friend at a French hotel, became fond of a boy who was staying there, as well. The child seemed unhappy, and Charity, the heroine, became embroiled in his affairs to an extreme and dangerous degree.

I was absorbed in the novel when my stomach began to growl, and I realized it was one thirty. I put down my book and glanced out the window where Derek was now grabbing some exercise with Hamlet. Derek threw a ball with impressive athleticism and Hamlet bounded after it like a happy puppy. I smiled, marveling at the idea that a creature so big could think himself so small. I decided to grab a quick sandwich before the meeting; I might need sustenance.

The Brontës had been reading with me. Emily was curled up on my lap, purring. Charlotte lay nestled against my right thigh, and Annie, ever the oddball, was sitting on my shoulder like a parrot.

"I'm hungry, girls. I bet you are, too. And today I think you've earned a treat for giving me feline therapy. Let's go open a can of the wet stuff!"

Alerted by my tone, the kittens had already jumped off the bed and scurried over to their bowls, crying piteously. The bowls were new, a gift from Dash; they were silver with white monogramed names, reading *Charlotte*, *Emily*, and *Annie*. Obviously the cats didn't stick to their assigned bowls, but I appreciated the sentiment of the gift anyway.

I laughed and followed them. I gave them the promised wet food, and they ate daintily, turning now and then to look at me—I liked to think in gratitude.

I left the room, locking the door, and jogged down to the kitchen, where Zana had anticipated the needs of the staffers and left out a buffet of sandwiches, chips, pickles, condiments, and soft drinks. I loaded up a plate and sat with it at the kitchen table, observing Zana.

"Did you get enough sleep?" I asked before taking a huge bite of my sub.

She nodded. "I don't need a ton of sleep, but, Lord, I was tired last night. Connie's bed is comfy, too."

"Do you have to be at the meeting?"

"Yeah." She sat down in the chair next to mine and took one of my chips. "I'm worried there will be layoffs." So Zana, too, had wondered about the effect of that event on an already strapped castle budget.

"Derek wouldn't do that today. Maybe in the future, but not today. That would be tacky, and Derek has class."

"True." Zana still looked nervous. "It's just— I love this job. I get to do my own thing, hang out in a castle. And I have good friends here."

"If he has to fire someone, it should be Dorian or Miranda. They're the lowest on the totem pole."

She studied my face. "You don't like Dorian, do you?"

"No," I admitted. "I feel bad, because there's no specific reason. I just—get a bad vibe from him."

She shook her head. "Give him a chance. He's really funny. He and I hit it off right away, mostly because he's always mooching food down here."

"Maybe that's not why he comes down," I said, raising my eyebrows. "You have made it clear that you're married, right?"

Zana laughed. "It's not like that."

"It might be. You're pretty, and he's . . . predatory."

I thought of the fox, looking so joyful as it pounced on some unsuspecting rodent.

Zana pursed her lips. "Give him a chance," she said again.

Paul jogged in and loaded two plates—one for him, one for Derek—and left again. Connie and Elspeth came in, deep in conversation, followed by Dorian and Miranda.

Finally, Renata strolled in, smiling at me. She came to

sit on my other side and said, "I've had a text from your brothers."

I groaned. "Are they bugging you?"

She laughed. "They are the bright spot of my day. I've told them they should never stop."

I nodded. Luke and Jay had that effect. Despite my complaints about them, I knew that they made people happy. They made me happy. A burst of homesickness overcame me for a moment, but then I was distracted by Dorian, who said, "Is anyone else kind of weirded out by this meeting? Should we bring our lawyers?"

"It's not that kind of meeting," Connie said. "Derek just wants to fill us in on the plans he's been making, mostly to try to anticipate and prevent bad press. He and Dash have been hashing out a—"

"Dash is here?" I asked.

Connie saw my face and said, "Yes, but Derek pulled him into a meeting the moment he got here, and they've been holed up in Derek's office. He hasn't had time to—"

"Has Derek had time to see you?" I asked. My voice sounded cold, and I felt cold.

Connie's face grew red, which answered my question, and she murmured something about how she "barely saw him."

I had no time to ponder the meaning of Dash's refusal to greet me when he had come to the castle because Derek's face appeared in the kitchen doorway.

"Hi, everyone. We'll have our meeting in the dining room, so if you could all just take your plates next door, we'll be ready to start."

Derek disappeared again and Dash replaced him in the doorway, his eyes scanning the room until they found me. Some of my indignation dried up when I saw how tired he was. Clearly, he had not slept all night, and there were purple smudges under his eyes. Compassion welled up in me;

then the beautiful Detective Bradley appeared in the door, looking not tired at all.

She touched Dash's shoulder and said, "John—a quick word?"

Dash nodded and went into the hall.

His companion gave a quick wave to Zana. "Hey, Z!" she called with a smile. Then she disappeared to have a conference with my boyfriend.

Renata's brown eyes were watching me. "Let's go next door," she said. "Later we can talk."

I nodded, miserable, and followed her into the dining room.

8

※

A Haunted Chamber

WE FILED INTO our spots at the dining room table, looking uneasily at one another. Derek and Dash stood against one wall. Detective Bradley was not present.

When we were all in place, Derek said, "Thanks, everyone. I wanted to give you some updates. I know many of us have terrible déjà vu because of what happened a few months ago. I know the similarity is disturbing, but we have to face reality, no matter how dreadful it may be." He cleared his throat.

I had a sudden memory of Ben helping Derek wrestle the Christmas tree onto the stage at the BC. They had laughed, and Ben made some joke about giants. I had felt festive, Christmassy, though it had been only September.

"The castle show will be canceled for the time being. We'll make an announcement to the press and offer rain checks to everyone."

His eyes flicked to the surface of the table. "The play at the Blue Curtain will go on. This is not really my decision.

I've signed contracts with Wood Glen officials to provide this fall event, and they don't want it canceled. The mayor in particular has said he has invited a large group for opening night."

Elspeth made an indignant sound, but Derek held up a hand. "They have every right to make this demand, and our affection for Ben doesn't change the fact that we have an obligation. So we'll continue with rehearsals, starting tomorrow.

"Ben's family said that they would let us know about funeral arrangements. Right now they are still processing the shock. I'll give the floor to Dash now."

Derek stepped away from the table and Dash stepped forward. "The police are very much on top of the investigation. We were all present when Ben died, and I know that you share my desire to have his killer found and punished. The difficult reality is that the killer is most definitely someone we know, and for that reason I need you all to keep your eyes open, to be vigilant about anything that seems suspicious or out of the ordinary. You all know how to reach me; please contact me with anything you think might be noteworthy."

His gaze skimmed over all our faces. "The other concern I want to mention is that the killer deliberately chose the castle as the place for the murder. This was not a momentary crime of passion, but a premeditated murder. Why the castle was selected as the setting remains unclear, but I think it is significant. Again, this means that you are all particularly situated to observe possible clues. I'm not asking anyone to be a detective. In fact, I must insist that you do not try to take that role, but I need you to be wary and remain safe. Don't travel anywhere alone. Walk in pairs or groups. Lock your doors at night."

Connie gasped softly. Dash looked at Zana. "For the

time being, Zana, I think you should plan to stay at your house, even on nights when your job goes long."

Paul said, "There won't be any of those for the foreseeable future. Zana can go home at a reasonable hour each day."

Dash nodded. "Finally, we have once again obtained a warrant to search the castle. We have officers searching your rooms right now along with the catacombs. We did not find the murder weapon last night, but it must be here, and we are determined to find that today."

Again, we sat in silence. How had someone stabbed Ben and then gotten away undetected? How had they managed to dispose of a weapon in the midst of a large group of people and in total darkness? I recalled the chaotic moment, tripping over something, or someone, and landing on Ben's legs. A shiver ran down my arms as I thought of it and the ghostly clinking sound. . . .

"The weapon is in the catacombs," I said with sudden certainty.

Everyone turned to look at me. "I was just thinking of that moment, how chaotic it was, and all the sensations that I experienced before I fully knew what had happened. And I remembered a sort of clanking sound."

"What do you mean?" asked Derek. "Like a weapon falling?"

"Yes, but why did the crime happen when the lights went out?"

Renata was catching on to my line of thought. "Because someone planned to commit a crime when the lights went out. Dash said it was premeditated."

I nodded. "And who knew when and where the lights would go out?"

"Well, all of us," Elspeth said.

"Anyone else?" Dash asked.

Paul looked thoughtful. "The theater group from Blue

Curtain knew, too. Derek led them through a simulation in advance because some of the members feared it would be too scary."

Dash had taken out his phone and was making swift notes, his thumbs moving.

I closed my eyes. "The way I remember it, something fell, but it fell kind of distantly. And we were all supposed to pause at that spot in the catacombs where there's a sort of beam across the ceiling and a hidden light switch by the left-hand skull. But there's something else right there; I noticed it because I was feeling a cold breeze."

"The vent," murmured Paul.

"There's a vent in the wall?"

Derek nodded. "Well camouflaged since there should be nothing modern in a crypt."

Dash finished typing and looked up at us. His sleepy look was gone, and now his hazel eyes were filled with something like triumph. "Nora, everyone, thank you. This is exactly what I mean about how you can help the police."

He held up a hand and moved swiftly out of the dining room. "Meeting dismissed," Derek said. "You're all free until rehearsal tomorrow at the BC."

He and Paul followed in John Dashiell's wake, and the rest of us sat in silence. Although no one mentioned Ben's name, I knew that we were all thinking of him, and the fact that someone, in twenty seconds of darkness, had pulled a knife from—where: a shirtsleeve, a pocket?—and plunged it into Ben's back, then moved swiftly to the wall where they had seen the vent (or searched for it)? And slid the weapon through the bars. Then they had bolted forward (or backward?) and blended in with the crowd so that he or she could be just as shocked as everyone else that Ben did not get up again after he fell, that blood was gathering around him on the stone floor. . . .

"Are you all right?" Renata asked, her hand touching my arm.

"Yes, thanks." I patted her hand with a grateful look. "But I think I'm going to take a walk."

I stood up, saw that people were still absorbed in their own thoughts, and left the room.

There was a coat closet near the main entrance, and Derek let us stow some of our cold-weather attire in there. I strode to it now and found my long autumn sweater-coat, pausing for a moment to breathe in the scent of Dash's familiar corduroy jacket. I donned the sweater and walked determinedly outside, bound for the woods. A few deep breaths of the cold air and I was already feeling better, healthier in mind and body. The sun was warm, and fall scents were in the air. Two large apple trees flanked the path that I took toward the western woods; some of the ripe yellow-gold apples had fallen on the ground, and I picked up a fat one. After a quick check for any bug intruders, I polished it on my sweater and took a bite. It was cold and delicious, and I munched it as I walked along, trying to banish any thoughts of murder.

My footfalls were quiet when I moved from the rutted path to the forest floor, but then my tread was silent, cushioned by moss and rotted leaves. Only the occasional snap of a twig might have alerted the local wildlife that I was in the vicinity.

I moved, following a well-trodden path that castle dwellers had taken before—perhaps even Philip Corby himself, the man who had envisioned and built a castle in a rural spot in Illinois. What had Corby really wanted from his dream of a castle? Had it met his expectations when it was finally built? And had he really hidden treasure somewhere within its walls? He had taken the time to compose a poem, something to intrigue the creative mind. He had been a patient man; the castle, Derek had told me, had taken seven years to construct. Had Corby been content to leave treasure to sit untouched over many years, even after his death, in the hopes that someone would one day find it? My path jogged slightly, and I rounded a giant elm to come face-to-face with a buck, his regal head crowned by a pair of giant antlers. He had just peeled some bark from a tree; I could see part of it jutting out of his mouth, but after a few motions of his strong jaw, the bark disappeared. He chewed meditatively, considering me while he enjoyed his lunch. I didn't dare breathe. I had seen deer from far away, usually through my window, but I'd never been this close to one in my life. I was transfixed by the size of him, and by the antlers that seemed nature's way of showing his strength and dominance.

Slowly, I reached for the phone in my pocket and, as unobtrusively as possible, put it into camera mode. I lifted the phone, half fearing the buck would charge me and gore me to death with his antlers. Instead, he turned back to the tree and ripped off another piece of bark. He might as well have shrugged at me; I was not considered a threat.

I took pictures, as many as I could, trying to make no sound at all.

After he munched his second meal, he pondered me again. Then, to the surprise of us both, he sneezed, and I smothered a laugh.

"Bless you," I whispered.

He made a snorting sound, and I wondered if a bug had flown up his nose. He lifted his head, shook his giant antlers, and then turned on the path, moving in an unhurried fashion down the mossy track and eventually into the undergrowth. Five minutes later, and it was as if he'd never been there.

My grandmother, who had been something of a naturalist, had always told me that every animal encounter was a special thing, a meeting of souls that was both inexplicable and important. "Animals have messages for us. It's up to us to interpret those messages and to receive the blessings that they bring."

My parents had told me to take her words with a grain of salt, but I had always been struck by them, and I did consider any encounter with a wild animal to be an almost enchanted moment.

And that was how one deer, with majestic antlers and a gentle manner, replenished my spirit, my courage, and my good humor. I hiked jubilantly back to the castle, excited to share my pictures with someone who might appreciate them. I revisited the apple trees, where Zana was gathering the fallen fruit in a basket.

"Good for pies," she called.

I had left my apple core for the deer in our secret spot. I waved at Zana, saying, "I look forward to the pie."

She laughed, and I traveled around the castle to the south entrance, where the naiad watched over the fountain, still plashing gently in the fall air. Paul sat at the table, typing something on an iPad.

"Hey," I said.

"You seem happy today."

"I'm euphoric. Do you want to see some amazing pictures?"

"I do," he said with a smile.

I bounded over to the table and took out my phone, then found the first photo and held it out to him. "Swipe right," I said.

He did, again and again, his brows near his hairline. "I can't believe you got this close. What a beautiful animal."

I nodded. "There's no hunting around here, right?"

"Not on castle grounds. We have signs posted, and the local officials are pretty good about monitoring and checking permits. Derek tries to encourage the deer we have to stay in the safe woods by putting out salt licks and various other deer-friendly treats."

"He is a soft touch." I marveled at the depths of Derek, a man I was still getting to know.

"He is. A good man. And a good brother." He cleared his throat. "I suppose it was you who put the poem on my desk?"

I blushed and nodded. "I didn't mean to pry. It was lying in the hall, and I saw her name, so I thought it was yours."

"It is."

"I didn't realize—how deep it went. You were together for such a short time. . . ."

"I know. It defies logic." Another brief, pained smile. "Anyway, thanks for keeping it out of the public view."

"Sure."

We sat together, contemplating the fountain and its mythological protector.

"It's a little cold for the fountain, isn't it?" I asked.

Paul nodded. "We usually turn off the timer on October first. Things have sort of gotten away from us."

"Yeah."

I watched some more. The water's gentle music was somehow mournful.

"I bought some sheet music," Paul said.

"You did?" My spirits soared again.

"Yeah. Stuff I was hoping to hear you sing."

Derek had a beautiful Steinway on the second floor, one of the best discoveries I'd ever made in the castle. He had worked my playing and singing into our last show, but lately I hadn't been finding as many excuses to go and play it.

"Oh, God, I could use some piano therapy right now."

Now Paul looked excited, too. "Let's go."

We stood up and moved swiftly to the rear entrance of the castle; Paul let us in, and we jogged up the back stairs to the second floor. Paul was striding to the piano, his right hand clamped on my sleeve. Like me, Paul loved to sing. He had confided months earlier that he was a fan of not only opera, but also of musicals and classical pieces. We reached the piano, and I spied a stack of sheet music sitting on top.

"Where did you find it?" I asked, sorting greedily through the pile.

"I picked it up when I went to Chicago."

"Ah." I held up a printed song and made a wry face at Paul. "Let me guess what you were thinking about when you went music shopping."

The song was "Love of My Life" by Queen.

"It's just a great song," he said, and I couldn't argue with that.

It was gorgeous. I was already on the bench, limbering my fingers on the keys.

"Sing with me," I said.

Paul shook his head. "I want to hear you sing this one."

He leaned on the piano and closed his eyes, and I began to sing, very softly, about the love of my life who had deserted me. It was impossible to capture the sweet, perfect melancholy that Freddie Mercury had given to the song, so I tried to give it my own spin. I thought of Dash, and our perfect August together, and Paul and Gen and every lover who somehow couldn't make things work.

When I finished, my eyes were closed and brimming with tears.

"Beautiful," he said in a husky voice.

Derek and Dash appeared then, emerging from the office in Derek's room, just down the hall from the piano. They approached us now. Dash's hazel eyes seemed locked onto mine, and his expression was almost sad.

They reached us and stood, hesitating. The air was charged with tension, whether caused by my song or something else, I could not determine.

Then Dash spoke, and the spell was broken. "We found the murder weapon," he said.

FOR A BLANK hour, I drifted around the castle, restless but unwilling to connect with anyone. Dash had said they located the murder weapon, but he hadn't said exactly what they found. Surely it had been a knife? We had heard no gunshot and Ben hadn't been strangled because that would not have caused bleeding. A part of me was curious, but another part was horrified just by the idea of a weapon. Finally, I went back up to my room, where I played in silence with the Brontës and then lay on my back on the floor, reading my book, which was becoming more and more suspenseful. The Brontës climbed on my stomach, and they nestled there for a nap.

Eventually a knock at the door roused me from my novel. "Yes?"

Connie peered in. "*Here* you are! I looked for you earlier and you weren't here, but you weren't anywhere else, either. I heard you singing a few hours ago and I finished my knitting and went to sing with you, but you were gone. Are you avoiding me?"

"No." I raised my brows at her. "Go back to the part about the knitting."

She bounded into the room, shutting the door behind her, then sat in front of me with her legs in the lotus position. "Renata and Elspeth are teaching me to knit. I want to make a sweater for Derek, for Christmas."

"That's really ambitious," I said.

"Yeah, but they said I'm doing well. It's a gorgeous blue yarn that will go with his eyes."

I wondered what sort of yarn would accentuate the eyes of John Dashiell.

"Anyway," Connie said, "everyone's kind of at a loss, so

I'm hosting a board-game gathering in my room. I stole a few of them from the recreation room, so we can vote on what we play. Zana said dinner will be portable, so we can bring our food up here."

I yawned. "That sounds nice. I have the problem of these cats, though."

Connie laughed and scooped them up, one at a time, relocating them to my bed.

"Ugh, I'm so stiff," I moaned. "I shouldn't have stayed in that position for so long." I stood up and rolled my neck.

I fed the cats their dinner and wandered over to Connie's to find that everyone else was already there—Elspeth, Renata, Dorian, and Miranda. Zana appeared a moment later, carrying a giant pizza box.

"There's another one downstairs," she said. "Compliments of Charlie Montini at Montini's Pizza. He and Derek are friends, and this is his way of showing support. So Zana got out of making dinner," she said with a grin.

"Well, you're not getting out of board-game night," Connie said firmly.

I laughed. "Connie, it's chilly in here. I'm going to run back and get my sweater."

I opened the door and Dorian called, "Come back, Nora! I'll keep you warm."

That was outrageous, but I had come to realize that Dorian wanted a reaction; he would have loved nothing better than if I had screamed at him or demanded an apology or reported him to Derek. He liked things chaotic.

Fuming quietly, I crossed to my room. A faint sound, a sort of sliding, scuffling sound, came from the Small Library. Suddenly fed up with both Dorian and whoever this intruder might be, I walked to the door and flung it open, turned on the light, then stood staring in disbelief. The room was entirely empty, but a tiny shred of paper was floating down toward the floor, light as a snowflake, eventually landing on the ground. The room had no windows, nor was there a fan, yet the paper was moving all by itself, as if by magical means.

Or supernatural ones.

9

Balfour Bakery

THE GAMES LASTED until well after midnight. Derek and Paul had come up for a final round, and then Derek had said pointedly that he needed to be fresh for rehearsals tomorrow, and that broke up the revelry.

When I got up the next day, I showered and put on some blue sweatpants and a Harvard sweatshirt my mother had purchased at a yard sale. I laced into my running shoes and set the kittens on the windowsill.

"Look at the leaves falling," I said.

Ever amenable, they did so, patting the glass with tiny and tentative paws.

I left my room and went to the second floor to find Derek. The door to his room was half open. I knocked on it and he called, "Come in!"

He was behind his desk, reading some mail and eating a piece of toast. The front part of his apartment was like a little office, and his desk faced the door. Beyond that space was his private suite.

"Derek, do you have a minute?" I asked.

He beamed. "Of course. Would you like some coffee?"

"No, I'm going down for breakfast in a second. I just wanted to ask—"

Connie wandered in from a back room, wearing a baby doll nightgown and rubbing her eyes. Her hair was rumpled but somehow sexy, and her expression was calm. She looked extremely—satisfied.

"Hi, Nora," she said, moving to Derek and sliding onto his lap.

Derek wore the dumb, euphoric expression of a man visited by an angel.

"Are you competing with me for Derek's affection?" she asked lightly. "Like I don't have enough competition from the beautiful Priscilla."

Derek waved that assertion away with a casual hand and fed Connie a corner of his toast.

"Blech," I said.

Connie laughed. "People need love, Nora." She gazed at Derek. "A lot of love in some cases."

"Okay, I should probably come back later after the hormones calm down."

Derek looked rueful. "I'm sorry. What did you want to talk to me about?"

He pushed Connie off of his lap with some reluctance, and she sighed theatrically. "I'll go get dressed," she said. She disappeared down the hall whence she had come.

Derek smiled at me. "I'm all yours."

"Okay—the thing is, last night I went into the Small Library. I've been hearing weird noises in there—"

"What kind of noises?" He was alert now.

"I don't know. I always think there's a person moving around in there, but there never is. So either the heating pipes are noisy, or there's an animal or something."

"Please, not an animal," he said under his breath.

"Last night I heard something again." I told him about the paper and its inexplicable floating.

He rubbed his jaw, thinking about this. "The paper tells me there's a hole somewhere, and a hole tells me there could be an animal. I'll need to get some guys out here to look at the roof. God, I hope we don't have rats. They're impossible to remove from what I've heard."

"Ick. I hope it's not rats, too. I never even thought—"

"Let's not get ahead of ourselves. I'll make a call. Thanks for letting me know, Nora."

"Sure. And sorry. You have enough going on."

"I told Paul sometimes I feel the way an actual lord of the manor must have felt. So many responsibilities." He grinned. "But I also kind of love that image." Derek was honest about his occasional egotism, which was ultimately endearing.

"I'll leave you to your amorous girlfriend."

I turned away to the sound of his laughter, but then he said, "Nora."

"Hmm?"

"I'm glad we are still doing the Ibsen play. I think it's going to be a great production and I think your Kristine is quite good. Nuanced and moving. I'm so glad I got you to take the role."

My face grew warm with the unexpected compliment.

"And I'd like to say that I have rarely worked with such a generous director. You really are a talented man, Derek."

Now it was his turn to blush. "Thank you, Nora," he said, looking at his hands.

I SAW MIRANDA on the first floor gliding in her serene way toward the front entrance.

She waved at me. "We're going to town for breakfast. Come with us."

The idea of leaving the castle was suddenly very appealing. "Okay. Who's 'we'?"

We reached the main entrance, and she pointed to the steps, where Elspeth and Renata waited with placid expressions.

"Oh, fun," I said. "Is this a girls-only jaunt?"

"Absolutely," said Renata. "I'll drive."

We were soon on our way, Renata navigating smoothly up the twisting driveway that eventually connected with Apprehension Road.

"I still can't get over that name," I said, squinting at the street sign through bright sunlight. "Does anyone know its origins?"

"No. I never thought about it," Elspeth said. "It is weird, though. Nora, you always notice the little things."

"So where are we dining this morning?" Miranda asked in her quiet voice.

"We thought we'd go to Balfour Bakery. In honor of Ben, I suppose." Renata's face, visible in the rearview mirror, looked thoughtful, sober.

"Do you think they'll even be open?"

"Jade told me they'd be opening today. They have a business to run. People want to stop life from moving on when someone dies, but they can't. It's a good thing and a bad thing."

We thought about Renata's words in silence as she drove into downtown Wood Glen. The town was decked with the obligatory haystacks and storefront scarecrows, with pots of marigolds and autumn-leaf garlands lining doors and windows. The small pine trees that lined the central parkway were lit with white lights that would stay on through Christmas. For now they merely conveyed a sense of fall and festivity.

There was an oak tree in front of Balfour Bakery, under which were a few tables for patrons. A few people sat at the tables, drinking coffee and munching pastries while reading the paper or, in one case, listening to an audiobook. I knew, because as we parked across the street, I heard a loud "Chapter twenty" intoned by a deep voice. The listener looked around guiltily and plugged in her earphones.

A large green ribbon was tied around the trunk of the tree, and other green ribbons hung in every window of Balfour. I noticed then that every merchant on the street had hung a green ribbon.

"Those must be for Ben," Elspeth whispered.

I would at that moment have thought that Wood Glen was the sweetest, loveliest, most wholesome little rural town if I had not witnessed two violent deaths since I had come to the castle in June. How could something like those crimes have happened there?

I was still pondering this question as we entered the little bakery and Renata led us to a table in the sunny window. Jade and her father were behind the counter, and Jade waved.

Soon she was at our table, looking solemn but not exhausted. She had not lost sleep over this, and I was glad to realize it.

"What can I get you guys?" she asked, pushing her black glasses higher on her little nose. "Do you all want coffee?"

"Tea for me, please," I said.

Miranda said she would also like tea. Jade nodded.

"Two coffees, two teas. Did you want to try my dad's egg pasties? Yummy breakfast, and they just came out of the oven. You can get them with bacon or without."

"That sounds fantastic," I said. "And I'll have bacon. Apologies to the vegetarians at the table."

Renata looked surprised. "Do we have any of those?"

Miranda raised her hand. "I am. But I don't mind if you eat bacon. I'll have a plain egg one."

Renata and Elspeth ordered, and Jade moved off.

"But everyone save room for donuts," Elspeth said. "That's the specialty here." She turned to Jade's father and waved. "Smells amazing in here as always," she said. "You're the best, Brian."

He nodded and waved his thanks, then moved into the back room on some errand.

Jade returned minutes later with our hot beverages, then came back moments after that with our pasties.

"Do you have a minute to pull up a chair?" I asked.

Jade looked around the room. There was only one other patron inside, a woman with a baby, and she seemed content to smile at her child while she slowly drank a cup of coffee. The baby's little legs kicked happily in the high chair and once in a while it made a little raspberry. The mother laughed every time.

One of the people outside had already left, and the other two looked absorbed in their chosen entertainments.

"Yeah, I guess so," Jade said. She pulled a chair from another table and sat at the end of ours.

"This pasty is amazing," I said with my mouth full. "Wow. So buttery."

"Butter is the secret to all flavor," Renata said. "But I speak as a woman who grew up with her mother's delicious baking and often visited Germany, with its torts and strudels."

I smiled, and Jade managed a little grin.

"Are the green ribbons for Ben?" I asked.

She nodded. "We wanted to do something for him. We still just— We can't believe it. I mean, I didn't often work the same shift as him, but he worked here for almost two years. We knew each other. We were friends. And he was such a lovable dork. How this happened"—she shook her head, not so much with sadness as with disbelief—"I do not know. No one does."

"It's terrible," Miranda said. "He was just a kid, wasn't he? Twenty or something?"

"He was twenty-five," Jade said. "He looked young." She turned to me. "I'm really glad you called me about his animals. We had a spare key to his place, which is just a couple blocks away. Those apartments on Alder. Do you know he had a whole menagerie? I knew he had a dog or two, but I went in there and found two dogs, a cat, a turtle, and a fish. He took in every stray. Well, I guess the fish wasn't a stray." She smiled at her joke. "And he just had this little tiny place, but it was neat and clean, and the animals had clean food and water bowls. They're all healthy and happy."

"What's going to happen to them?" I asked.

"We're working on it. My friend Shana has a huge fish tank. Her dad looked at the fish and said it was fine to put with the other population. So they dumped it in there, and she said it seems really happy. Ben just had it in a little bowl with the ol' castle, but now it's in this, like, underwater city with about twenty other fish."

"That's good."

"Right now we have the dogs, the cat, and the turtle. My mom has said that she was not going to take on all those pets since we already have several cats, but the problem is we can't decide which ones to rehome. The dogs are super well trained and both really cute. Just mutts but adorable. The cat is like a little dog himself—an orange tabby with a super-affectionate attitude. He sits on my dad all night, so of course my dad wants to keep him. My mom has taken to the dogs, and everyone loves the turtle. He's hilarious. He plays with the other animals, and he's, like, this drama queen. If the others get fed before he does, he gets this look on his face like he's some reincarnated king. It cracks me up. So noble and infuriated. Sometimes the cat sits on his shell, and he just sits there blinking like he enjoys it."

"Sounds like you have some new family," Renata said.

"I don't know. They certainly aren't a problem so far, and obviously Ben took such good care of them—" Tears filled her eyes then, surprising her, and she shook her head. "Sorry," she murmured, wiping her eyes. "I don't know where that came from."

I leaned over and hugged her against my side. "It's hard. There's no getting over it in an instant. You just have to walk the miles."

"Yeah. That's true." She let out a shuddering sigh. "His family is coming today. They're going to make the arrangements. It's just his mom and his sister. I feel so bad for them."

Jade's father returned and saw Jade at our table. He walked over and greeted us. I had never actually met him before.

"I'm Nora," I said, shaking his hand.

"Ah," he said, smiling. "Jade has told me all about you."

Miranda introduced herself, as well.

"I understand you have a new cat," I said.

He grinned. "His name is Tiger, and we are best friends. My wife is offended because she thought she was my best friend, but no—turns out it's this cat."

We laughed. He scratched his arm with an absent air. "You all been talking about Ben?"

We nodded.

"He was a good kid." He cleared his throat and scratched his arm again, uncomfortable with his own grief. "What they're going to find at the end of this is that there was no motive. It was just someone insane who wanted to be violent. Ben just happened to be there. You mark my words. That poor kid died for nothing."

AFTER JADE AND her father left our table, I said, "You know, I lived in downtown Chicago for ten years and a nearby suburb before that. I never knew someone who was killed, and I certainly never witnessed a murder. Then I came to this idyllic little town, and—"

"It's crazy," said Elspeth. "And I swear, Nora, before June, there really was no violence here."

Renata had been looking thoughtful. "There's a problem," she said, "with the whole investigation."

"What's that?" Miranda asked, tearing another piece off of her pasty.

"We have a boy who had no enemies. He is killed, and everyone around him says there is no motive. We come to his place of work, where everyone loved him and said there could be no possible motive. So we have a murdered boy and no motive for murdering him."

I nodded. "That's true. But keep in mind that Ben could have been the nicest person in the world and still have had an enemy. Maybe even an enemy he didn't know about? Who knows why people hold grudges? What bothers me is that person has to be someone we know. Aside from a couple of people from the theater club that I didn't recognize, I knew everyone in that room. So did all of you. How do we come to terms with that?"

Miranda looked at me; for the first time, I realized that she had two different-colored eyes: one blue and one brown. For some reason it did not look strange, but it did make her distinctive and somehow lovelier for the difference.

Renata shook her head. "Your boyfriend needs to find the killer soon. We all need to breathe easily again. I feel as though I've been holding my breath since the night Ben died."

This brought silence again, and I decided it was time for a subject change. I faced Elspeth and Renata. "Connie told me you're teaching her to knit, that she's making Derek a Christmas present."

Elspeth nodded. "You know, I didn't think she would have the patience, but she's doing quite well."

"Well, what if I want to learn to knit?"

Elspeth smiled. "We always have room for more students. You, too, Miranda, if you want."

Miranda smiled and shook her head. "No time, I'm afraid. Plus, I've always been dreadful at needle arts."

Elspeth smiled at me. "And do you want to make your boyfriend a sweater, Nora?"

"Maybe," I said, feeling sulky.

Miranda turned to me. "Who's your boyfriend?"

I stared at her, surprised. I thought everyone in the castle knew my history with Dash. But Miranda had been there such a short time, and she was always gone. . . .

"She's going out with the cop," Elspeth said with a satisfied expression. "The dreamy one who ran our meeting."

Miranda's brows rose. "You're going out with him?" She turned to Elspeth, nodding in confirmation. "You're right. He is dreamy."

My smile was wry, but I was saved from the necessity of responding by the arrival of Renata, who had slipped away moments earlier; now she bore a variety of donuts on a platter and said, "My treat."

I selected a Boston cream and took a huge bite, hoping the conversation would flow on around me, which it did. The custard in the pastry was so delicious that it brought me brief comfort. "Food is love," my brothers always joked when they took second and third helpings. And Zana insisted that food was comfort. Perhaps they were all right. If so, this was Renata's way of showing affection, and I smiled at her and patted my tummy. She laughed.

In that instant I was struck by how pretty Renata really was. I had always found her rather stern-looking, but when she laughed, I could see her excellent bone structure, her even white teeth, the attractive wrinkles around her eyes. Her hair was still brown and glossy, though she was in her early fifties, and I realized why the mysterious man in town wanted to date her, and why his ex, Barbara, resented her.

I lost track of what the others were saying as I let my thoughts drift and ate my treat in silence. Once I was finished, I contemplated just how much pastry and sugar I'd consumed; I was incredibly full.

"I have to get up and walk," I said finally. "I'm stuffed."

Miranda looked at her watch. "Yeah, I've got to get going. Thanks for introducing me to the bakery, though."

We stood up and began to make our way toward the door. The bill for everything, Renata assured us, had already been paid. We offered her our thanks, and Jade appeared. She pointed at a bucket near the door, where a variety of flowers sat in six inches of water. "You can grab one on your way out if you want to leave one at Ben's memorial."

I wasn't sure what she meant but I selected a pink rose and moved out to the large tree and its green ribbon. Only from that vantage point did I see the little plaque—Ben's picture decoupaged onto a wooden board along with a touching tribute in an elegant font:

> *In memory of Benjamin John Boyle, aged twenty-five. Devoted son and brother and friend to all. Ben, we will remember you.*

The picture of Ben had clearly been taken at the Blue Curtain. It was a slightly blurry and heartbreaking shot of Ben goofing around, his head thrown back, his hair rumpled. He wore a huge smile and he looked about six years old.

Wiping away tears, I set my flowers in a vase in front of the tree, then signed a visitors' book that the Balfours had put on a little table nearby. This gesture of love and respect was more moving to me than perhaps a full funeral mass would have been. Just people who loved him acknowledging him with silent affection. There were already at least twenty blooms in the large vase, and by the time we four left, it was bulging with flowers.

10

The Mysterious Mr. Corby

WE RECEIVED A text from Derek during our drive home:

> Elspeth and Allie have completed the tentative
> costumes for the production. Please see them
> today between ten and twelve for your fitting.
> Lunch at noon, then BC rehearsal.

"I guess I'd better get my butt up to the fitting room," Elspeth joked. "I assume Allie is already there."

Allie Fisher was the other costume designer for the production; she taught home economics at Wood Glen High School, and she loved collaborating with Elspeth. They had worked together, Elspeth told us proudly, on five productions.

When we reached the castle, Renata let us out at the door and drove on to the small parking lot against the building. I climbed up the stairs, hoping to work off some of the thousands of calories I had just consumed. I went into my room, saw that the Brontës were sleeping in a gray heap on the windowsill, and tiptoed to the bathroom to comb my hair and wash my face.

Then I moved down the hall to the costume room. Elspeth and Allie were deep in conversation, staring at a piece of silk and admiring it in the way only a seamstress could. Allie looked up at me and smiled. She was fortyish, with red curls and a face full of freckles.

"Hey, Nora! I hear you're rocking the role of Kristine. Els and I are going to make you look very modest and Norwegian, but with just a touch of rebellion."

"Good. Kristine has hidden depths," I said with a grin.

Allie nodded. "Okay, here's the thing. There's nothing in Ibsen's stage directions about Kristine's clothing, other than that she's wearing traveling clothes. But many productions put her in widow's weeds."

"Funny," I said, "since Kristine tells Nora she didn't love her husband and he died three years earlier."

Elspeth snorted. "I have some issues with that costuming. Why would people assume that a widow would wear black for three years? Was that really the social expectation?"

"I don't know. If it was, it reinforces Ibsen's idea that these women lived in an oppressive society."

My gaze traveled over the costume room, with its brightly colored dresses and suits, its masks and boas and hats and shoes. How glad I was that I could shed all the personas except my own.

"So we decided to go with a black skirt, with a nod toward that oppressive expectation," Allie said. She held up a long black skirt, attractive but simple in what seemed a cotton blend. "But we decided on this nice blouse and— wait for it"—she turned around to a little table full of prop jewelry and swung back with a pretty pearl and black cameo—"this!"

"Oh, I love it. Kristine probably wore it as a memento of her late mother," I extemporized. I loved to build backstory with the costumers.

Elspeth stepped forward with a nubby coat in an unusual shade of green. "And we thought we'd add a spot of color with this traveling coat. Muted but pretty."

"I love it. You two have such vision. I know Derek will appreciate these choices."

They nodded; clearly they were confident, as well.

"Now, we still need Kristine's outfits for Acts Two and Three. We'll have those ready tomorrow. We're thinking we'll do up that long dark hair in a kind of pretzel braid, and we'll weave in those silver highlights. In Act One, Derek says they should lend her a look of exhaustion. But by Act Three, they will make her look enchanting."

"Exactly," I said. "The ironic reversal. It will be the beautiful Nora Helmer who looks tired and haggard by then."

They led me to the jewelry table to show me their choices for Connie's costumes, and a voice behind us said, "Am I interrupting?" It was Miranda.

Elspeth looked surprised. "No, but—I was under the impression—"

"Oh, I'm not here for a fitting," she said, "But my room's right across, and I wanted to see some of the costumes. Is that okay?"

"Of course, doll," Allie said. She had swept another costume off the rack and was removing some pins from the hem.

We crowded around it. "Is this for Connie's first scene?" I asked.

"Yes! And look at the coat she comes in with," Elspeth said. "I got it at the antiques shop."

She held up a black woolen coat with gray fur cuffs and collar and a matching gray fur muff.

"Ohhh," I breathed. "Connie will loooove this."

We four admired the perfection of the coat and muff for a moment, stroking the faux fur and picturing the outfit on the stage.

"Are you girls drooling over clothes?" Dorian asked, sounding bored.

Allie turned. "Yes, we are. And yours is nothing to drool over, I'm afraid. You're poor, and you've been struggling for a decade. So Els and I went for a simple pair of dark pants, a slightly raggedy-looking shirt, and a gray vest. Derek wants it to underscore your unhealthy look. We're going to give your skin a kind of gray tone, too."

To my surprise, Dorian perked up. "Good. Make me look old and haggard. But I would tone down the gray in Act Three when I find happiness again."

"Yeah. Like Nora said, that's the ironic reversal. The makeup will underscore that."

We chatted some more about the imminent performance. I peeked at my phone, checking for texts, but found nothing.

"Nora, one more thing," Elspeth said. "I asked Derek for permission to give Kristine just a little sparkle on Christmas Day—nothing to suggest she is wasteful or vain. He let me indulge in these tiny earrings. He says she may well have worn them on Christmas."

I saw a twinkling and set down my phone, reaching for the bits of starshine. "These can't be real diamonds?" I asked.

Elspeth laughed. "Cubic zirconia. But they were pretty expensive. We bought them back when—well, when I had a slightly larger budget."

"Ah." I studied the earrings in my palm, wondering how Kristine would have felt wearing them, back home again after ten years, hoping for a new start. . . .

"I'm here!" Connie yelled, bustling in with her puppy-like energy. "Let's see these costumes."

Allie laughed. "Nora, you can try yours on in that fitting room. Tell me if anything needs adjusting. Connie, let me show you what we've got for Mrs. Helmer. . . ."

When I left twenty minutes later, I felt buoyed by the energy of the rest of the cast. The room was filled with people who were ready to collaborate on a production, to share a vision that was born in 1879 with Ibsen himself. We were starting to feel the thrill of the drama, despite our terrible loss.

I went straight down to lunch; despite my large breakfast, I was feeling the need for some protein and hoped to find one of Zana's sub sandwiches. As soon as I peeked in the kitchen, I saw Zana there washing some dishes and talking on her phone. I moved into the dining room and saw a cold buffet, the sort that people could come and get at any time. I filled a little plate and peered in once more at Zana. She was still talking on the phone, so I wandered out with my plate and decided to bother Paul. Connie and I routinely harassed him in his office, and he was always gracious and sometimes even glad for the distraction. He would say, "Oh, no, it's the chocoholics," or "Here come the dessert desperadoes," or something else he made up on the spot.

I reached his office and peeked in. He was frowning at a printout in his hand.

"Hey," I said.

He put it down and smiled. "Hey."

"There's lunch in case you're interested."

"Have a seat. Want some chocolate?"

"No. We had breakfast at Balfour Bakery." I held up my plate. "So of course, I'm eating again."

"It won't do you any harm."

He kept his eyes on my face; I happened to know that

Dorian, after the same words, would have let his gaze travel over my body. And that was a crucial distinction.

"Are you busy? I can bug you later," I said,

"No, it's fine. I'm finished with these reports, so I probably will stretch my legs in a few minutes."

"I know things are . . . challenging right now."

He sighed. "Yeah. But life is all challenge."

I thought about this. "That's true. And daunting."

He shrugged.

"I hate to repeat an idea that Dorian had"—Paul laughed, and I continued—"but did you and Derek ever consider pursuing the idea that the poem from your great-great-uncle Philip might be literal?" I pointed at the little framed verse on the wall.

"The door they cannot see?" Paul said, smiling. "We thought about it, as I said. When we first got the castle and had some renovations done, we found some of those hidden passages. I suppose there could be more. But even the hunting would be expensive, and we don't have extra funds right now."

We sat in silence for a moment, and Paul said, unsmiling, "I should probably tell you—"

Oh, God, he's going to fire me, I thought with a pounding heart.

"—that Derek is thinking of selling the piano."

"Oh, no!" I cried. He might as well have told me that Derek was going to euthanize one of my family members.

"It's getting to that point. We've got a couple of irons in the fire, some feelers from a couple of production companies who might film something here. If those work out, the old Steinway is safe."

"I know I'm being selfish," I said. "It's not mine. It's his to do with what he wants, and of course he must do what he needs to do." I felt, absurdly, on the verge of tears.

Paul nodded. "I told him I'd rather he sell any of the other antiques before that one. He knows we both love it."

"I'm being silly. Ignore me. And don't tell Derek I acted like a child."

"You didn't. You acted like a woman who loves music and who has been befriending a piano."

"You're sweet," I said. "Tell me more about Uncle Philip while I eat my grapes."

He leaned back in his chair. "Derek and I have talked about him a lot. He was eccentric, yes, and some people probably thought he had one screw loose. But I think he was actually creative, maybe even a Renaissance man. He had so many interests and so much money to pursue them. He had two advanced degrees—in engineering and I think philosophy. There's a journal of his in a museum in Chicago. We viewed it online, and it says that he loved chess, all puzzles, and a woman named Kelsey, whom he never married but who I think lived here with him until he died. He was very generous with his money—gave to many local charities. He was a shrewd investor always, and no matter how much he gave away, he seemed to make more."

"I'll bet you guys wish *you* had that problem."

Paul laughed. "Yeah. But Derek and I think we share a lot with Uncle Phil. You know we're both creative souls. We love the castle, we love drama and music and literature, and we're also both very mathematical."

"You must have aced your SATs," I mused.

Paul grinned. "We got identical SAT results. People thought we cheated."

"But you just have similar brains."

"We do." He stood up and stretched, then said, "Walk me to the kitchen. Your grapes look good, and I'm going to get a plate of my own. It will be a long rehearsal today, I think."

"I hope I get to run lines with you. Dorian doesn't have

the empathy to play Krogstad the way you do, and I've barely gotten to work with you."

"True. I've been bugging Derek about it. Priscilla is chafing for more stage time, as well. Understudies need practice, too."

"You're no understudy," I said to Paul, and he sent me an appreciative glance.

"It was better for this production. And Dorian is good in his way."

"Yeah."

"You don't like him," he observed, looking at my face.

We stepped into the hall and he locked his door.

"He's okay. We're not going to be best friends or anything."

We walked companionably back to the kitchen and found Connie, Dorian, and Miranda in the adjoining dining room.

"Nora, I was just looking for you. Did you come from upstairs?" Connie said. "I wanted to tell you that your phone was in the costume room." She held it up. "You sure are fast, because I just heard you up there!"

"What?"

"I heard you in your room, and I called and asked if you wanted to go downstairs with me, but you didn't answer. Your door was open, so I figured you'd be out in a minute."

I stared at her blankly. "My door? Not the Small Library?"

Connie spoke patiently. "Your door," she said. "The one across from mine."

I looked at Paul and said, "I haven't been up there in half an hour."

I set my plate down on the table, and Paul and I ran up to my room. We got there out of breath (I more so than Paul), and I said, "God, I hope the kittens didn't get—"

We swept through my slightly open door, and in a rush

of relief, I saw the Brontës stretched out on my bed like a pride of lions, looking at us with affectionate disdain.

I ran forward to kiss their little heads and to murmur appreciation into tiny fuzzy faces. "You were good girls, very good, to stay in the room!"

Paul was moving around, peering into my bathroom, my kitchenette, my closets. He checked the locks on my windows. "No one else has your room key? Dash, maybe?"

"No. He has one to the castle, but not to my room."

"And no one else—"

"No." I felt anger rising in me and a hefty dose of fear.

"We'll lock up tightly when we go. We'll talk to Derek and Dash, maybe think about getting the lock changed again."

"But someone's been next door, too. Someone or something." I told him about the racoon, or the ghost, or whatever it was.

"Do you want us to relocate you?"

"I— No, not really. But maybe I could ask someone to—"

Whom would I ask? I didn't have a spare bed. Dash was too busy now to be my bodyguard, and it would feel strange asking any of my colleagues to sleep in my room because I was frightened. And then the answer came to me.

"I wonder, Paul. Could I have my brothers come? They would be good company for me, and I haven't seen them in a couple of months."

"Perfect," he said. "From what I remember of the Blake twins, no one's going to want to come near this room."

I laughed, and I instantly felt better. Whatever happened, I could figure it out with the boys. They had rescued me before, with their violent teenage-boy advice, and I might need to use their bravado as a shield.

On the other hand, would I be endangering them? Ben

had been only seven years older than they were. Would it be tempting fate to invite them to the castle, which was the scene of a crime?

As fate would have it, I didn't have to make that decision. My brothers would make it for me.

11

Getting into Character

THAT AFTERNOON WAS a long one. We started by
sitting and waiting while Derek fussed on the stage,
talking about the set with his carpenter and about costumes
with Elspeth and Allie. Normally we would have chattered
during these moments, filling the wait with camaraderie or
impromptu practice of small scenes. Now, as if by mutual
agreement, we sat in silence. We were all missing the ebul-
lient presence of Ben, who usually bounded onstage at the
start and said, "Time to deliver the Christmas tree!"

I looked around at my castmates furtively, pretending to
be looking at my phone. Andrew and Millie looked pale
and shell-shocked. Jack did not have the swagger we usually saw; he seemed vulnerable to me for the first time.
Barbara was biting her nails, looking anxious, and Elspeth
and Renata sat knitting, knitting like twin Madame De-
farges telling their terrible secrets.

Connie plopped down beside me. "Well, this is a fun
group," she murmured quietly.

I met her gaze. "It's going to be a long day, I think."

Even Connie, with her irrepressible good humor, seemed sad, like a wilting flower. And Derek, who had been joined onstage by Paul, had a certain grimness about his mouth as he gave instructions and consulted his brother about props.

Finally, Derek turned to the group.

"Okay, let's get started. Elspeth, Connie, Jack, places, please. Nora and Dorian, be on standby. We're starting with Act I and running all the way through."

Priscilla, whose face had begun to look stormy, her pale skin red with some strong emotion, suddenly burst out. She jumped out of her chair and said, "Are we all just going to pretend, then? We'll just imagine that our friend Ben wasn't murdered mere days ago? And that he wasn't knifed to death by someone in this room?"

The theater was silent. No one had a response to this, and Priscilla added with a shrill edge to her voice, "I love drama, but I don't think my acting skills extend to that."

Millie and Andrew sat near her, looking scandalized, their eyes wide, their mouths in little o's, like salt and pepper shakers depicting choirboys.

Andrew stood up and patted Priscilla's shoulder. "We loved him," he said gently. "We all loved him."

Priscilla turned and threw herself into his arms, weeping on his shoulder. He patted her back as though he were burping a baby.

Derek came to the edge of the stage.

"Okay, cast meeting," he said. We gathered around him, and he said, "Priscilla is right, of course. And it's good that she brought it out into the open. It is beyond belief that this happened to Ben. Unlike Priscilla, though, I don't think he was attacked by anyone in this room. There were others there, people we don't know, as well. And there's always the outside chance there was an intruder who took advantage of the darkness."

I didn't believe that. A quick look around told me that no one else did, either.

"Meanwhile," Derek said, "we have a play to perform. Ibsen himself would have understood our grim task. Let's not forget that his career was spent examining and indicting the darker aspects of human nature. And look at the way he deals with death in our play: Nora's father and mother, Kristine's husband, and Krogstad's wife are already dead when the play begins, but they remain important characters. In their absence. Torvald was dying, Rank is dying, and Nora intends to die. Ibsen never lets us stray too far from the reality of death. We can be honest about our pain and grief because they are already embedded into the lines of the play. We can do this. I can't speak for Ben, but I'd like to think he would want us to do it. And one more thing: Paul has arranged for the program to say that the performance is dedicated to his memory."

Silence reigned again. Priscilla had stopped crying and had been listening carefully to Derek's words. Now she nodded at him.

"Thank you, Derek. I know you're in a difficult position, and that actually helped a lot. Especially knowing that our performance will be in Ben's honor."

"Yes, thank you, Derek," Renata agreed. "We are lucky to have you at this difficult time."

Derek bowed his head in response, then said, "Do we need some time, or are we ready?"

"I'm ready," Connie said.

The rest of the cast agreed, either with a nod or a verbal response.

Connie went behind her stage door. Elspeth was behind her, cast now as the delivery girl and new prop master.

I turned to look for Dorian, who had a scene with me in a few minutes, and saw that someone was sitting at the back of the theater in a row not touched by the stage lights. Eventually my eyes adjusted and I realized that it was Dash and that he had probably heard everything Priscilla said, along with Derek's eloquent speech. I didn't immediately go to him, even though we were looking at each other. I had the momentary illusion that I could not cross from the light into the darkness, could not reach him in his place of shadow. The moment passed, and I hurried down the aisle to find him standing up to greet me.

Behind me, Connie was asking, "How much?" of the delivery girl.

Elspeth said, "Fifty, ma'am," in a bright childlike tone.

Dash hugged me, and I inhaled his scent. Then I whispered into his ear, "We can't talk; they're running through the whole scene without stopping, and—"

He surprised me by clasping my face in his hands and kissing me more deeply than a hello kiss required. It was outrageously exciting, and when he pulled away, I looked at him in surprise.

"That was nice," I whispered.

"Nora—," he began, and his phone buzzed.

With an impatient sound he pulled it from his pocket and I got a glimpse of the caller's name. Even though his phone was upside down, I could tell that it read Robin Bradley. Something inside me turned cold, even as my brain told me, *She's his colleague. They have to talk to each other.*

Dorian appeared behind me while Dash murmured into his phone.

"Nora, come on. We need to be backstage. Your dialogue with Connie is coming up."

He was right, but I disliked his intrusion, his assumption that I needed him to tell me my cues, to order me back to the stage. Dash ended his call and his face reflected a similar resentment.

"I'll be there," I said. "I'm talking to Dash."

Dorian curled his lip at Dash. "Found the killer yet or are you guys just hoping someone will confess?"

Dash's face, in a trick of the shadows, seemed to be filled with dislike. "No," he murmured. "Shouldn't you be sitting in front of a makeup mirror somewhere?" Dorian smirked at Dash and clamped a hand on my arm, trying to pull me toward the stage.

"In a minute," I said, sending him a cold look.

He held up his hands in surrender and said, "Okay, okay."

He walked down the aisle, passing Derek, who was hurrying toward us.

"Dash, a quick word, if you have a minute."

I barely got to touch Dash's fingertips before Derek pulled him away for a conference.

I hurried back to the stage, then climbed the side stairs and went into the wings. Then I moved into my spot in the Helmers' sitting room; the maid had just told Connie/Nora that she had a visitor.

Connie swept in, looking young and happy. "Hello— I'm sorry. I don't— Kristine? Kristine, is it really you?"

WE MADE IT through the whole play, and Derek said he was pleased. We sat on the edge of the stage as Derek went through his production notes.

"Helene, I need you to open the door wider when you admit visitors. There are some seats from which you can't see them. Krogstad, you're a little too much like a cartoon villain when you make your threat about Nora's unhappy Christmas. Tone that down. Dr. Rank." He looked at Andrew. "You are ill, but there's no mention in the stage directions of you having a limp. Just moving slowly should do the trick."

Andrew nodded, laughing.

Derek bent over his notes, his dark hair hanging over one eye. I looked at Connie, who was in fact gazing at her lover with a blissful expression.

"Nora Helmer, I want you a little more buoyant during your happy scenes, to contrast with your stillness later. Maybe even skip now and then or twirl around."

"Fun," Connie said.

"Kristine, I want you to make it clear through body language that you are uncomfortable around Torvald. Not necessarily judging him, but definitely chafing under his condescension in a way that Nora has been unable to do."

I nodded.

"And, Torvald, you've got the condescending tone down, but when you make that final forgiveness speech to Nora, you're sounding too magnanimous. The speech is supposed to highlight his hypocrisy."

"Got it," Jack said.

Derek went on with his notes for some time; I realized that my stomach was growling. I think Derek might have actually heard it, because he looked up at me and smiled, then said, "We'll break for today. Castle Troupe, there's dinner waiting at home. Wood Glen group, thanks for all your work today. I know it was hard, and you were brave."

As we were filing down the aisles toward the lobby, my phone buzzed. To my surprise, it was my mother's name that appeared on the screen. I swiped on it. "Mom? What's up?"

"Hi, honey. I wonder if we could ask you a favor. Dad's old aunt Joan died. Remember her?"

"I think so. We just met her that once, right? She looked like a tiny little mummy."

"Nora! But yes, she was old when you met her, and now she has died. Dad feels obligated to go to the funeral in Florida, and he wants me to go, too. The boys have made it quite clear that they do not wish to go and that they would like to 'hang at the castle' until we get back. Would this be too inconvenient? Dad and I would be back on Monday."

Since I had been about to call home and ask if the boys could come to visit, I said, "I think that should be fine."

We chatted for a while, and by the time I reached the castle, we had arranged for the twins to arrive later that night.

So it happened that after I had eaten my dinner and welcomed my brothers, and after they had mooched food from Zana; flirted with Connie; thrown a rubber football back and forth with Derek and Paul; pounded on Renata's door, making her evening with their obnoxious jokes; visited Elspeth and her cat; and clomped around the costume room, trying on hats and boas and taking pictures of each other to post on Instagram, we finally settled down in my room. I was tucked into my bed, and the boys lay on a large air mattress on the floor that Elspeth had produced from somewhere. I had found extra sheets and blankets, and the room flickered with firelight. The Brontës had abandoned me for the new arrivals, and the three of them climbed on my brothers and purred while they investigated.

"These are great cats," Luke said, holding Charlotte up for inspection. She dangled in the air, still purring.

"I think tomorrow we might have to build a small village that they can destroy. We can film it and let them be monsters. That could work for our film assignment on perspective," Jay added.

"We're doing it," Luke agreed.

He was lying still because Annie had flopped on his neck and half closed her eyes. Emily had done the same on his stomach.

Luke looked at the ceiling and sighed. "This is the life,

Nor. You've got this great room, the fuzz balls, free food, roaming privileges in a castle and its grounds."

"Yeah, it's pretty perfect," Jay agreed.

"Except that murderers like doing their evil work here."

I had told my brothers about Ben and warned them that he was off-limits to their endless joking. There was nothing funny about murder.

"We'll help Dash solve it," Jay said with a yawn. "Shouldn't be hard. It's a standard locked-room mystery. You were all in there, in that tiny space. Your friend ended up dead. The question was who had the motive."

"Yes. The problem is, no one had a motive. Everyone loved Ben."

"No one had a motive that you know of," said Luke, raising a finger in the air. "Jay, she's standing on my eye. Get a picture."

There was some muffled giggling while they captured Annie's goofiness on film.

Then Jay said, "Yeah, didn't you say he wasn't from around here?"

"Well, he was, but only for two years or so. I think he grew up on a farm somewhere. Southern Illinois, maybe or Iowa. I can't remember."

"So maybe he had another life there. Maybe he came here to escape it," Jay said.

Luke liked this idea. "Yeah! What if he came here with a new identity? What if he was in witness protection?"

I sighed. They had never met Ben, so they didn't know how ridiculous that sounded. "I don't think so," I said softly.

Eventually the boys and the cats settled down, and I heard deep breathing (and some distant purring).

I thought of Ben's face as I had last seen it, smiling and excited to take part in the castle show. He had told Millie that he would protect her in the catacombs. Or had it been Barbara?

Ben's smile, guileless and sweet, had not suggested anything beyond simple goodness. He had not been a man with secrets—I was willing to stake my castle job on that.

But if Ben had no secrets, someone else did. This dark thought kept me awake for another hour.

12

The Wolves of Wood Glen

THE NEXT MORNING, I was shaken awake by my brothers, a nostalgic pastime for us all, since they had done this ever since toddlerhood; they still cared not a whit whether they were depriving me of much-needed sleep. Their brotherly harassment was standard procedure.

"Norbert!" shouted Jay, putting his palms on my face. "Wake up and attend to our needs."

I rolled away from him, and he leaned over me, blowing his breath in my face.

"Agh! Jay, brush your teeth. What did you eat yesterday, a raw onion?"

"We had gyros," he said, mildly hurt.

Luke had found my shower bucket and put the kittens inside it. He dumped them on my supine torso, then picked them up, put them in again, and dumped them again. The kittens, who had proven amenable to most of the boys' manhandling, submitted to the capturing and dumping with what looked like mild curiosity.

I sat up, shoving both brothers away so I had some semblance of personal space. "Jay, brush your teeth, take a shower, do whatever you need to do to get ready. Luke, leave those cats alone or I will train them to bite you. You take a shower after Jay does, and then I will."

"Boring," Luke said.

Jay sat on the edge of the bed and steepled his fingers. "I will counter with this offer: rustle us up some breakfast and tell us the itinerary for the day."

I smothered a laugh. Their obnoxiousness was so over-the-top that it always cracked me up, which they well knew.

"I'll show you an itinerary," I said, trying to sound threatening.

Jay and Luke exchanged a disappointed glance. "You shouldn't try to be funny," Luke said.

"Okay, here's the deal: get ready in twenty minutes, or I won't tell you about Renata's special treat."

"We'll just go harass Renata," said Jay, narrowing his eyes at me.

"She's not there. She's out making arrangements."

She and I had discussed the boys the day before, prior to their arrival.

"Give us a hint," Luke said.

"Nothing until you're ready."

That got them in action. Jay jogged to the bathroom while Luke went rifling through his suitcase for clothing. Much to my amazement, they were indeed ready in twenty minutes, their fair hair damp and combed as if they were bound for church.

"Lovely," I said. "Now I get a shower. There's juice and coffee in my little kitchen. I'll be out in ten and we can go down to the kitchen, see if Zana is there yet."

When I emerged, clean and dressed and more awake than I had been, the boys were posing the Brontës for various photographs that they captured on their phones.

"Finally, Norbert," Jay said lazily.

"Stop calling me Norbert."

"Nora the Explorer," Luke suggested.

"Ignora," his brother countered.

"Nah, that's no good."

They tried other versions of my name as we marched noisily down the main staircase. We found people in the dining room, and a lovely buffet that Zana had already put out, though it was not yet eight o'clock. My brothers greeted Elspeth and I introduced them to Miranda and Dorian.

The latter looked surprised, then delighted. "I didn't know you had twin brothers, Nora!"

"Well, here is the evidence," I said, moving to the sideboard.

Dorian questioned them while I took some eggs and toast.

"I'll bet you guys get up to a lot of shenanigans," he said. "Do you ever trade places and fool people?"

I turned to see the twins looking at me with cautious expressions. "Sometimes," Luke said.

"What?" I yelled.

"Calm down," Jay said. "It's not like we're being secret agents or anything. Last week we just did it to annoy our biology teacher."

I was developing a low-grade headache. "God, they don't pay teachers enough to deal with you two."

"No," Luke agreed with a solemn expression. "It's a tragedy, really, what they're paid."

Elspeth snorted into her coffee. I sat down, shaking my head, and the boys loaded their plates as though they'd been stranded on an island for days.

They plunked down next to me and Renata walked in, her eyes sparkling. "There they are! My comedians."

The boys preened under this description, and Luke said, "Hey, Renata." He took a huge bite of coffee cake and mumbled with his mouth full, "What's the plan for today?"

Renata sat down across from us.

"You know each other?" Miranda asked; she had been observing my brothers as though they were zoo animals we'd brought in for entertainment.

"Oh, yes, the twins and I keep in touch," Renata said, winking at them. Then she said, "So, boys, down the road a ways is a riding stable. They rent out horses for people to ride down a lovely trail through the forest. Would you like to do that? We had horses when we were girls, my sister and I. My horse's name was Beata, and she was a beautiful white mare. Sometimes I go to the stable and ride a horse there who looks like her."

Jay pointed at her. "Do they have mighty steeds? We're really only interested in mighty steeds."

Luke nodded. "Will they provide the jousting lances, or do we need to bring our own?"

Renata laughed merrily, wiping at her eyes. She loved my brothers and their nonsense.

"I think you can keep your jousting swords at home," she said, pouring some coffee into a mug set at her place. "And yes, they have some very large horses if you feel brave."

I finished my breakfast in relative peace while the boys entertained my castle colleagues. Derek and Connie wandered in blushing, and Derek asked if the twins might like to help him carry some antiques down from a storage room later in the day.

"No problem," said Jay magnanimously, eating the last crumbs of his coffee cake. "Whatever you need, Derek."

I rolled my eyes and brushed the toast from my fingers. "They're going out with Renata, Derek, but they should be available after that."

Luke stood up with his empty plate. "Our schedule looks pretty flex after a morning of riding."

"Invigorating," Jay said.

"Have your people call our people," Luke said, holding up his hand for a high five.

Derek slapped it, grinning.

Much to my pleasure, my brothers took their dishes into the kitchen, and I heard them thanking Zana for their breakfast, which meant that everyone else heard it, too.

"Nice kids," Elspeth said.

"They're hilarious," Dorian corrected. "They remind me of my brother and me."

Everything reminded Dorian of himself. I shot Connie an evil little smile, and she read my thoughts, nodding emphatically.

Renata stood up as well after one more gulp of coffee. "Are you ready, equestrians?"

The boys came back, jostling each other in the doorway like eager puppies.

"We're ready, *Tante* Renata. We have looked up selected German words to impress you," said Luke.

"But we should warn you," Jay said with an expression of faux concern. "We've both eaten large quantities of food. The up-and-down motion of riding might cause things to— spurt out of us. You might not want to ride behind us."

They moved out of the door as Luke added, "Or in front of us."

Renata cackled at their gross humor and said, "I can teach you German words for that, too."

"Nice!" yelled one of my brothers as their voices drifted toward the main entrance.

"I'm exhausted," I said. "I don't know how my parents do it."

Derek laughed. "If they're anything like my parents when I was a teen, they just say, 'Go far away or be quiet.' That worked pretty well."

Miranda, who had been silent throughout the twins' improvisations, said, "They're really cute, Nora. And handsome. I would never guess you were related because they're so fair, and your hair is so dark. But then again, who am I to talk about hair color? Nobody thinks I'm related to anyone in my family." She grinned and fluffed her pretty white hair.

"Yeah, why is your hair white?" Dorian asked, ever rude.

Miranda shrugged. "It just turned white when I was young. I guess some of my ancestors went white early, as well."

"It's pretty," Elspeth said, "and distinctive."

She stood up and accompanied Miranda to the kitchen, each carrying her dish. Then the two of them went into the hall, seemingly to head back to the third floor together.

Dorian left, too, after telling Derek that he could make money doing a reality show in the castle. "I for one would love to be in that," he said in his brash way.

Derek nodded and thanked him for the suggestion. After Dorian left, he shook his head at my querying expression. "I hate reality TV. Nothing real about it. And I wouldn't exploit the castle that way."

"Good," I said.

Derek looked at his watch. "I have to run."

He bent to kiss Connie, then whispered something in her ear. She giggled, and a bolt of pure envy ran through me. Dash and I had been like that—in August.

Inspired, I took out my phone and typed:

Help! I'm being harassed by two men.

A minute later I got his response: What?

I sent a picture I had taken of the twins that morning. Luke, with a villainous expression, was pretending to strangle Jay, whose tongue protruded under his comically crossed eyes.

Dash responded a moment later:

The twins! I'll try to find time to see them. How long are they here?

One more day, I responded.

He sent back a smiley face and a heart emoji. That was it. With a sudden sense of exhaustion, I wondered how long we would keep dragging on like this in our new, hollow relationship before Dash said he was too busy to keep it up. I sighed.

Connie's voice was suddenly in my ear. I had not noticed her leaning closer to me. "Derek has a favor he wants us to do. Feel like going into town?"

"Yes," I said, once again feeling claustrophobic in the castle, especially without the twins' distractions.

I arranged to meet Connie at the main entrance in twenty minutes. I ran upstairs and freshened up, making sure that I looked presentable in my faded jeans and gold turtleneck. I told each Brontë that I would return soon and warned them that my brothers would probably return, too. They accepted this with peaceful expressions; Annie purred. I gave them a snack and locked them in my room, making sure I pulled the door shut tightly.

When I left the main entrance, Connie was waiting in her car. I climbed in and said, "Hey, partner. What mission does Derek have for us?

Connie's sunny expression sobered. "Poor Derek. He has so much stress right now, and Priscilla's outburst really got to him. I mean, he doesn't know who did this to poor Ben, either, and it's gnawing at him. A second murder in the castle. And now of course it's been in the papers and on the news again—"

"Oh, shoot," I said. "My mom is going to freak. I didn't tell her. And I let her send the twins here."

"She'll be okay with it. Dash will solve it quickly and that will be that." She looked at my face, which remained expressionless, and added, "He was quoted in the paper, too. He sounded super professional and he made it seem unconnected to the castle. Without actually saying that. Derek was really grateful."

"He can count on Dash," I said.

I knew I hadn't escaped Connie's hawklike gaze. "So you haven't told me—what does Derek need?"

She sighed. "Well, he wants us to kind of get a sense of morale. Of the whole group, really, but especially Priscilla. If she quits this production, it will hurt Derek's feelings. It's not the end of the world, but he wants to work with her again in the future, and this whole thing might make her opt to take herself off to Lane Park."

This was the only other community theater within fifty miles, and Derek had assured me that it put on respectable productions, but that the Blue Curtain had a longer history and was the premier choice for rising actors.

"Plus," Connie added, "the others tend to be influenced by Priscilla. You probably noticed last night. She's persuasive, and it doesn't hurt that she looks like that. Even the women want to be on her side. There's some sort of psychology about beautiful people, isn't there? How people want to be near them, to please them?"

She said this in all innocence, and I said, "Well, look how I've been drawn to you since my first day here."

Connie turned, surprised. "I wasn't fishing for compliments, although thank you," she said with a sweet smile. "I know that you and I are attractive, and that people do look twice at us. But there's something different about her. I don't know if it's sex appeal or what. Thank God Derek seems immune."

"Because he sees only one woman," I said.

"Now why does that make you look sad? Tell me what is going on right now, Nora." She pulled the car over on a leafy shoulder of Apprehension Road, under a beautiful orange- and yellow-leafed tree that swayed in the October wind. "We're not moving until you do."

I shrugged, aware that I looked like a surly teen, and stared out my window. "I still want Dash. I still think he's great, and I'm still attracted to him. Significantly so." I thought of the way he had kissed me for the first time, on a little bridge over the creek on castle grounds, and my face grew hot.

"But?"

"But ever since I took the role at BC, things haven't been right. We're all awkward with each other, and it used to be so easy and comfortable. And there are these long silences. It's like we have to work to make pleasant conversation, the way you do with a stranger or someone you don't like that much."

Connie thought about this while I looked at the trees. We seemed to be approaching a peak color weekend, and the forested road ahead of us looked as inviting as an autumn postcard. Dash and I had talked about going to Michigan or Wisconsin, somewhere woodsy. Renting a cabin and hiking through the autumn foliage . . .

"There's obviously been a misunderstanding," Connie said. "One of you has the wrong impression."

"About what?"

"I don't know. But I know that when I had problems with Derek, a certain Nora advised me to talk to him. To be honest about how I felt."

"I've tried," I said.

"How?" Connie was like a stern teacher now, looking at me over the top of her sunglasses. "What exactly did you say?"

"I don't know—saying I'd like to get together. I sent him a picture of the twins. I said— I think I've said I miss him a couple times."

"You need to be *way* more dramatic than that," said the very dramatic Connie. "You have to convince him that he's the center of your world. Because he is, right?"

"He was becoming that way. It felt like we were on the verge of—something. Back in August."

She studied me for a while, then relented. "We'll sort this out." She pulled back onto the road. "Meanwhile, you could use some fudge or a Balfour Bar or something."

"I have to stop eating my feelings," I complained.

Connie laughed, and we talked about other things for the rest of the journey. When she pulled up to a parking meter on Birch Road, my spirits were restored. Connie joined me on the sidewalk, and she said, "I guess we can start with Andrew and Millie. This is their store."

Surprised, I looked up at the red awning that read *Portnoy's Gifts*. I knew that all of the community theater people had local businesses, but I had never frequented them.

"Oooh—I might be able to do some gift shopping here."

"For whom?" asked Constance Lancaster, who had impeccable grammar.

I grinned. "My parents have an anniversary coming up. And I think Paul has a birthday coming, too, doesn't he? And some other things."

We went through the doors and into a cute touristy store with sundry gift items. A table along one wall seemed to have samples of jams, crackers, and cheeses.

"More food," I murmured.

Andrew appeared behind the table and spied us.

"Why, hello!" he cried in an avuncular manner. "What can I get you two ladies today?"

"We're just browsing," Connie said. "Nora's never been in here."

"Ah, well, I'll be happy to show you around. Would you like to try some samples?"

We drifted over to the table, and he offered us crackers on a plate.

"There are sample knives in all the jams. You can spread them on your crackers."

We did so, sampling apricot, raspberry, strawberry, and blueberry.

"These are delicious," I said. "Oooh—how much is that?"

I had spied a basket filled with all sorts of jams, crackers, cheeses, and a bottle of wine. It would make a lovely gift for my parents.

"Fifty dollars," said Andrew. "Millie puts those together herself."

For the amount of food I saw within, it was an extremely reasonable price. "I'll take one," I said. "But I want to keep looking."

"Of course," he said smoothly. "I'll just put this by the register for you."

He lifted the basket to which I had pointed and moved smoothly to the front of the store.

Connie wandered closer to the register, studying some wind socks on a brightly colored shelf. "How are you and Millie doing, Andy?"

Andrew knew what she meant immediately. I set my sample knife back in its jar and went to join Connie.

"We're still processing," he said. "Like everyone." He heaved a giant sigh. "We loved that boy." His eyes filled with tears. "We were going to take him to Chicago to show him our favorite haunts. We had it planned for next week." He shook his head. "He was like our son. His mom lived far away, and his dad had died. We just kind of adopted him into our family not long after he arrived in town."

Connie had empathetic tears in her own eyes. "We were all saying that there's just no possible motive. I would believe that it was a random madman, except that we knew everyone in the room," she said.

We all just kept repeating the same things, unable to fathom the terrible act. Andrew had turned away, I suspected to hide his tears.

"It is truly devastating," he said. He busied himself taking the price tag off of my gift basket.

"Where's Millie?" Connie asked, looking around.

"She went to get us some coffee. Ah, here she is." He smiled at his wife as she came through the door with a cardboard cup carrier.

Millie saw us and said, "Oh, hello! I wish I had known you were coming. I would have grabbed you both a coffee."

"We're fine," I said. "Do you need help with that?"

"No, Andy's got it," she said, handing him the whole thing over the counter.

Connie persisted with her morale check. "How are you doing, Millie?"

At the sign of sympathy, Millie immediately grew teary-eyed.

"Hanging in. Going through the motions, you know." She wiped at her eyes, poking a finger underneath her glasses to do so. "Have you seen the shrine over at the bakery? It's out on the street."

"Oh, yes. It's beautiful. His family will see it and know he was loved."

"Yes." Millie went to a cabinet, pulled out a bottle of window cleaner and a rag, and began cleaning some glass display cases. "I heard the family will be keeping the ceremony private," Millie said, sounding slightly resentful. "So no chance to pay our respects, aside from the shrine. Andy and I left a bouquet, and I took pictures." A sudden thought seemed to terrify her. "Oh, I hope they bury him in the Wood Glen cemetery and not that farmland where he came from. We'd never get to visit him there."

Her growing distress made me eager to change the subject. "You have a nice store here. How long have you been running this place?"

Andy rattled out the history as if on automatic replay. "We opened our doors in August of 2003. Haven't had a year in the red since. It's not like Wood Glen is necessarily a tourist site, but somehow we get a lot of overflow traffic from people who find Chicago too expensive, so they see the sites and then stay in one of our more reasonable bed-and-breakfasts. And Millie and I reap the benefits. We supply the Maple Inn with jams and teas for the rooms."

"Symbiotic relationship," I said, and Andrew grinned.

"What are your bestsellers?" Connie asked, looking at some T-shirts.

"All the gourmet foods sell well, even with locals. They make great gifts. But we also do well with books and of course with the wine and spirits. And we also sell a lot of Glennie," Millie said.

"Glennie?"

Millie's eyes brightened. "Andrew and I wanted a signature product. We found these teddy bears that we could buy in bulk. They're quality material, though, not like dollar-store stuff. Then we commissioned Barbara to knit little sweaters and embroider the word 'Glennie' on the front, and on the back, 'I'm from Wood Glen, Illinois.'"

She pointed to the display window, where several bears in bright red, orange, and blue sweaters sat ready to lure customers. There were more Glennie Bears sitting on shelves, most of them dressed in autumn finery and leaning on little pumpkins.

I grinned. "I would totally want one of those if I were a little girl."

"I kind of want one, anyway," Connie said.

The bears were in fact quite attractive, with smooth brown fur and brown button eyes that looked soft with love.

The paws were made of felt, a slightly lighter brown color. The little sweaters were adorable, and I saw that some of the bears had little booties, as well.

"How long does it take Barbara to make all those things?" I asked.

Millie waved a hand. "She's amazing. Visit her yarn store; it's like a wonderland."

Connie turned, her face lovely and bright. "I went there! It's where I got the yarn for Derek's sweater. That's top secret by the way."

Andy turned salesman. "You could get him a Glennie in a matching sweater."

"Oh, that's such a great idea!" Connie eyed the bears for a while and said, "First I'll make sure I can finish the sweater. Then I'll come back."

"Do it well before Christmas," Millie warned. "We'll run out even with extra supplies."

I wondered what Dash would think if I bought him a bear, perhaps wearing a little police uniform. I had no idea if it would charm him or horrify him. Did I really know Dash at all?

"We should probably get going," Connie said. "Just let me visit the book aisle."

We both browsed the bestsellers; Connie found a suspense novel and a book about knitting and brought them to the front. I told Andy I would just get the basket for now.

"Great purchases," Andy said while he rang us up and Millie readied our bags. They worked well in concert, obviously from years of practice.

"Do come again," Andy said. "Millie will put our business cards in the bag, and they have our hours on them. We've gotten many a person out of a jam when they needed a present."

We thanked him and turned to leave, but I spied a framed photograph on a windowsill near the counter.

"Is this our group?" I asked, moving closer.

Connie joined me to peer at the picture.

"This is the photo from the catacombs! The one Millie took on the night that—"

"Yes," Millie said sadly. "I love the picture; Ben looks so happy. He loved being in the drama group."

"Do you mind if I take a picture of it?"

Millie shook her head. "It will be better quality if I send you a copy. Here, I'll do it right now."

"Send me one, too?" Connie said. She and I gave our email addresses to Millie, who promptly sent the photo.

We thanked her and said goodbye before marching out. I stowed my basket in the back of Connie's car, and she tucked her bag in there, too.

"Since we talked about Barbara's yarn, we should visit. You'll be amazed," she said.

We went back to the sidewalk and I glanced in the window of Portnoy's Gifts as we walked past. Andrew sat in a chair, his head in his hands, and Millie patted his shoulder while she dabbed at her eyes with a tissue.

BARBARA'S STORE WAS called Skein Street, and the moment we opened the door, I found myself lusting after yarn. I, who had never knitted or crocheted in my life, wanted everything I saw. The shelves were filled with large white bushel baskets bursting with yarns in rich rainbows of color that she had divided into warm and cool. One area was shades of blue, then green, yellow, orange, and red. The other wall contained lavender, pink, white, silver, brown, and black. The effect was lovely, but what made the room amazing was that she had crocheted loose nets of silver and mermaid blue and hung them across the ceiling; into these were tucked twinkling Italian lights. Several easy chairs were grouped in corners so that knitters could work with their new yarn. Some women sat in the back, knitting quietly and drinking tea. The center of the room held spinning racks with needles of all sorts, books with patterns and ideas, knitting magazines, and various notions like buttons, ribbons, and lace. Finally, two mannequins wore crocheted clothing that looked surprisingly fashionable. Both were dressed for fall; one wore a knitted black jumper with a plum-colored turtleneck and tights beneath it, along with a long silver chain that held a lovely stone pendant, bright with swirls of blue, purple, and black.

"I would wear that outfit," I said.

"The jumper? I like this one," Connie said, pointing at the other mannequin, which wore a knitted orange sweater with a black leather miniskirt and black leggings dotted with pumpkins.

Barbara appeared through a little curtained doorway and said, "Nora, Connie—hi. Are you out shopping?"

"I am," Connie said. "I'm working on that sweater for Derek, but I might get some yarn for other projects."

"Do you sell these knitted clothes?" I asked, pointing at the jumper.

"You would have to commission them," she said. "And then I'd give you a time estimate. I would make it or one of the artisans I work with."

"You're amazing," I said. "Not just the knitting, but the decor. This shop is kind of magical."

Barbara smiled, and for the first time, she really drew my interest. Before, she had kept to the fringes and seemed to be a natural introvert, but now I had seen her talent and her obvious passion, and her eyes had grown bright with my compliment.

"Thanks. I've knitted since I was a kid. Crocheted, too, and macramé, embroidery . . . basically anything with a needle. I dreamed up the idea of this shop in college when I majored in business."

"Wow—I admire people with a plan," Connie said, fingering some soft, fuzzy white yarn. "My gosh, this looks like it came right off the most darling sheep."

Barbara laughed. "Would you like some tea while you shop?"

We thanked her and said yes. She disappeared again, and I flipped through a book called *Knitting Made Easy.*

"Do you think I could do it, Connie? It seems very complicated. I've never had much patience for—sitting-down things."

Connie laughed. "Nor have I, but you should see Derek's sweater. It's one-eighth finished." She looked triumphant about this.

"Maybe I'll join the next knitting lesson with Elspeth and Renata."

Barbara appeared with teacups and a pot on a tray. "We also have lessons here at the store, on Friday afternoons."

"Oh, I might check that out, too," I said.

Connie thanked Barbara again for the tea and gave her an innocent blue gaze. "How are you doing? Since the—event?"

Barbara didn't cry, but she grew a bit more pale. "I'm fine. It was a horrible thing to witness and my heart goes out to his family. What a loss. What a stupid, inexplicable loss." She looked a bit angry then.

"When was the last time you saw him? Before our practice that night, I mean."

She shrugged. "I'm not sure. The bakery is at the end of the street. I'd see him go by a lot—sometimes alone, sometimes with Zana."

This shocked me. "Zana, like our Zana? From the castle?"

Barbara nodded. There seemed to be a little gleam of malice in her eyes, but it might have been a trick of the Italian lights that twinkled above us.

"Yes. Odd, right? A married woman hanging around

with a guy ten years her junior? I never knew what to make of that. Anyway, I probably saw him the day before, one way or another."

"Did he ever come into the shop?" Connie asked.

Barbara opened the teapot and peered inside, then put the lid back on. "Once in a while. He liked the colors and the lights; he said he found it restful. Sometimes he'd sit in that armchair by the window and drink tea. We'd chat if no one else was in the store. It tends to be pretty busy, believe it or not."

I raised my eyebrows. I didn't know anyone in Chicago who knitted; Renata and Elspeth were the first people I'd met who actually did it.

Barbara saw my skepticism and said, "It's always been popular. But after that huge women's march, when all the women were knitting pink hats? I was overrun then with people who wanted yarn. Suddenly knitting was more popular than ever. And it never really calmed down, which is great for me."

As if to verify her words, some people bustled in the door and started oohing over the yarn.

"Would you like some tea?" Barbara asked them.

Connie convinced me to buy a pair of knitting needles and some soft yarn in a chocolate brown that I could imagine becoming a sweater for my boyfriend. A little voice in my head said that if I wasn't still with Dash by Christmas, I could give it to my father.

Barbara rang us up, keeping up a charming hostess dialogue while her eyes remained alert and roamed the store. I realized that she was quite good at being a proprietor, too, because she projected a calm, friendly demeanor while negotiating visitors and keeping an eye on her wares.

"Well, have a nice day, Barb," Connie called. "We'll see you at practice tomorrow."

"Yes," Barbara said. "Dress rehearsal is coming soon."

This was both a chilling and exciting thought. We had only three more rehearsals before we began dress rehearsals—at least two of them, perhaps more—to get us used to costumes, props, and staging.

Once again Connie and I jogged to the car; the air seemed to have grown colder, and I was wishing I had brought a jacket.

"Feels like October now, doesn't it?" asked Connie with a smile. "I love cold weather." She spun around on the sidewalk, looking at the sky.

"You love everything," I said. "And remember how you just twirled. That's what Derek wants you to do onstage."

"I know. I've been practicing."

I laughed, and Connie led us down the sidewalk and around the corner, then across Balsam Street. I looked across the gentle flow of traffic and spotted Dorian on the opposite sidewalk, sort of slouching along and looking generally disreputable. For once he wasn't wearing a smirking expression; his eyes were darting around as though he were hunting for someone.

"Dorian alert," I murmured.

Connie looked up and sniffed. "He's starting to look scruffy. I think he believes that's how Krogstad would look, but it's the wrong look for our castle show. Look how long he's let his hair grow! I think Derek should make him cut it."

I felt a mild admiration for method acting; I'd had no idea Dorian was that devoted to the role.

As if he knew we were watching him, he darted suddenly into an alley that seemed to lead to the garages of actual Wood Glen residences. I watched him with my eyes narrowed until he disappeared from view.

"Shall we move on?" asked Connie.

I shrugged and said, "Lead on, Cruise Director."

We turned the corner and proceeded to Priscilla's store, which was called Light in the Glen. Under this legend on a gray-blue awning were the words "Distinctive and Elegant Gifts."

"You'll love it here," Connie breathed. "It's so fancy."

We entered the store; a tiny bell tinkled, and we were immediately enveloped in a pleasurable sensory experience: soft classical music played, and a delectable autumn scent permeated the air. People strolling around the store occasionally bumped into a display of wind chimes, which tinkled and gonged in various pleasing tones.

Priscilla appeared before us, smiling. She was wearing a silky blue pantsuit that shimmered in the shop lights; she wore a tangle of silver chains and matching silver sandals. Her hair was twisted up in a casual yet elegant pouf on her head. She held a tray of chocolates in various shapes and shades of brown.

"Would you like to sample some of my signature candy? It's made by a wonderful chocolatier. The company is called Castle Chocolates."

"What a coincidence," I said. I was inexplicably troubled by the name.

Priscilla turned her amazing eyes on me. "The family name is Castle," she said. "So no conflict of interest." She had read my thoughts, apparently.

"Oh, my gosh," Connie said. "These are delicious! Try one, Nora."

I took a piece of chocolate from Priscilla's tray and bit into it. It was indeed wonderful. A blend of dark chocolate, caramel, and something crunchy—

"Nuts?"

"Pretzels," she said with a smile. "They're great at flavor combinations. These are called Castle Crunchies. Andrew is in love with them. He's always coming in here for another box, saying that I'm feeding his addiction. Sometimes he sends Millie." She grinned. "But who hasn't eaten more chocolate than they should now and then?"

"Guilty," I said.

Connie began her interrogation of Priscilla, asking how she was holding up, and I wandered away, browsed up and down aisles filled with lovely things: candles and candleholders, potpourri and room spray, glass decanters and serving trays, jewelry that was out of my price range but that I found attractive. In one corner were some beautiful touch lamps in an art deco style. I drifted to the display, wondering how one would look in my room at Castle Dark.

Priscilla left Connie's side and came to me. "Aren't they pretty? I love lamps. I love light—hence the name of my store."

"They're terrific. You have a real eye for merchandise."

"Thank you. This store is a labor of love." She looked genuinely gratified by my compliment. "Look at this one. Maybe my favorite."

She walked to a lamp that seemed to be just a tangle of dark trees, sculpted of some dark resin. The trees were bleak, leafless, and somehow poetic, clustered together in wintry commiseration. Priscilla lifted the cord, which had a switch on it.

"Flip it on," she said.

I did so, and only then did I see the wolf inside the trees, his body crouching, his eyes glowing gold.

"Ooh! That's gorgeous, but I wouldn't want it at my bedside," I said.

"I love wolves," said Connie. "They're so beautiful."

"You love everything," I repeated. "And you wouldn't want to hear one of them howling under your window."

"They say that wolves aren't visible until just before they attack," Priscilla said with a strangely pleased look. "They're good at hiding. I just love this lamp. It's already sold, though. Someone's coming to pick it up tomorrow."

She looked regretful for a moment, then brightened and said, "The music you hear is for sale; the CDs are along that wall." She pointed. "And that lovely scent is called Autumn Romance. I have it in candle and potpourri form if you'd like a fall scent for your room."

"I think I will get some," I said. "But I also want to look at that clothing rack over there."

"Designs by Claudia," she said. "I've worked with her for years. She's a wonder."

I moved to the dresses and pantsuits, all of which looked slinky. I realized Priscilla was wearing one of the outfits, and there couldn't have been a much better model.

The clothing was elegant and deceptively simple. Again, it was expensive, yet I longed for something that would make me look as sophisticated as Priscilla did without even trying. I kept coming back to a pantsuit in a rich green, somewhere between jade and sea green. It was silk, solid green except for the cuffs of the shirt and pants, and the collar, all of which were a pattern reminiscent of a Tiffany lamp in green, black, and gold. It was lovely.

"Connie," I whispered, "I want this."

"Get it," she said, joining me. "It would look perfect on you. Your dark hair against that green? And the black in the collar would marry everything together."

"I don't really have the money to—"

She glanced at the price tag. "It's not that bad. And you're normally very frugal. I think it's time to treat yourself."

"Keep talking, temptress."

Connie laughed. "If you end up using it as a costume, you can write it off on your taxes."

"Sold," I said, lifting it from the rack. "I have some jade earrings from a former boyfriend. I never wear them much, but they would go perfectly with this."

"Get it. She has perfume, too. For the full sensory experience. Come here."

I put the silky outfit over my arm, and Connie led me to

a table filled with perfume samplers. "This one is called Chinese Garden," she said.

I held out my hand, and she spritzed on some perfume. I sniffed it. "Oh, that's stunning," I said. It was delicate, yet somehow musky and mysterious, flowery and innocent yet sensual and suggestive. "That's the best thing I've ever smelled."

Priscilla appeared behind us. "Isn't it? My bestseller."

"Do you have it in a small size?" I asked.

"An ounce, yes. At a price that won't break your bank."

"I can't look at any more, Priscilla," I complained, "or I'll just want to buy more. This place is a treasure trove."

"I do love my store," she said.

"Did Ben ever visit you here?" Connie asked. "Barbara said he used to sit in her place drinking tea."

Priscilla's face didn't change. "Sometimes. On his lunch hour or whatever. He liked the candles, and the toy aisle." She pointed at a small aisle for children with appealing-looking toys. "He was a kid at heart."

She smoothed her face with both hands as though ironing out her previous expression. "Can I ring that up for you?"

When we left—I with potpourri, a silky new pantsuit, and some alluring perfume, and Connie with several candles, some Castle chocolates, and a scarf that brought out the sky blue of her eyes—we marched to the car, and I said, "We have to go back. I'm out of money."

She laughed. "It was a good trip, though. No one seems overly sad about Ben—just the normal amount. I think things will be okay."

On the way back to the car, we passed Jack's establishment, simply named Jack's Pub. Jack stood outside, smoking a cigarette. Connie and I approached him, but before we could talk to him, a vendor appeared from inside to discuss something on his clipboard, so we decided not to interrupt.

We climbed into her warm car and began driving back through the autumn foliage. Connie's mood had improved, but mine had moved to a darker place. Yes, we had checked in with everyone—the Portnoys, Barbara, Priscilla. We had seen Dorian lurking and heard that Zana spent a lot of time with Ben. Yet we seemed no closer to knowing what had happened to him.

I recalled Priscilla saying that wolves stayed hidden until they attacked.

And in my mind's eye, I saw again the glowing gold eyes of the wolf in the barren trees, watching and waiting, a beautiful, invisible predator.

13

Twin Trouble

ABOUT HALF AN hour after Connie and I returned, the boys got back from the stables. They came galumphing down the hall, then burst into my room with tales of their ride.

"It was pretty cool, Norbert," Jay said. "I rode an impressive charger named Lancelot. He was stately and dignified, as opposed to Luke's horse, who was an embarrassment."

Luke nodded, chagrined. "Horace and I are still good friends, but he did something absolutely shameful on the path, Nor. And I noticed that he couldn't meet my eyes when we parted ways."

I laughed. "So you had a good time."

They agreed, saying that Renata had taught them many basics of riding and that she had promised to take them again.

"Now, we brought a little something for your Brontës," Luke said. "Renata took us to a toy store on the way back." He rustled through his backpack and found a little bag of blocks. "Jay and I will construct a town for them to destroy. We will film it, create subtitles, and display it in slow motion. It will win all the prizes at Cannes."

"Great. Don't forget you promised to help Derek."

"Of course," Jay said. He had put Emily inside his sweatshirt and she sat on a fold of material, her little head poking out of his collar with a sleepy expression. "She's nice and snug in there."

"Yeah, despite your personalities, they like you," I admitted.

Luke said, "Will lunch be soon or—"

"I think you have time to help Derek first."

"Fine."

My brothers donned tragic expressions.

"We must earn our victuals, then," Jay said. "Cats, we shall return. Sharpen your claws and get ready to sack a village."

I shook my head as the boys went thumping to the stairs, heading for the second floor and Derek's apartment.

I decided to go to the kitchen a bit early in search of Zana. She was there preparing a salad and individual pizza breads.

"Hey," I said, "can I help?"

She shook her head. "I think I'm ready. I'll just text everyone to be ready to eat in half an hour, and then I'll slide these in the oven in about ten minutes."

"I can set the table or something."

"Well, thanks. You can put these napkins out there for starters. One on every place mat."

I went into the dining room with a pile of napkins and did as she requested. Then I came back, and she handed me a pitcher of water, then a stack of glasses. I continued my journey with the various table settings until everything was in place. Then I went back and saw her putting her pizzas in the oven.

"Now we wait," she said, smiling and pushing her glasses up on her nose.

"So I owe you an apology," I said.

"What? Why?"

"The night that Ben—was attacked—you were comforting all of us, feeding us, and we didn't pay much attention to your grief." I turned to look into her eyes. "Today I learned that he was your friend."

Now it was Zana who had to wipe away sudden tears. "Yeah," she said, "a funny friendship, but there you go."

"How did you two—?"

"I used to work at the bakery if you recall."

I did remember now: Zana had told me, back in July, that she had worked at Balfour before taking the job at the castle. "Yes, of course."

"I worked with Ben for about six months before I moved to this job. We hit it off right away. We liked the same kind of music, the same sort of jokes, the same TV shows. We were both kind of sci-fi geeks, and that gave us a lot to talk about. When we were behind the counter in the bakery or back by the ovens, we would pretend to write our own science fiction book, but it was really just a satire of others we had read. Oh, my God, I never laughed so hard as I did when we were making up those introductory paragraphs."

"It sounds fun."

"It was. He was a fun, good guy. He didn't have a mean bone in his body." She looked at me, her expression half sad and half worried. "And that's what concerns me, Nora. There's something evil at work when a kid like that is victimized. By one of his own friends, no less."

"Obviously not a friend."

We sat pondering this. Zana eventually roused herself to send a castle-wide text telling people that lunch was ready.

"Nora, can you put out the salad while I get these out of the oven?"

I did so, placing the salad on the sideboard. I texted my brothers to make sure they got the message, and predictably they were the first ones at the table.

"Did you wash your hands?" I asked them.

Jay and Luke looked at me with despairing expressions. Jay said, "Nora, that is such a plebeian expression, a commonplace query of a midcentury housewife. . . ."

"Which means no," I said calmly. "Go. Zana will let you use the kitchen sink."

They dragged themselves into the kitchen without lifting their feet, trying to annoy me and succeeding.

Soon I heard Zana laughing at something they said, and I was briefly glad that they had lifted her spirits.

Renata and Elspeth came in, followed by Miranda, who scrolled on her phone. Renata grinned happily. "We had a lovely morning," she said, taking her dish to the sideboard and helping herself to some salad.

"Thank you," I said in a low voice. "They had a great time."

"As did I," she replied. "They are such delightful boys really."

I nodded. "By the way, I went to Skein Street today."

"Ah. Lovely, no?"

"Yes. I think I might want to join Connie in the knitting lessons."

"We would be glad to welcome you," she said, sitting down at the table.

The twins came back in, looking cleaner, and they began some sprightly badinage with their honorary aunt.

Elspeth and Miranda had also found the salad, and they sat down near the chattering group. Paul and Derek came in, speaking in low voices, then Connie, looking slightly worried, then Dorian, with his ever-present smirk.

Connie murmured something to Dorian when she saw

him behind her, and he slung a casual arm around her shoulder as he answered her. Connie didn't react to the gesture, but I was insulted on her behalf. What made him think he could be so personal with her? With her boyfriend standing just in front of them—a boyfriend who was his employer?

He looked up and saw my face, and his smile widened. He had come to view me as a prim and puritanical woman, uptight and shrewish, and so anything that upset me tended to amuse him.

Zana came in with a tray of pizzas, and Derek set it in the middle of the table.

"Join us, Zana," he said.

"I have one more pan, and then I will." She zipped back into the kitchen.

We were all seated and munching hungrily for a while when Derek said, "Since I have you all here, I will mention that Friday is our first dress rehearsal, and I want all lines solidly memorized. Things are sounding pretty good, but some of you need to study the scripts more attentively. The play will go more smoothly, and more quickly, if we have those lines ready. It's also more authentic dialogue when it trips quickly off the tongue."

We all agreed to this with nods of the head.

"Do you need Luke and me to be ushers? We could also stand in front of the curtains and warm up the crowd with some comedy," Jay offered.

Derek grinned. "If you're in town and you want to pass out programs, that would be great."

I waited for them to call Derek plebeian, but they meekly accepted his offer.

I wished Jade Balfour had been there. "That's patriarchy for you," she had told me when I adopted the Brontës. They were all female and Jade had pointed out that the males had been taken first. She would recognize a double standard when she saw one. And that gave me an idea. I texted her under the table, telling her to stop by, if she had a chance, to meet my brothers.

How are the animals? I asked.

She wrote back, with emojis representing all five of them, including the fish. Then: They're stuck with us, it looks like.

For some reason it made me happy to know that the animals would stay together, especially with animal lovers like the Balfours.

Paul caught my eye when I finished texting. "I would love to run lines with you, Nora, if you ever have a chance."

"Yes, of course," I said. "We can do it this afternoon."

We finished lunch rather hilariously; my brothers did in fact have the desired effect of cheering everyone who had been melancholy. When they had stuffed themselves, they stuck out their bellies and groaned, like old men after Christmas dinner, and said, "Zana, what have you done to us?" and other annoying things as they patted their falsely huge stomachs.

Eventually they stood up, once again taking their plates to the kitchen. They saluted me and said, "We're finishing with Derek, and then we have a project up in the room. See you then, Nor."

They bustled out as if they owned the castle, and I saw Derek and Paul exchange an amused glance. Maybe the boys reminded them of themselves as teens.

I finished my lunch, lost in thought and not paying much attention to the conversation around me. Finally, after eating a cookie from a tray Zana had put down, I met Paul's eyes.

I stood up and went to the door, and Paul met me there and asked, "Now a good time?"

"Yes, perfect. The boys will find me if they need me."

"Let's use my office. No one will bother us there."

We walked down the main hall; it had grown overcast outside, suggesting that a storm was imminent. This made the hallway dark and shadowy, and the lighted pumpkins Derek had scattered here and there shone brightly in the gloom.

We reached Paul's office and I sat down across from his desk.

He studied me with concern as though he were a doctor and I a patient waiting for a diagnosis. "How have you been?" he asked.

I grinned. "Since you saw me at the lunch table?"

"I mean since you found your door open. Are your brothers a good distraction?"

I shrugged. "The question is, a distraction from what? I don't even know why it was open or what Connie heard in there. Maybe it all has an innocent explanation."

"I hope so. But I've spoken to Derek about the locks."

I sighed. "Anyway, let's get started on our lines. I think this is my favorite scene in the play, this dialogue between Kristine and Krogstad in Act Three."

"Mine, too," he said.

I stood up, faced the wall for a moment, and tried to channel Kristine's feelings: her long-buried love for Krogstad; her sadness at seeing him so defeated, so weary and angry and bitter; her desire to make some little happiness for herself in the life she had left. . . .

I turned and sat down, facing Paul with a steely expression. "All right, Krogstad, let's talk."

Paul looked at me with a blend of anger and disbelief. "I wouldn't have thought that we two had anything to talk about."

"No, because you never understood me," I said, mournful.

He stood up and began to pace. "What is there to understand? A grasping woman throws over a man the moment a better prospect comes along. . . ."

He turned back, and I saw that he had captured what Dorian had not managed to find in the character of Krogstad: that beneath the anger, there was pain. Paul's eyes were spiked with tears.

We continued to talk: I patiently explaining why I had married a man I did not love for the sake of my family, and Krogstad explaining his loss, his grief, his embittered life.

"I'm like a half-drowned man clinging to a wreck," he said, wiping his eyes and then turning to face me with sudden fury. He accused me of trying to take his job at the bank, something he'd worked for in a desperate bid to earn back his lost reputation.

I assured him that I did not want that, nor was I there only on behalf of my friend Nora. "Why do you think I came back to town, Nils?"

He stared at me, dumbstruck. "Kristine, did you really have some thought of me?"

Like the sun coming from behind a dreadful cloud, his smile emerged, making him look like a child who has been reunited with a long-lost parent.

"I need someone to work for," I said, my voice weary but hopeful. "Your boys need a mother. Give me something, someone to work for."

We moved closer together, and he took my hands. Derek had suggested that despite the fact that no kiss was in the stage directions, he thought there would be one between Kristine and Krogstad now, something soft and sweet and full of promise. So Paul and I kissed chastely, our eyes wet with unshed tears, and as Paul walked away and into the hall, he turned and said, "I've never been so happy!"

In that moment, for whatever reason, I knew what I was going to get Paul for his birthday.

I would convince my sister, Genevieve, to come out for the performance.

* * *

JADE STOPPED BY that evening after dinner. My brothers had finished their film of the kittens, and after I introduced them to Jade, they debuted the film for all of us on my computer. They had filmed all three kittens, first vying for a spot at the one window cut into an upside-down card-board box. Their caption read: Imprisoned but furious, the monsters cannot be contained.

Then, in slow motion, the cats squeezed through the window, one by one, their mouths occasionally opening in a meow, at which point Luke had zoomed in to show their teeth.

Jay had been dangling a string on the other side of a "town" they had built with blocks, and naturally the kittens had blundered right in. The caption read: They rampage. Humanity is not spared. The screams are quickly silenced. Lots of slow-motion footage of the kittens, curious about the blocks they were knocking down, pausing to knock down some more. By the end, thanks to the boys' framing, they did look like creatures bent on destruction.

"I envision an A plus," Jay said, pleased.

"It's pretty cool. Did you film that on an iPad?" Jade asked.

"No, on Luke's phone," Jay said. "But he has Movie Maker software."

"Have you used Spark?" Jade asked. "It makes pretty good movies, with music and video capability."

I stared at them. I was twenty-seven—not exactly old—but they seemed to know vastly more about technology than I did.

"We used to make posters," I said.

They looked at me with blank expressions, and I shrugged. "Whatever. What did you guys want to do tonight?"

"Our last night in the castle," Jay said mournfully, pushing back some of his longish hair.

"Don't despair. We'll make it fun," I said. "I have a special surprise. Paul told me that he and Derek have one, too."

"Yeah?" they said in unison.

Jade laughed. "Gee, I wish someone would give me a special surprise."

"We'll work on it," I said, giving her a half hug. "Meanwhile, you're invited to dinner and our post-dinner activity: a movie and s'mores."

"Oooh, s'mores!" Jay said. "Are we going to make a bonfire?"

"No, we're just going to make a fire," I said, pointing at my fireplace.

"Awesome!" Luke said. He stood up and put a hand on my shoulder. "That's the best idea you've ever had in your life."

"That sounds more like an insult than a compliment."

"It is what it is," he said, and Jade giggled.

That evening, as we roasted marshmallows in front of my fireplace and the boys told ridiculous ghost stories, I said, "Oh—I have my own ghost, did you know?"

I told them about the noises, and the piece of paper, and my slightly open door, about Connie hearing something in my room while I was downstairs. My brothers stared at me.

"Why didn't you tell us this earlier?" shouted Luke.

In a shot they had handed their barbecue spears to Jade and run to the room next door. A minute later Luke peeked in.

"We're going to make some noises. You tell us if you hear them."

Jade and I waited, and then some muffled sounds came through the wall—pounding, scraping, dragging. Some of them sounded quite similar to the ones I'd already heard.

Eventually the twins returned. "What did you hear?"

"Various noises," I said. "Some of them sounded familiar."

Jay stroked an imaginary beard, thinking. "We mostly just moved around in there. Knocked on the wall, moved books, dragged each other across the floor."

"Well, maybe that's what the ghost does," I said lightly.

Jade said, "It's not a ghost. Why would it haunt a room where no one goes?"

I didn't have an answer for that, and suddenly I didn't want to talk about it. When I called my brothers back to their snacks, they returned willingly, ready to consume more sugar.

Jade contemplated them while licking sticky marshmallow from her fingers. "You guys are hilarious," she said. "You should have your own podcast or something. Or your own YouTube channel."

"We're working on it," Luke said, surprising me.

"Wha—," I began, but Derek knocked at the open door.

"Hey," he said, "do you guys have a minute?"

"Sure," I called. "Would you like a s'more?"

Derek shook his head. "Connie just fed me chocolates that she got in town. Sinful."

"Oh, yeah, that was from Priscilla's store. It's amazing."

"Yeah, I've gotten Connie a few presents there," he said. "Meanwhile, I have something for you two. This is from Paul and me."

He held up a box, and the twins lunged at him to accept it.

"Wow, thanks," Jay said, already tearing at the paper.

"Constance wrapped it," Derek said to me over the heads of the twins.

I nodded, watching my brothers. Memories of Christmases and birthdays floated through my mind. Luke and Jay, pudgy, funny, smart. Adorable as they were now.

Their efforts revealed a box, which they opened, tossing out tissue paper and pulling out two black T-shirts with capital white letters that read *Castle Security*.

"Awesome! This is outrageously good!" Luke yelled.

"Derek, my good man, I honor you," Jay said, bowing to him. "We will wear them with pride."

Jade looked at me. "Do they ever talk like normal people?"

"No."

She nodded. "That's cool."

The twins had already put on the shirts over their clothing; they went lunging down the hall, knocking on doors and saying, "Everything okay here? Castle security."

Then, a moment later: "Just stay in your room until we deal with this—don't worry, ma'am. We're castle security."

From down the hall I could hear the sound of Renata's hearty laughter.

THE TWINS LEFT the following morning. Dash pulled up as we were saying goodbye and handed both boys a children's badge that read *Volunteer Police Officer, Wood Glen PD*.

The boys immediately put them on their coats and stood bantering with Dash while I hugged my parents.

"Thanks for sharing them," I said. "The whole castle loves them even though they're incredibly annoying."

"Yeah," my mom said fondly.

"Well, I'll see you all soon, right? On opening night?"

My mother nodded. "We're thinking we might stay at a B and B in town, in case I want to see more than one performance."

"Cool. Also, I'm going to try to get Gen to come down. She needs a break, right?"

My mother liked that idea. "Oh, that would be lovely! We could take our family Christmas card photo."

I laughed. "Yeah, that would work. Okay, I'm going to invite her today."

My dad pulled me aside before they left and said, "We read about the murder. Inside the castle, wasn't it? Again?"

I nodded. "But the two aren't related in any way. It's just—some horrible person taking advantage of a carefully timed show to plan a murder." I pointed at Dash. "The police are on it, believe me. They'll get whoever it was."

He nodded. "See that Dash keeps an eye on all of you. Mom and I don't want to worry, but you know we will." He touched my hair. "We're proud of you. You made the best of things when you lost that part, and now you found this great job and a nice boyfriend. Just be safe."

"Thanks, Dad."

My brothers approached and pretended to strangle me, then accepted my hugs and kisses.

"See you soon," I said.

I watched them drive away, and Dash put his arm around me. When the car had disappeared down the long driveway, I said, "Hey," to him.

"Hey."

"You look tired."

"Yeah." He cleared his throat. "We've been doing a lot of interviewing."

"So I heard."

"And I'm here to do some more."

"Oh?"

"Everyone in the castle. Derek is going to text people a schedule. We'll be meeting in the sunroom."

"Okay. Does that include me?"

"Yes," he said, not meeting my eyes.

14

The Man with No Enemies

THE SUNROOM WAS long and narrow, extending across the eastern corner of the castle. Dash was not alone; some people were being sent to Detective Bradley, who sat coolly in a wicker chair, sipping from a cup of tea and studying some notes in her hand. For obvious reasons, Dash said, I would be interviewed by Detective Bradley.

I approached her at my allotted time right after lunch.

She looked up and said, "Nora, right?"

"Yes."

She was even prettier close up; her skin was flawless, and her lashes were long.

"I'd just like to go over the night of Ben's death if that's all right with you."

"Of course." I settled across from her in another wicker chair, padded with a floral pillow.

She took a sip of her tea. Then: "Did your group all go in together, or did you go in small clusters? Do you recall?"

I closed my eyes, trying to remember the night: the chattering, the excitement. Millie's picture at the door.

"We posed for a photo," I said. "Millie took it. I saw a copy of it in her store."

"Ah. And the whole group was in the picture?"

"Everyone from the Blue Curtain play, yes. Except Millie, who took it."

"And right after taking the picture you entered the catacombs."

"Yes. It was— There was some trepidation, but only because some people were worried about being scared. People have different thresholds for fear."

She frowned. "And everyone in your group knew when the lights would go off and where?"

"Well—apparently yes. The people from the castle knew because we had rehearsed it. And the people from the theater knew because Derek had done a dry run with them to manage their expectations."

"You were the closest to Ben when he fell, by your own admission."

"Yes, I fell with him. Or over him, I guess."

"And can you think back to determine who was behind or in front of you?"

I closed my eyes but remembered only motion. Shifting bodies in the darkness . . . tripping over Ben's leg and falling on top of him . . . laughing, at first, because I thought we had both tripped. And then the distant clang of the weapon falling into the vent.

I told Bradley this. "It was surreal. Disorienting. If I try to guess where people were, I am afraid that I might be making it up after the fact."

"Understood." She stretched elegant arms above her head for a moment. I thought of a swan. "Sorry," she said with an apologetic grin. "I haven't slept much lately."

A burst of hot suspicion fired up my core and into my throat. Dash was tired, and she was tired. Dash could barely be bothered to text me these days. And coincidentally a beautiful detective had started working with him.

She leaned back and the wicker creaked slightly. "Who would you say had a grudge against Ben?"

"No one," I said promptly. "It's something we all agree on. No one had a motive. His death just seems impossible. It feels like theater."

"But his body is very real, I'm afraid," Bradley said.

When I shivered, she asked, "Would you like some tea?"

"No. Are we finished or—?"

"No, not yet. What sort of conflicts did people have at rehearsal? People in the cast?"

"The cast? Nothing much. Just little drama issues sniped about by dramatic people. We all talked behind someone's back at some point."

"Whose back did you talk behind?"

I shrugged. "I haven't made a secret of the fact that I'm not a big fan of Dorian's. I've griped about him sometimes."

"What's the problem with him?"

"I can't put my finger on it. He's just . . . sort of phony. And he assumes that every woman wants his company. I guess a lot of actors do that."

"What about Jack? Is he the same way?"

"Yes—and no. Jack has an ego, which he'll be the first to admit, but he's still a nice guy. Funny. I know that sounds like a double standard. Maybe it is."

"How long have you dated Dash?" she asked.

I sat up. "What?"

"The length of your relationship?"

"Why is that important?"

Her warm brown eyes met mine. "You are a link between the police and the castle. And two murders have been committed in the short time since you were hired here."

"Are you calling me a murderer?" I heard some ice creeping into my tone.

She smiled. "Not at all. I'm trying to identify any connections that might be significant."

"I started dating Dash in July."

"And your castle colleagues, did you know any of them before getting hired?"

"No. I met them all on my first day."

She flipped through some notes. "Can you tell me anything else about Miranda Pratt?"

"No," I said, realizing this truth with surprise. "I—just know her name. We've hung out together a couple of times, but we haven't discussed anything personal. Except that she has two jobs."

"Ah?" She made a note of that. "Thank you. And Dorian? Anything you can tell me about him?"

"No. I've spent less time with him than I have with Miranda."

"All right." More notes. Another sip of tea. Then, in another jump of subject, she said, "Why did you take the job at the castle?"

"What? I—lost a role that I thought would pay my bills for several months. The director sent my audition tape to Derek, who was impressed. He lured me out here for an interview, and I fell for the whole vibe. I've been here ever since."

"If you had to guess who killed Ben, whose name would come to mind? Speak without thinking."

"Dorian," I said, and then I felt ashamed.

I FELT DRAINED after my interview. Bradley was sharp, and she had tried to keep me off-balance throughout. My eyes had wandered over to Dash when she finally dismissed me, and I saw that he was interviewing Zana, who sat straight in her chair with a terrified expression. Had someone told Dash about Zana's friendship with Ben?

Dash jogged up to meet me in the hall. "Nora," he said, taking my hand.

"Yes?"

"I'm sorry. We have to interview everyone."

"Well, your lady friend certainly does a thorough grilling."

Dash looked at me, surprised and almost smiling.

Then Derek loomed up out of the shadows. "Nora, Dash, I'm glad I caught you. Nora, I had Randy Whittaker come out to check the west wall and roof. He said it all looks sound as a drum. No sign of holes or of animals."

"Well that's good, right?" I said, feeling bitterly disappointed.

"What do you mean, looking for holes?" Dash said.

I started to answer, but Derek said, "Just a structural issue. Do you have to go right back in, or can I talk to you for a minute in the castle office?"

Dash touched my shoulder with a warm hand and then Derek led him away, speaking rapidly into his ear.

Now I wandered, at loose ends, and decided to go to my room and read my book. Just as I shut the door, I heard a scrabbling sound outside. I grinned and opened the door again to step back into the hall and watch the show. Hamlet, Derek's big black Labrador came bursting out of the stairwell and began to run at full speed toward the costume room. Then he turned and came rapidly back toward me. I only had time to touch his head, laughing, before he turned again and galloped back down the hall. Elspeth peeked out of her room. "Hamlet's got the zoomies," I called, still giggling.

Elspeth, laughing now too, tried to pet him, but he wasn't finished running. "I'm guessing Derek didn't get to exercise him very much today," she called back. We had seen him do this before, though not often on our floor.

"I think he's winding down now," I said. Hamlet finally ran out of gas and stopped in front of me, butting my leg with his big head while I petted him.

"Goofy dog," Elspeth said, waving and closing her door.

I bent to say good night to Hamlet and he touched my nose with his cold wet one. "Go back down to your master," I said, with a final pat on his back.

Hamlet sniffed me for a few moments longer, then turned and strode to the staircase, where he disappeared.

Once I got back in my room, I read a few more chapters of the very suspenseful (and now romantic) Mary Stewart book, then put it aside and closed my eyes. Emily Brontë sat tucked up against my right side, Charlotte was tucked behind my head, and Annie sat on my belly. I lay still, thinking about all the people that I worked with onstage. Which of them seemed suspicious?

Connie? Ridiculous. It would have been like suspecting one of the Brontës of murder.

Derek or Paul? No. I had ultimate trust in them.

Miranda or Dorian? Both mysterious, and as I had told Bradley, I knew nothing about either one.

Jack? I had never felt suspicious of him or even uncomfortable around him, although I had criticized him now and then. As far as I knew, he didn't have any secrets. He was the one person whose business we had not visited when we were in town. Connie assured me that Jack's Pub was a tasteful place that did a good business, not only at the bar, but in the attached restaurant, where they served lunch and dinner to the locals.

Priscilla? There seemed to be something behind her elegant demeanor, her silky sexiness, her inexplicable charisma. I sensed an emotion behind it all, but I could have been imagining drama for her. I was good at that.

Millie or Andrew? Millie seemed almost invisible, with her mousy hair and passive look. Andrew, always benevolent, had loved Ben. So had Millie. I wondered what "girl" Andy had been talking to Ben about when I'd seen them joking around together.

Barbara? She had surprised me with her artistry and her business acumen. Her store was a marvel of design, and her talents would not have been something one could guess by meeting her out of her milieu.

Elspeth or Renata? No.

Zana? No.

There was no bringing myself to suspect the castle crowd; clearly, I was prejudiced in their favor, but I also felt I knew them well now, and I felt confident that they could not commit an act of violence, not one of them. I had once seen Zana stand on a chair to let a moth out the kitchen window, and Paul had walked the length of the main hall to put a spider outside. Derek put food out for the deer, and Connie volunteered to read bedtime stories to children via her old school in South Bend. Elspeth dressed her as a princess for the occasions, and she called the weekly readings "Story Time with Princess Goodbook."

I sighed again, and the next thing I knew I was waking up. The Brontës were milling around on the bed, trying to hint about their empty bowls.

"Okay," I said groggily. "Time for dinner, right?"

But I lay there a bit longer, thinking about Dash, and Derek and his financial troubles, and the twins. An image of my brothers came to me from a time I had taken them to the Brookfield Zoo on my own. I had pulled them in a wagon and they had sat in their little safari suits (they had loved costumes from toddlerhood) and gazed through their baby sunglasses at the passing scenery. When we reached the elephants, their first request, I lifted one of them in each arm and propped them on the bottom rung of the enclosure fence, standing behind them so that they wouldn't fall. I still remember the size of the elephant in front of us, the wonder of the little boys, the sun on their hair. Jay's had been longer than Luke's, as it was now, curling in baby ringlets on his little explorer jacket—

A noise in the room next door.

The raccoon noise with no raccoons; Derek had said so. I had been thinking about something just now—the boys at the zoo, Jay with his curling hair . . . Dorian with long hair lurking in the alley near Barbara's store. Dorian at the castle seeming somehow different. Dorian saying about my siblings, "They remind me of my brother and me."

Suddenly I remembered Dorian on the game night in Connie's room saying, "Come back, Nora!" Had that been just another of his jokes or had he been trying to keep me away from the room next to mine—the Small Library?

And then one final image: Dorian appearing on the stairs next to Connie and me after a "midnight snack" when we'd just seen him emerging from the run-through on the day before Ben's death.

Quietly, I slipped off my bed and went to the side table to retrieve my phone. I turned it on and flipped it to camera mode.

The soft noises next door continued.

On silent socked feet, I glided across my floor. I turned my knob slowly and opened my door gingerly to avoid making it creak. In the hall I moved swiftly to the door of the Small Library. I took a deep breath and flung the door open.

Dorian sat at the table, sorting books. Across from him another man sat doing the same thing as though Dorian was watching himself in the mirror. Except that one of the men had slightly longer hair . . .

They looked up, shocked.

"Say cheese," I said. I snapped their faces.

I ran back to my room and locked the door. Moments later Dorian knocked at it, saying "Nora, can we talk?"

"No," I said.

I found a group chat I used for Paul and Derek, and typed, Come upstairs ASAP. Caught raccoon in the act.

The hall was silent now. I pressed my ear to the door and heard nothing; either Dorian was standing there, waiting me out, or he had gone away. I didn't want to risk opening the door in case he was still there. What was going on? Dorian had a twin, and he was in the castle, as well! Did Derek know that?

I took some deep breaths, realizing that I was safe until Derek and Paul came. I went back to my bed and sat on the edge, trying to relax. Then I heard a sound behind me—a scraping, sliding sound.

I swung around to see Dorian—no, not Dorian—emerging from the wall beside my closet. "Time to have a chat," he said, smiling.

I screamed.

15

The Forest Dark

"GET OUT OF my room," I said. It was hard to breathe, suddenly.

"I'm not going to hurt you," he said. "Just give me the camera, and I'll disappear." He advanced toward me, and I held up a shaking hand.

"Don't come near me." I stepped back, closer to the door. But Dorian was out there. . . .

"What's your name?" I asked, curious despite my fear.

His brows rose, and then he smiled. "It's Drake. And you're Nora. I feel like I know you so well. I've heard you in here, chatting to your little cats."

That invasion of privacy brought a burst of anger that temporarily banished my fear. "What the hell are you two doing? Derek is going to murder you both."

Murder. A cold feeling spread through my veins, effective as a drug. I felt ready to collapse. They were being secretive, pretending to be one man. Dorian had been at the front of the crowd in the catacombs, but what if his brother had waited at a convenient spot so that he could emerge when the lights went out, stab Ben, and then disappear? Was I in the room with a murderer?

I was distracted by a movement in the same spot from which Drake had emerged. Dorian suddenly appeared, stepping out of the open panel in my wall. "Nora, don't look so scared," he said. "We're not evil. We're just dishonest." He spoke with a charming smile that did, in fact, look evil to me.

"Get out of my room," I said, my voice icy with fury, my hands trembling with fear. "Get out *now*."

Dorian smiled. "Just give me the phone, and forget you saw us, okay? I can promise you a really nice present if you do."

"What?" I said in disbelief. "Are you insane?"

The brothers exchanged a glance that seemed sinister at that moment. At the same time, my brain finally started working again, pushing logic past my fear. I wasn't locked in, it said. I could leave.

I marched to my door and unlocked it.

"Nora," one of them cried as I flung wide the door.

The elevator opened to my left, and Paul and Derek stepped out.

"What's going on?" Derek said. He saw my expression and turned three shades paler. I pointed at my open door, and he and Paul lunged in.

"Well, this is a surprise." It was Paul's voice, clearly stunned.

Derek's voice then. "Dorian, what the hell is going on here?"

I didn't go back to my room. Connie's door opened and she thrust out her sleepy face; I realized she had been taking a nap. "What's—?"

I glided past her, sat down at her dining table, and told her what had just happened. Opening my photos, I held up the picture of Dorian and Drake.

"What the heck!" she cried.

We heard voices now, men's voices raised in anger.

"Oh, no," Connie said. "Derek's temper is a well-kept secret, but when he gets mad, he gets really mad." She looked half proud, half nervous.

"—and how *exactly* did you know about this hidden passage? Paul and I had no idea—"

Some quiet murmuring from one of the twins. Then Derek again: "So you traded places in there, going through my things, terrorizing Nora, slithering around my castle like duplicitous snakes!"

My hands had stopped shaking, and though I was still fearful, a part of me was enjoying this dressing down delivered by a very angry Derek.

"Duplicitous snakes," I said. "I like that."

Connie managed a grin.

Paul's voice now. "What exactly did you think you would accomplish, deceiving everyone like this?"

Dorian's voice, starting to regain some of its smarmy charm. "Guys, come on. You're brothers. You know that it's fun sometimes to get a little wild, have a little adventure. I can't believe that story doesn't tantalize you every single day. I can't understand why you don't have this whole place turned upside down."

"What story?" Derek's voice was blank.

Dorian sounded amazed. "The poem! The legend! There's treasure in this place, and Drake and I couldn't resist looking for it. Why don't you guys have treasure fever?"

Paul's voice, cold and final: "Because we're adults."

Derek had regained his composure or some of it. "I want you out," he said. "Both of you. Turn in your keys to me immediately. Naturally I will be changing the locks, so don't bother to try sneaking in again. I think it goes without saying that I'm disappointed in you, Dorian. You're a good actor, and I thought you were becoming a friend. Oh, and

I'm firing you from the Ibsen production, as well. I can't work with someone I don't trust."

There was real distress in Dorian's voice. "Derek, man, come on—"

His brother spoke up then. "It was my idea, not his. Don't punish Dorian for what I did."

I could almost feel the fury of Paul and Derek flowing across the hall.

"Are you suggesting I'm the one in the wrong here?" Derek asked quietly.

Some mumbled words from the twins. I wondered how often their parents had told them off in a similar manner. Or maybe they'd been allowed to get away with misbehavior, facing no consequences, no punishment . . . and now they would have to accept both.

A tiny glimmer of pity rose in me, mainly because I realized Dorian was a person who made stupid choices, and he most likely didn't realize it. His handsomeness had probably taken him far without much effort from him.

Still, when I heard Derek say, "I want you out by tomorrow," I felt only relief.

I looked at Connie; predictably, she looked slightly aroused by her boyfriend's show of strictness.

"Oh, you are unbelievable," I said, and she blushed even more.

Then we both laughed, perhaps longer than was healthy. The relief of one mystery solved, the "raccoon" exposed for what it was, the revelation of a hidden door in my wall that could now be sealed—all of those facts would make for a much better sleep in my bed tonight. I realized that even if Derek had changed the lock on my door, the twin intruders would have still had total access to my room through the Small Library and the hidden panel. I trembled with a sudden chill.

Connie was wiping tears of laughter out of her eyes. "Are you okay?" she asked.

"Yeah. It's just so weird, thinking of them creeping around, covering for each other so they could keep hunting for some mysterious and most likely fictional treasure."

"It's great to daydream about. But it seems like they made a job out of it. That's crazy."

"Maybe they grew up reading the Hardy Boys," I said. "Don't all of those titles have something to do with smuggling or treasure or locked rooms?"

Connie laughed again. "Maybe I should read one of those as Princess Goodbook."

"Stick with the classics."

Paul appeared in Connie's doorway. "Nora, thank you for alerting us. Naturally, we are dumbfounded—"

"No one could have expected you to know," I said.

"They actually went to the town hall to look up old building plans on microfiche," he said. "That's how they knew about the hidden panel. Do you want to see it?"

I followed him, Connie at my heels, and went into the hall, where Derek was just returning with Annie and Emily Brontë, who had escaped and apparently run a little way down the hallway.

"Naughty," he said.

I grinned at him. "Is Charlotte okay?" I asked a bit nervously.

I peered into my room and saw Charlotte sitting sleepily on my bed, her paws placed neatly together below her white chest patch. Clearly all the commotion had awakened her.

Derek set the cats on the bed and walked me over to the panel in the wall. It was still open, and I stepped into the narrow space behind it, perhaps four feet wide, which composed a tiny hallway.

"If you walk to the right there," Derek said, "you can

see the panel that leads into the Small Library. But if you keep walking, you'll see an opening at the end of the hall. There are stairs."

We looked at each other in disbelief.

He nodded. "Yeah. They go all the way down to the first floor, and apparently there's an exit hidden behind the trellis and ivy on the west wall."

Connie, ever the romantic, peered through the doorway in my room. "Imagine if you were locked in here, forbidden by your parents to see your lover. And then you discovered this door and found you could see him as much as you wanted, with no one the wiser.

Paul's head appeared next to hers. "That's an awfully positive spin to put on the whole thing."

Connie smiled. "Nora, you can use it to run off with Dash."

"Or we could just use the front door," I said.

"Not romantic," she said, shaking her head sadly. "Not romantic at all."

TUESDAY'S DRESS REHEARSAL went well, all things considered. I had gone down for a brief breakfast to find Dorian, pale but composed, sitting in the dining room. Zana sat beside him, patting his hand while he ate some coffee cake.

"Good morning," I said, realizing that I couldn't escape a meeting once they saw me.

"Hey, Nora," Zana said.

Dorian, ever resilient, smirked at me. "Zana's feeding me my last meal."

"I'm sorry you lost your role," I said, mostly meaning it.

"Yeah, that one hurt," he said, chagrined. "But I'll get another job. They're auditioning at Lane Park. Something by Strindberg. I think I have a good chance; I audition well."

He didn't add *because I'm handsome*, but we all seemed to understand that was what he meant. Even Dorian seemed to feel his looks were more useful than his talent.

"Will Drake be going with you?"

His eyes darted away from mine. "No, he's got some things to tie up in town. He'll probably keep his place here, and I'll commute to Lane Park while I'm staying with him."

There was something shifty, surreptitious in his manner that made me think he and Drake had deceived us about more than the treasure hunt. How else could twin faces have benefitted them? One would, of course, be able to give the other an alibi. . . .

"Anyway, thanks for taking pity on me, Zana. You're a pal. I hope I'll see you around. Maybe we can meet at the bakery or the pub."

"Sure," Zana said. Then, concerned, she added, "Will you and Drake be able to afford the rented house now?"

He shrugged. "For a while."

"There are affordable apartments in town," she said consolingly. "It's nice to have the yard and the garage and the garden, but you guys can do without that, right?"

He looked at his plate, picking at the last few crumbs. "Eventually."

I had poured myself a cup of coffee, and now I headed to the door. "I promised Connie I'd meet her on the patio," I lied. "Good luck to you, Dorian."

"You, too, Nora. No hard feelings, right?"

I turned to meet his eyes, which held not genuine remorse, but something between flirtation and resentment. "Right," I said.

I left the dining room and moved swiftly to the elevator, which I took up to the third floor and my room. In my room, I decided it was time to fill Dash in on what had been happening in the castle. I had been on verge of texting him the day before, right after our discovery of the Pierce brothers, but perversely, I had felt that the next text should come from him. Now that seemed childish, so I texted Dash:

> Dorian's been fired. Long story. But he has a twin brother, and they were using their resemblance to cover for each other as they made mischief. I wonder if they could also be involved in your burglaries? Dorian's brother, Drake, has a house in town, with a garage.

I sent the text before I could talk myself out of my unsubstantiated suspicion that was just a hunch based much more on Dorian's aura, his facial expressions, and his history of deception.

The Brontës were milling around their bowls, and I went off to feed them, my mind troubled by the idea of deception and the masks that people wore, especially actors, who wore the best masks of all.

WHEN WE FINALLY donned our costumes and picked up our first props, the world of Ibsen's play felt much more real. Connie had dropped me off while she parked her car, and I found that no one was yet there except for Jack, dressed in Torvald's middle-class suit, with a pocket watch attached to his vest and a pair of tiny reading glasses resting on his nose.

"You look perfect," I said. "Nice to meet you in the flesh, Torvald."

He patted the seat beside him. "Sit down, Miss Linde. I must apologize for all the obnoxious things I'm about to say to you on that stage," he joked.

I laughed. "All in a day's work."

His eyes met mine, and I saw some sadness in them. "It's changed us, hasn't it?"

I nodded. "It has."

He sighed. "Priscilla's been coming to the pub every day after she closes up. I'm her sounding board, and she's mine. We vent and complain and process all of our feelings. I guess it's been healthy. Like therapy. We've both had this 'life is long' philosophy all our lives. Now this kid, this boy, gets cut down out of nowhere. Anyone can die any-time. We've been admitting that to each other, to ourselves. It's—shifted some things in our worldview."

"I understand," I said.

Connie came drifting down the aisle, a sunny Nora Helmer dressed in a green gown with a black collar, and a little red flower pinned to the lapel. "What are we talking about?" she asked.

"How great this production will be," Jack said in a heartening tone. "Shall we take our places, Mrs. Helmer?"

Connie laughed as he stood up and proffered his hand. Derek was delighted to see them already onstage and ex-amining the newly completed set, lush with carpets and a flickering light in the fireplace and bookshelves filled with books. Ibsen's doll's house looked cozy and ready for the holidays; the large Christmas tree that Ben had helped put on the stage now glimmered with white lights and red rib-bons. Though it was only October, I had a sudden festive feeling, as though Christmas really was around the corner.

And then, within minutes, we had begun. Nora and Tor-vald discussing her purchases; Torvald warning her that she must never be in debt; my arrival; Nora confiding to me that she had a very large debt, but that she'd taken it on to save Torvald's life. Krogstad's appearance in Connie's sit-ting room, warning her, "It's up to you how merry a Christ-mas you'll have, Mrs. Helmer." Then the end of Act I, and Nora's reversal, from happy and excited to sick and terri-fied. The curtains closing.

Then Act II, with a new Nora pacing around a Christ-

mas tree with "burned-out" candles, "stripped of orna-
ment," just as Nora had been stripped of her happiness, her
innocence, her confidence, because she was at the mercy of
a blackmailer. She had more interviews with Torvald,
Krogstad, Kristine, but before them with Ann-Marie,
played by a wise and indulgent Renata, who consoled Nora.

Finally, Act III: the act of revelations. Rank confided
that he was dying; Kristine and Krogstad had their meeting, and Kristine insisted on the direct communication that
the Helmers had avoided for eight years. Because she was
honest, she saved her relationship with Krogstad, and her
future happiness was likely. "It is worth the try," I said in
one of my final lines. Paul's face, when he turned to me and
said he had never been so happy, convinced me that he was
the better man for the role. He and I shared the sweet kiss
that Derek had wanted, and Paul walked offstage. I stayed
long enough to see my friend in her masquerade costume,
at which point Torvald hurried me out the door. He had
romance on his mind, but his wife, who intended to commit
suicide, said they needed to talk.

Then the final dialogue, with confrontations and accusations and apologies and statements of disbelief. And then a
final severing, and a slamming of the door.

WHEN THE REHEARSAL was over, we gathered on the
edge of the stage and sat down in our costumes, legs dangling. Derek turned on the houselights, and when he came
back, his eyes were shining.

"We have some work to do," he said. "But I have never
felt more confident about a show."

We clapped for him, and he clapped for us.

Despite everything, the joy of performance was once
again in my bones. I closed my eyes and lifted my face to
the hot stage lights.

*   *   *

BY THE TIME we drove home, it was dark and nearing ten o'clock. Connie chatted happily while she drove, and I gazed out at the moon, which was almost full and had a slightly orange tinge that made it look particularly beautiful.

We reached the turnoff onto the castle driveway, and I said, "You know what? It's gorgeous out tonight. I think I'd like to walk up. I can look at the moon and smell the forest. It will do me good."

Connie hesitated, stopping the car. "Well—I don't know if Dash wants us wandering—"

I laughed. "Even if a murderer was lurking, there's no reason why they would just stand around in the woods at night on the off chance that one of us might come along to be attacked. Besides, what motive would there be? We don't know anything, sad to say."

Connie gave in. "It is beautiful tonight."

"Feel like taking a moonlight walk this time?"

"Maybe," she said with a grin. "But Derek's going to want to dissect every aspect of the play, so there might not be time. You should get some sleep, because tomorrow is a dress rehearsal with the understudies."

"True. All the more reason for some fresh air. It will help me sleep." I opened my door and said, "See you inside."

"Okay. Enjoy the moon," Connie said.

I climbed out and slammed the door. Connie's car moved quietly up the rutted road, then wound out of sight.

I took a deep breath of night air, and as I had hoped, I was rewarded with some delicious night scents. Rotted leaves, that universal autumn smell, joined with aromas of pine and moss, and the slightly damp bark of mist-shrouded trees. I began to walk, veering onto the footpath that led through the forest, gazing up occasionally at the tangerine moon framed by sighing trees. I was perhaps halfway back when I heard something behind me: a twig snapping. Pausing, I listened but heard nothing more. I began walking again, and this time there was no denying it; I heard branches breaking behind me. I was moving faster now, and the pace of the footsteps behind me seemed to quicken, as well. My mind veered in crazy directions. The moon now seemed not a lovely orange but a blood-tinged cream. Hadn't I just told Connie that no murderer would lurk in the dark? Would I die here, having never performed the play, never resolved things with Dash, never learned what had happened to Ben?

I broke into a jog, trying not to trip over vines or jutting logs. The person behind me began to run, too, and I could hear heavy breathing. They had closed the gap between us, had gotten closer, mere feet away.

My mouth was dry, my heart beating rapidly, and I ran, fearful of a hand on my shoulder, a knife in my back. . . .

Moments later, it was there: a cold hand on my arm, squeezing. "Nora—"

I screamed. "No!" and tried to tear away the hand that clutched me.

"Nora, it's me," said a quiet voice. "It's me. I'm just walking home."

I swung around and saw Miranda, her white hair glinting in the moonlight. She looked almost ethereal there in the woods, the wind lifting her hair.

"Miranda," I breathed.

"Did I scare you? I'm sorry. I wanted to catch up with you because I didn't want to walk alone."

Suspicion shimmered in me. "Where are you coming from?"

"My other job. My friend picks me up, and then she drops me off on Apprehension Road. She still has a half-hour drive ahead of her, so I can't blame her."

"Your friend?" I said. The anonymity of the other person troubled me.

"Yeah. Her name is Sally. She and I have performed together before, so I—" She stopped, looking as though she had said too much. "Anyway, I was glad to run into you. You scared me at first, with that flowing black hair. It looked spooky."

"So does yours," I admitted with a small smile.

"Yeah, I don't think you and I were meant to walk in dark woods. We don't have the constitution for it."

I nodded. "I thought it would be lovely, but too many things have happened lately. It was not good timing."

We walked for a moment in companionable silence. "So what's your other job?" I finally asked.

Miranda was silent for a moment. Then she said, "I dance at a club." She sensed rather than saw my expression and said, "It's not a seedy place. And I'm not a stripper. But the costumes are pretty skimpy. However, I have a great boss, and I love dancing. And you wouldn't believe the pay, Nora."

I thought about this. "Well, I'm glad you're getting a lot of money for your talent. Artists so rarely do."

This cheered her. "My boyfriend and I want to travel Europe for a year. We're trying to sock away as much money as we can. Between my castle job and this dancing gig, I'm making way more than I would in a standard nine-to-five job."

"But there's no danger that some audience members would—stalk you, or get too fresh, or—"

She shook her head; she looked ghostly there in the dark.

"That's why I love my boss. Do you know what he told us at the last meeting? We have these bouncers named Steve and Spike."

I laughed.

"Yeah, I know. Crazy name, but he's a doll. Anyway, my boss Richard told us last week that Steve and Spike were there not just to protect our physical selves, but to protect our dignity. He said, 'Yeah, they're coming because you're attractive and you dance well, but that doesn't give them any rights, none, to come anywhere near you. This is made clear to them in our sign at the door, and it also says we are within our legal rights to protect our employees by whatever means necessary.'"

"Wow. That's great. I've heard stories—"

"Oh, women are treated terribly in a lot of clubs and strip joints: their bosses swearing at them, treating them like crap, hinting that they should give the customer whatever he wants." She looked disgusted. "That's not Richard. Last month, a guy tried to grab my skirt and pull me toward him. Spike shoved him so hard, he fell back and fractured his elbow. He said he would sue us, and Spike said, 'We welcome your attempt.'"

I laughed.

"The girls all started clapping, and even some of the guys in the audience joined in. Can you imagine? Going to a judge and saying that you were just trying to pull a girl's skirt off and a guy dared to try to stop you? Can you imagine explaining that lawsuit to your wife or your girlfriend? As you might imagine, no lawsuit ever materialized. But Richard said it would actually be good for the business. 'First of all, I'm confident we'd win,' he told us. 'And secondly, a public understanding that we are a respectable club that shows a healthy esteem for women and their rights can only be a good thing.'"

I stopped walking. "Is that for real? Because I think I want to marry him."

Miranda laughed. "He's married. And has like a hundred kids."

"Well, his daughters should be proud."

"I know his wife is proud. She comes in now and then. She knows us all by name. She and I share recipes."

"Is this the sort of place that I could come to? To see you dance?"

She brightened again. "Absolutely! Lots of couples come. We work hard on our choreography. We're not just pole dancers. We're all trained dancers. Grew up doing *The Nutcracker* at Christmas and stuff like that. I'll miss the job when we travel, but Richard told me I can come back whenever."

We had reached the castle, and I said, "You must get tired at night."

"Exhausted," she said. "But I'm still going out. My boyfriend is picking me up in about twenty minutes."

"Seriously?"

She laughed. "We agreed that we would make time for each other, even with our weird schedules, so we have a lot of late dinners. He's taking me to Jack's Pub. It's open till midnight on Tuesdays."

"I am full of admiration for you both," I said. "Sincerely."

"Thanks," she said. "Hey, how did the dress rehearsal go?"

"It went well. Derek is happy, so I'm happy."

We started to climb the steps to the main entrance. "I heard Dorian got sacked."

I nodded. "Derek did the right thing."

I unlocked the door, and we entered our castle home, turning toward the elevator as if by mutual consent. We climbed aboard and pressed "3."

"Oh, I know. I've always felt a little weird around Dorian. There's just something about him, you know?"

I knew. And as I said good night to Miranda on the third floor, I found myself remembering that gleam of resentment in Dorian's eyes.

16

At Midnight

I WAS SUDDENLY WEARY and wanted nothing more than a long bath and a good book. I told the Brontës I was going to take a bath—something that would now interest them, since I had bought some little plastic ducks that they liked to bat from the tub ledge while I was bathing.

I ran a bath, pouring in some floral-scented bath oil that Connie had given me on some silly day she'd found on her calendar—National Best Friends Day or something like that. Connie just loved giving gifts, something I tried to reciprocate when possible.

Now I enjoyed the benefits of Connie's generosity, submerging in warm scented water and watching the Brontës slap at the ducks, which persisted in bobbing back up again. I giggled as I watched them, then leaned back, closed my eyes, and relaxed. I banished all thoughts for five blissful minutes. Eventually, bathed and peaceful, I emerged from the bath and set the three ducks on the mat, where the cats could examine them.

On a whim, I strolled out into the main room, no longer

fearful of "raccoons" that might interrupt my privacy, and found the green silk pantsuit that I had purchased from Priscilla. I slipped the top over my head, then pulled on the loose and flowing slacks. The material, expensive and luxurious, felt wonderful against my skin. I strolled to the mirror, fluffing my hair, and looked at myself. I had chosen a color that accentuated my skin, and my face seemed to glow against the jewel-toned silk.

"Ah," I said, remembering.

I went to my little jewelry box and found the jade earrings I had received four years ago from an amorous but ultimately unfaithful boyfriend. I slid them into my ears and saw that they matched the outfit perfectly.

Sighing, I walked to my bed, and my gaze fell on the basket I'd bought from the Portnoys, which I had forgotten to give to my parents when they picked up the twins. I heard Miranda's voice in my ear, saying, *We agreed that we would make time for each other. . . . I'm still going out. . . .*

Suddenly wide-awake and consumed by a strong whim, I took the basket and tore off the plastic wrap. I laid some items out on my bed—the wine, some cheeses, crackers, and jams. I found two blue-rimmed wineglasses on my little sideboard and leaned them against the wine bottle. Emily Brontë, gray and fluffy, came and sat beside my impromptu picnic, her paws pressed neatly together in front of her.

"I should hire you out for commercials," I said, admiring her perfection. "But I wouldn't want you to get spoiled by Hollywood."

She made a small contented sound, and I said, "Wish me luck, Emily."

I picked up my phone and texted Dash. I miss you. I've missed you for weeks. Any chance you'd like a midnight snack? I sent the text before I could regret it, along with a picture I took of Emily and the midnight picnic.

I put the things back in the basket, not wanting the cats to play with them. The wine and the glasses went back on the sideboard, and I waited for my phone to buzz.

He was exhausted; he'd been working nonstop since Ben had died. He was probably asleep.

He probably hadn't heard the text, and I shouldn't feel rejected if he didn't respond.

He most definitely wasn't with the beautiful Robin Bradley, comparing notes in some shadowy corner of Jack's Pub. . . .

Emily meowed at me rather sternly, and I said, "I know, I know. I'm being ridiculous. This is Dash we're talking about, right?"

Curious, the other Brontës jumped on the bed, and all three of them waited with me, their expressions patient.

"I can learn a lot from you," I said, scratching each little head with separate thanks. "But I can also confide in you, right? That I'm worried—"

My phone buzzed. I looked at my cats, whose expressions encouraged me to pick up the phone. I feared a text that would depress me, make me cry, ruin the liquid feeling of peace that I'd enjoyed for the last hour.

"Screw your courage to the sticking place," I quoted to them. "Renata would be proud of me, quoting Lady Macbeth. Here goes."

I tapped on Dash's text and read a simple response.

Twenty minutes.

I grinned; my body seemed to be filling with air, or helium, something light and ticklish.

I WAS WAITING at the front door when he pulled up. He drove up too fast, stopped his car, seemingly intent on parking it on the sweep of gravel and mulch that eventually turned into the front lawn. It was not a parking spot, as he well knew, having posed as the castle gardener for a significant amount of time a few months earlier.

His door swung open and he stepped out, slamming it behind him without looking back. He wore dark slacks and a shirt that he seemed to have buttoned hastily, something white or pale blue that shone in the moonlight. He and I both moved swiftly, meeting at the bottom of the stairs, and I threw myself into his arms, which wrapped around me, viselike and pleasing. I smiled against his mouth, which was pressing insistently against mine, warm and urgent and interested.

"Inside," he managed to murmur. "Elevator."

Somehow, we got up the stairs, still kissing, and somehow we staggered to the elevator, the door opened with a quiet sliding sound, and I pushed Dash inside; I managed to press "3" before he pushed me against the elevator wall, kissing my neck, running his hands up and down the silky material on my body. He broke away for a moment, looking confused and excited.

"What is this?"

"New outfit," I murmured, pulling his face back to mine.

On the third floor, I held a finger to my lips. "Everyone's sleeping," I said, although I had no idea if that was true. But I wanted total solitude—no greetings, no distractions, no visitors.

Dash was mine.

I opened my door, which I had left unlocked, and we rushed forward.

I didn't have any conscious thought at that moment except that I wanted, I needed, and I was determined to embrace the man who had raced across town to find me, whose dark hair had fallen slightly over one eye, and whose hands were rubbing persistently over my silky limbs.

He slid his hands into my hair and said, "Nora."

Then the Brontës were scattering off the bed as we dove onto it together, quiet, determined, and blind to anything but sensation.

PERHAPS TWO HOURS later I lay in my bed next to Dash. I got up on one elbow, lazily, and touched his hair. He had been smiling dazedly at the ceiling, but now his lovely brown-gold eyes turned their gaze on me.

"Hey," he said.

"Hey. Thanks for coming over."

He sent me a mischievous glance. "I thought you were going to feed me. "

"Oh, my gosh!" I jumped up and moved across the room, almost slipping on the silky material that lay pooled upon the floor. "I have wine, cheese and crackers, and jam."

I brought the food and wine to the bed in two trips and instructed Dash to open and pour the wine. He did so, and I found a plate to hold all the crackers, which I was sure we would eat. Then I opened the cheeses and the jams, standing with my back to Dash.

"I read in the castle brochure that the view is amazing, and I have to agree."

I laughed. "Thanks. But now you're making me self-conscious."

I turned back with the tray, and Dash looked solemn. "You should be conscious of the fact that your self is beautiful."

I set down the tray on my quilted coverlet and climbed back into bed. "Very sweet."

"Very true."

He handed me a glass of wine, and we toasted each other in silence. And then we ate, suddenly ravenous, every speck of food on the plate.

"Try this jam," I said, holding a cracker to his mouth.

"Mmmm. Try this cheese. I think it's Gouda."

"Is this what is meant by a bacchanal?" I asked when I finally stopped eating and sat against my pillow, swirling my wine.

Dash laughed. "If it is, then I am converting to Bacchanalia."

"Me, too."

We sat in silence for a while; eventually Dash put the tray on my bedside table and leaned back next to me.

"Dash?"

"Yeah."

"Tell me now what's been going on with you."

He looked remorseful. "I'm sorry. I—thought I was losing you. It messed me up."

I put down my wine and turned to him in surprise. "Why did you think that?"

He shrugged. "Whenever I came to visit, you were always laughing with Derek or Paul, and then Dorian came—"

"*Dorian?* I never—"

"But you did. He was always near you when I came. He's very good-looking, and he's younger than I am."

I'm sure my eyes were bulging out of my head. "Dash, I hate Dorian. He was always so slimy and intrusive. He and his brother spied on me, and they came in my room when I—"

He sat up. "What?"

"In a minute," I said, holding up a hand. "Why in the world would you think—he was interested in me or I was interested in him?"

It was his turn to look disbelieving. "Because he *was* interested in you, Nora. He liked you. And he managed to drop hints, in my hearing, about the perks of the castle, and one of them was all the beautiful women, and how he liked a challenge. Crap like that."

I laughed. "And that's exactly what makes him so repulsive."

His lips curled. "Go on."

I laughed, but then I gave Dash a little slap on the arm. "You know me. And I think I have made my devotion clear. I think I made it clear in August."

"In any case, I think your instincts about Dorian were right on target. I passed your tip about the Pierce brothers' garage to Robin. She was very interested to hear it."

I absorbed this in silence and said, "But back to your lack of trust?"

Now he looked regretful. "I know I shouldn't have—receded like that. But you're this beautiful, vibrant woman in an environment full of talented, extroverted, handsome—"

"And what is your point?" I asked, a touch coldly.

He studied the ceiling. "I'm just a quiet man."

I didn't know whether to be relieved or happy or angry. "And it never dawned on you that after ten years of working with handsome, extroverted narcissists I might be drawn to a man who is handsome and smart and sexy and quiet? That those are the very qualities that made me fall for you?"

"No," he said, not meeting my gaze. "But of course I see it now, and now I'm a narcissist, too."

I laughed. Then I put my face close to his. "I will forgive you for misjudging me if you promise never to do it again."

He pulled me against him and gave me a lingering, newly confident kiss. "I will never do it again. And don't think I don't realize how perfect you are, Nora."

"Not perfect. But maybe perfect for you."

"Definitely perfect for me. More wine?"

I flopped back on my pillow. "No, I am sufficiently high on relief."

"Me, too."

The Brontës had decided it was safe to return, and they strolled around between us, demanding attention. Dash laughed and petted the Brontës for a while, murmuring, "I missed you, ladies."

He looked solemn when he said, "You want to tell me what you meant about Dorian spying on you?"

With a sigh, I began the long story: the raccoon, the inspector, my brothers and their hair, the glimpse of a different Dorian in town. The hidden passage, their intrusion into my space.

"Unbelievable," he said. He climbed out of bed and began to put on his clothes. "I'm going to check out this secret passage."

I watched him contentedly, then laughed and said, "You wore two different shoes!"

His eyes met mine. "I was in a hurry."

I got up, stretched, and slipped back into my silks.

"I love that outfit, by the way," Dash said, already feeling around on the wall near my closet.

"Good to know. Here, I'll show you." I pointed out the piece of painted trim that was actually a button, and we heard the door unlock. "Now slide it," I said.

He did so, eyes wide, and moved into the tiny hallway behind. He walked to the end.

"There's a stairway there," I said. "It leads all the way to the first floor, where a well-camouflaged door lets out onto the west lawn."

He turned to me, shaking his head. "This castle never stops with the surprises."

"And right here is another door that goes into the Small Library."

He moved back toward me, and I said, "You can see the latch there."

He opened it and walked into the small book-lined room. "So one of them sat in here, poring through books in hopes of finding treasure?"

"Yes."

"Why this room?"

I shook my head. "I don't know. Something to do with the poem." He looked blank, so I recited the poem for him, telling him about the whimsical nature of Uncle Philip.

"So those two literally switched places so that one of them was always on book duty?"

"As often as possible. I don't think Drake learned Dorian's lines, but I did get the sense, once or twice, that Dorian was different at mealtime. They probably both came down to eat, the wily buggers."

There was a soft knock at the door. "Nora? Are you okay?" Connie's voice.

I went to the door and flung it open. "Yeah. I invited my boyfriend over for a midnight snack."

Connie's brows rose; she looked past me at Dash: his rumpled hair, his mismatched shoes, his happy face.

"Ah," she said. "I heard voices and feared that somehow those jerks got in again—"

"No. Derek has padlocked the ground-floor door."

"Good. I thought so, but—things have been so weird around here."

"You can say that again," I said. "Want to come in?"

"For a minute. I'm supposed to go visit Derek soon." She looked at her watch. "It's after two in the morning."

I went to my little kitchen and pointed to the chairs. "Sit here. We have some wine if you want. It's very good. I'm impressed with the Portnoys' store."

"Yeah, this is a good town for tourist food. Wait until you taste the Balfour Bars that Renata bought when we were at the bakery together. Remember when she walked out with a bag?"

"Oh, yes. I've been waiting," I said.

Dash and I sat across from her, close together, and she smirked. "So I assume you two have worked out whatever silly thing was causing your drama?"

We looked at each other. Dash said, "Absolutely. Nora has apologized, and everything is fine."

With a surprised laugh, I smacked his hand, and he grinned.

Connie yawned. "Derek has asked me to move in with him. Just one floor down, but still kind of a momentous thing."

"Of course it is!" I said. "Are you thrilled?"

Connie smiled, peaceful and happy. "I already live there most of the time now. But I told him I want to call both rooms home. I need my Nora time, too. He understands that."

"Wow, I'm really popular this evening," I joked.

Connie looked at me with wide eyes. "Nora, you are an essential part of my life. I can't remember Wood Glen before you came here."

"Nor can I," said John Dashiell, brushing a stray lock of my hair back into place with tender fingers.

17

The Animal Guide

THE NEXT MORNING I woke up with a smile. Dash wasn't in the room, but he had left a note that read *Back soon, Dash*. Those words was followed by about ten Xs. I grinned stupidly at the note, which he had left on his pillow, and then wandered into the bathroom. When I emerged, showered and wrapped in a towel to feed the squalling Brontës, Dash came back in, holding a tray with some breakfast breads and coffee. He looked at me as he set down the tray on my little dining table.

"I like the green silk outfit best, but this one comes in a close second."

I smiled, setting down the food and removing the towel from my hair.

He came closer. "You look like a mermaid when your hair is wet. Remember when we went to the beach . . . ?"

"And you kissed me every time I swam past you? Yes. I remember it all the time. Along with the time you kissed me in that parking lot and said you'd never met someone like me."

"Not original but true."

"It was the look on your face, not what you said."

He nodded. "Shall I help you dry off?"

I laughed, and once again we found ourselves in my bed without intending to sleep. Eventually, sated and smiling, I made a lazy grab for my phone to see if I had any texts. Dash did the same, and I saw him texting something rapidly, looking at his watch.

"Don't say you have to go."

"Not quite yet," he said.

On a whim I took out my phone and snapped his picture. "You look very sexy with your hair all messed up like that."

"Hmmm." He smiled.

"Did they give you a hard time in the kitchen when they saw your mismatched shoes?"

He scowled. "They hassled me even more for the way I parked my car. Paul demanded my keys and said he'd park it in a rational way, rather than like a man muddled by lust."

"He makes a good point," I said.

"Yeah."

I thought of "Fair Genevieve," and wondered if Paul felt envious of Dash and Derek. I felt more determined than ever to get Gen out for opening night; she had texted back and said she would "check her calendar."

Dash lifted his phone. "Now it's my turn; I'm going to capture your mermaid hair."

I laughed, and his phone buzzed. He looked down. "Oh, good, it's Robin."

"Robin." I stared at him. "Interesting that you give me the cold shoulder for simply existing near handsome men, but you work every day with that gorgeous specimen of femaleness."

He blinked. "Robin?"

"Yes, Robin. Don't lie and say you haven't noticed she's attractive."

"Well—I just think of her as a cop."

His face held no irony, and I narrowed my eyes.

"And what does Robin have to say to you at"—I consulted the clock—"seven thirty in the morning?"

"That she'll take the first part of my shift so I can be here with you."

A small silence. "I love Robin," I said, and Dash laughed.

I looked down at my phone, still open to photos, and said, "Oh, Dash! I wanted to show you this the other day, but you were—"

"Yeah, I know."

"Anyway, I was walking in the forest, clearing my head, and I met a friend."

I scrolled to the pictures of the beautiful buck. Dash took the camera and flipped through.

"Wow. I can't believe how close you got."

"I couldn't, either. He was so lovely. And—sort of friendly. I hope he never leaves the castle woods; he's safe there, but not necessarily in the forest outside."

"Huh—this is really cool. Let's take a walk soon and see if we can find him again." He swiped some more, and said, "When was this taken?"

I looked at it; it was Millie's picture of our group. "The night of the murder," I said. "I don't know if you were there or still parking the car. Millie Portnoy said she wanted to take a picture of the group."

Dash enlarged it slightly and studied it. I leaned in, doing the same.

There we were again, smiling dutifully at Millie's camera: I had my arms around Connie and Renata. Priscilla was between Ben and Andy, her mouth pursed slightly as though she were talking, and Andy was in the middle of a laugh, leaning toward her and ready to retort. Elspeth, tall and slender, stood next to Jack, and Barbara and Miranda stood on either side of Dorian, though Miranda had turned to look at Derek, who was at the end of the row and looking as though wanted to consult his watch. Paul had dived in front of the first row, lying across the ground, his head propped on one elbow, grinning in his sweet Paul way.

"Everyone looked happy," I said. "How do you go from this to murderous?"

"I don't know."

The picture was bringing back memories of that night, the clustering crowd in the narrow hallway, the confusion of the dim lighting, the distracting skulls, and then the total darkness—tripping, falling, thinking that this was somehow part of the performance. I studied the people in the picture, trying to remember who had been in what location when we began to walk. And then I saw something I had never seen before; it seemed to leap out at me, chiding me for being blind.

"Oh, my God," I whispered.

He turned, his body tense. "What? What is it?"

I pointed at the photo. "That night, it was so dark in the catacombs that it was hard to know who was where. I was sure I was behind Jack, but then the crowd shifted, and I was behind Ben. Or maybe the crowd didn't shift after all."

"Meaning what?" But recognition was dawning in his eyes.

"Look at Jack. He was wearing a blue button-down shirt. He's about Ben's height, with similar hair color. Look at Ben. Also a blue shirt but a polo."

Dash let the phone slip out of his grasp and onto the bed in shock. He leaned his head back on the pillow and closed his eyes.

"I don't think Ben was the target," I said quietly.

He nodded, his eyes still closed. "That's such an important catch, Nora. And I didn't see it. Thank God you did."

"I only just did. You would have seen it in a minute."

He got up and began to put on his clothes. "I need to

contact Jack, put him under protection. Meanwhile, let's think about who might have a motive."

"Jack's a nice guy. But I can see more motive to kill him than I could to kill poor Ben."

"Such as?"

"He likes women, and he likes his reputation as a lothario." I thought of my talk with Jack in the empty theater. "At least, he did. He's very sober these days."

"Any idea if he's seeing someone?"

"Not that I know of. I mean, he and Priscilla talk a lot, but I think they're just friends."

Dash began to button his shirt. I watched his fingers. "Any possibility of a woman scorned among that group in the catacombs?"

"Not that I know of. I mean, no gossip reached me. But I don't always hear the gossip. I'm like a nun in this castle, alone in my room and meditating."

He sent me a glance that suggested I had recently broken a vow, and I grinned. "A nun in a very liberal order."

"What other motives? Is he in debt? Did someone else want his role in the play? Who's his understudy?

"I don't think roles in a play can be a motive for murder," I said.

He sat down on the bed, holding his mismatched shoes. "When you lost that role in *Evita*, did you resent the woman who won it?"

"Yes. But I didn't wish her ill. I just resented her."

"Yes, and you're a mentally healthy person. What if you weren't and you had your heart set on the role? Actors are—dramatic people. Have you ever known one to overreact when they lost a role, got a bad review, or received criticism?"

Examples began to occur to me, bursting into my mind like popcorn. "Well—yes."

"Another possible motive. And that's not dipping into

his family relationships, his recent arguments, any resentful bar patrons. . . ."

"Just make sure he knows to protect himself. And not to trust any of us in the group."

Dash, his face solemn, assured me that he would not let another man die. "I feel bad enough about Ben, who was attacked right in front of me."

"As if you or anyone could have known."

He bent to kiss me. "I'm sorry I have to leave early. But thank you for helping me to see this, Nora. You've got me on the right path." He kissed me again, lingeringly. "In a lot of ways."

"Direct communication from now on?"

"Definitely. And more midnight snacks?"

"I'm counting on it."

We smiled at each other. Then he blew me a kiss and bent to scratch the Brontës, who lay in a gray pile of fuzz in front of the fireplace, and then he was gone.

I flopped back on the bed and sighed. Despite the talk of murder, my happiness at being on sound footing with Dash lingered like a lovely scent in the room. I felt grateful to Miranda, who had appeared suddenly in the forest and said those crucial words to me: *We agreed that we would make time for each other, even with our weird schedules.* Why had I assumed that we were locked into time constraints?

Miranda's appearance in the forest made me think of the deer, my new friend and animal guide. And he *had* guided me, because the pictures of him had led to Dash's discovery of the group photo, and my realization about the matching blue shirts. Twins again . . .

Dash was on the job now, and I had every confidence that my boyfriend would both protect Jack and find the perpetrator. I only hoped it was going to happen soon. I hated suspecting my fellow actors, and yet I had to suspect them as a form of protection.

Today I wore a sweater I'd bought in my precastle life. A checkerboard pattern of blue, green, and black, it had always been a favorite. I wore it with black jeans and a pair of blue hiking boots. I was about to jog downstairs when there was a knock at my door.

"Who is it?" I moved closer; I thought I heard murmuring.

"It's Derek. And Paul and Connie."

I flung the door open and said, "Is something wrong?"

Connie bounded into my room and scooped up Annie, who had already finished her food. Connie held her like a baby and scratched her full tummy. Annie's purr was so loud, it made us all laugh.

"Come on over to the easy chair," I said. "I can bring over the dining room chairs. Sorry my bed isn't made."

"I'll get the chairs," Paul said.

Soon we were seated in a little triangle near my long, lovely windows.

I looked at Derek. "Did you talk to Dash before he left?"

"No. Why?"

"He's following a possible new lead. We ran across it this morning when we were looking at pictures on my phone, and I happened to run across this one."

I lifted my phone from the table and showed them the group picture from Millie and Andy's store.

"Okay," Connie said. "What's the lead?"

"Look at Ben." They did so. "Now look at Jack."

Paul saw it first. He whistled. Derek and Connie got it a minute later.

"We were right," Connie said. "There was no motive to murder Ben."

"I don't think so," I said. "Not to insult Jack, but he's far more likely—"

"Of course he is." Derek nodded. "Is Dash going to tell Jack?"

"Yes. He's also going to put a guard on him."

"Maybe this means they'll wrap things up soon." Paul's tone was hopeful, and it lifted my spirits.

"Let's hope so." I realized then that I didn't know why they'd come to my room. "Um—what did you guys—"

Connie was excited again, suddenly bursting at the seams. "Derek had the best idea. You're never going to want to leave the castle again!"

"That sounds kind of disturbing," I said, and Paul and Derek laughed.

Derek beamed his gray eyes at me. "Paul and I were talking about the unfortunate incidents with Dorian and his brother, and their invasion of your privacy. We should have been on top of it when you said you heard noises. Before they frightened you in your own room." Derek looked angry.

"We're very sorry that happened," Paul said.

"You couldn't have known—," I began, but Derek held up a hand.

"We should have made it our business. Again, we apologize."

"It's okay," I said. "It's over now."

"Yes." Derek cleared his throat. "So Paul and I were thinking we could turn a negative into a positive. Something nice for you."

"What? I don't need—"

Now Connie interrupted. "Nora, you have to have to listen to them!"

I laughed. "Okay, I'm all ears."

Derek jumped up. "Come on over here," he said, moving to the wall with the false passage. He opened it and beckoned to me.

I moved forward, saying, "I know you said you're going to seal these up or something. Or put giant locks on them, which I appreciate."

Paul joined us at the door. "We actually had a different idea."

Connie was grinning like a fool but said nothing.

"Okay, what were you thinking?" I asked.

Paul walked into the hallway and went as far as the descending staircase. "We'll have to figure out what to do with this. You can let us know if you want to keep it, so that you have a direct entrance to your room, or whether we should get rid of it. But as for the rest, we thought we might put a window in this hallway, to bring in a little more light. Maybe carpet the floor, and then turn the doorway into the Small Library into an actual doorway. Same as the door in your wall."

"What do you—"

"We thought you might like it if we added a wing to your room. To make the Small Library a part of your living quarters. We'd make it so you can lock it from the inside, and you can rearrange furniture, make it like your little study—"

"And the Brontës would have more roaming space!" Connie added, knowing that this would delight me.

I stared at them all; I felt as though I couldn't blink. My eyes were dry, and then they were suddenly very wet.

"You like the idea?" Derek asked.

"I love it," I whispered. "I love it so much I can't even tell you. That library—I love it so much, and I love all of you!" I wiped at my eyes.

Paul moved forward and pulled me into a big hug; I clung to him.

Derek and Connie exchanged a high five.

"Connie told us you would get emotional," Derek said.

"Connie knows me well," I said into Paul's sleeve.

Finally, Paul pushed me away and grinned into my face. "Let's take a look at your new space and talk about the possibilities."

I nodded, and we moved single file into the Small Library.

"Oh, and, Nora?" Paul said. "Regarding the secret door and your unwanted visitors—I'll need you to fill out an incident report."

Connie rolled her eyes behind his back, and I laughed. "Okay. I'll come down and do it in your office later so I can steal some chocolate."

18

To the Death

SEVERAL DAYS PASSED without incident. The October air had remained calendar-appropriate cold, but the sun had shone for days, and Wood Glen was alive with the scents of autumn—leaves and grasses, pumpkin bread in Zana's kitchen, sweet-smelling hay bales brought to our front porch by the landscaper, woodsmoke from fireplaces up and down Apprehension Road.

"I love fall," Connie said as we took a hike down an unfamiliar path.

I had told her about my deer, too, and she said she'd like to find him with me, but it wasn't likely because, being Connie, she couldn't stop talking.

"What is Nora going to say now?" I said.

Connie made a face at me. "That I love everything."

"But I'm glad you do. Otherwise you wouldn't be my sweet friend Connie."

This pleased her. "Derek says after the final performance at the BC, he'll start working on your room. They don't have money for a big renovation, but he says they can do some fancy stuff with the doorway and a do-it-yourself window installation."

"I'm so excited. It's the nicest gift I've ever been given. Dash is happy for me, but he's also nervous because he says he'll never top it."

Connie laughed. "I'll brainstorm with him."

"Speaking of gifts," I said, "my sister, Gen, said she's made arrangements so that she can come down for opening night."

Connie's blue eyes widened. "So—we've got some matchmaking to do."

"No, we have to be really subtle. I'm just going to put her in the front row, and Paul won't know she's going to be there. She'll see from his performance that he is a special man, sensitive enough to find the layers of Krogstad, and she'll fall a little deeper into infatuation."

"Romantic," Connie said appreciatively. "Hey, look!"

We had reached a little opening in the trees, wide enough that we could see the castle in the distance.

"It's such a beautiful building," I said. "I wonder if it met all the expectations of Uncle Philip."

"How could it not?" Connie said. She touched my arm. "Remember the first day you came, and you told me you had feared the castle would be some cheap, gimmicky place?"

"And you said that I would love it, which I do. I'm so glad you were there to convince me."

We walked some more, and she said, "Who do you think would want to kill Jack?"

I shook my head. "I don't know enough about Jack's life. A woman, I'm thinking."

"Wouldn't it take a lot of strength to stab that hard?"

"But think about it. Did you ever see women get violent over a man?"

She nodded, her eyes widening as memories occurred to

her. "Yeah, okay, but that was usually women against women fighting over the guy they both loved."

"Hmmm. Maybe it was a case of 'If I can't have him, no one can.' In any case, Jack has been informed, and he's got a cop assigned to the bar and to his house."

"Wow."

We walked some more, making far too much noise to lure a deer closer, but it was a joy to crunch through the various twigs and leaves, smelling the fall air.

Connie said, "Oh, we're doing knitting class in the costume room tonight. Renata is bringing the Balfour Bars."

"Ah, the legendary Balfour Bars! I am ready to be wowed."

"You will be," said Connie.

The trail forked in front of us. Connie stopped, inhaling the air and looking at the sky.

"Ah. We should probably get back. Derek wants to run through the revised castle show so we can start next week. He's moved it from the catacombs to the library. He says Elspeth is going to make it look very creepy in there."

"What a great idea! That kind of versatility will keep him in business."

Connie looked sideways at me. "I hope so. Nora, I can't bear for them to lose the castle!"

"Is there a danger of that?" My bones felt cold.

She shook her head. "Not in the near future. But he and Paul have been trying to create a five- and ten-year plan, and—they don't know if it's sustainable, the way they've set things up."

"They're too generous. And they love ambience too much. So many purchases just to create a great set or a perfect meal."

"Yeah. But that's what I love about Derek. His generosity and his big vision for everything. He really should have been a king, with a room full of precious gems, because he would take care of all his people," Connie said, looking pensive. "But back to the matter at hand. Bring your yarn tonight. Elspeth and Renata have some pattern books for beginners, and you can pick out what you'd like to make."

"I feel like a sweater might be kind of advanced," I said. "Maybe a scarf to start with."

"Anything handmade makes a great gift. Dash will love it."

"I think he will," I said, smiling.

When we got back to the castle, Elspeth and Renata were at work on the main entrance stairs, creating a Halloween tableau with pumpkins, fake cobwebs, and plastic ravens, complete with faux feathers and realistic eyes.

"Looks spooky," Connie said. "I like this even better than last year's vision."

Renata nodded. "Elspeth always has ideas. I am merely a laborer."

"I'm excited about tonight," I said, "and being initiated not only into the knitting club, but into a particular echelon of chocolate connoisseurship."

Renata laughed and said, "We'll be pleased to have you there, and the initiations will be enjoyable ones."

Connie and I went upstairs, and she said she would see me at lunch. "I promised Derek I would help him deal with some of his correspondence."

"Is that a euphemism?" I joked.

She grinned. "Not this time. He's pretty busy in that office."

She waved and disappeared into her room to "freshen up." I detoured briefly into the Small Library, my heart brimming with gladness. I let my hand trail along the lovely wood table, imagining the Brontës sitting there. How fun for them to have a whole big room and mysterious hallway to explore without danger of getting lost in the big castle.

Suddenly I longed to buy something to put in this new room, something to give it distinction and personality, to make it "Nora's study" rather than just the Small Library. I could go to Relics, the antiques store Derek loved, and find some tasteful antique to stand in a corner; or perhaps I could find something bright and lovely at Priscilla's store, or at Portnoy's Gifts. I wanted to get another basket for my parents, anyway, since Dash and I had laid waste to the other one. I smiled at that memory for a moment, then left the library by the hallway door and unlocked my own door. I made sure my kittens had everything they needed, then grabbed my keys and my purse and set out on my shopping adventure.

When I reached downtown Wood Glen, the wind had picked up, and leaves were blowing back and forth across the roads in poetic flurries, their colors vibrant in the October sun. I parked in front of Balfour Bakery, which was two doors down from Portnoy's Gifts. I could walk through the lovely leaves to Priscilla's store and then to Relics if I didn't find anything I liked.

I climbed out of the car, paid the meter, and observed the vast shrine of flowers that had amassed in Ben's memory. The sight lifted my spirits, as did the warm scent of baking bread in Balfour Bakery.

"Good morning," I said to Jade's parents, who were dealing with a line of customers.

Mara waved, and I moved around the shop, looking at the wares they sold that were not behind the bakery glass or on racks behind the counter. In one corner they sold coffee made by a local brewer; in another some presliced loaves of pumpkin bread and jack-o'-lantern cookies. On a table under the window, I saw boxes of chocolates. I went closer and saw that the Balfours, too, carried Castle chocolates. Impressed by the Wood Glen merchants' willingness to support one another, I looked at the different flavors. The Balfours had one of the flavors Connie liked, along with the one Andrew loved.

I got in line with everyone and gazed out the window in vague abstraction until it was my turn.

"Hello, Nora," Mara said. "Jade can't stop talking about your brothers. How funny they are, how cute they are, how they should have their own YouTube channel."

"I'm glad they hit it off. The twins said Jade was 'very cool.'"

Her mother laughed. "Well, Jade is having a Halloween party in a few weeks, and I know she'll want to invite them. Maybe pass that on to see if they're available. I'd love to meet them." She smiled. "Meanwhile, what can I get you?"

"I'm spoiled with Zana in the castle. I shouldn't need one bit more to eat. But I like the look of those autumn spice donuts. I was thinking I'd bring some to the police station for my boyfriend and his colleagues."

"Oh, how nice."

"So I'll get a dozen, please."

"None for you?"

"Okay, thirteen. But leave mine out of the box."

"Sure thing," she said, grinning.

"I see you carry Castle chocolates, as well. I saw them in Priscilla's store."

"Oh, yes, several of us carry those. They're a popular brand, and the owner is local. In fact, he and Brian went to high school together." She pointed at her husband, who nodded.

"One of my best pals," he said, "so we like to support him."

"That's great. Oh, yes, those look delicious," I said as Mara began putting donuts into a box. "The scent of them is intoxicating."

"They're a fall favorite," she said, her expression placid.

I thanked the Balfours and took my purchases to the car. I set the box on the passenger seat, along with the little bag that held my donut. I paused for a moment by the tree, saying a few silent words in memory of Ben. Then I began to walk. Portnoy's Gifts had a sign on the door that read *Back in a minute!*

"New plan," I murmured, and headed toward Light in the Glen.

At the end of the street was Lucy's Diner; to my surprise, I saw Millie peering in the window. Perhaps she was looking at the lunch specials. She stepped away from the window and looked uncertainly down the street, first one way, then the other. Her gray-brown hair was blowing in the raw wind, and her nose looked red.

I had come within feet of her when I said, "Hi, Millie."

"Oh, hello, dear." She looked distracted, and I had the sense that she didn't even see me.

"I was about to buy another of your lovely gift baskets, but the store was closed," I said.

Millie looked glum. "Oh, yes. I'll just go back and open up. Come back when you wish."

"Thanks. I will."

I watched as Millie walked back toward her own place of business, her posture somehow defeated.

I wondered if she was depressed, perhaps about Ben. She did not seem emotionally healthy—unless I was reading more into her expression than was really there.

I kept walking, past the diner and around the corner, then about halfway down the block to Priscilla's store. When I was still three storefronts away, I saw Andrew coming out with a bag. Probably his bag of chocolates, I realized, and I wondered just how addicted he was. But who was I to talk? I had just bought a donut, and I was going to be eating Balfour Bars tonight. Not to mention that my boyfriend had fed me a croissant in bed that very morning. I was grinning when I passed Andy.

"Hey, chocoholic," I said.

He grinned. "Can't resist 'em. I tend to munch behind

the counter, you know. Nothing like a good piece of chocolate."

"Can't disagree with that," I said, laughing.

He went on in the direction of his store, and I entered Priscilla's place.

Once again, I was struck by the beautiful scents and sounds of her elegant haven. Priscilla was talking on her cell phone.

I studied a rack of scarves near her and heard her say in a low voice, "But you don't know that, Jack." She listened some more, then said, "Okay. Me, too. See you tonight."

She ended the call and said, "A repeat visitor?"

"I'm just looking, but I am so happy with the things I bought from you. I love them."

"Wonderful." She stood looking at me for a moment. "Can I help you find something?"

"No, I'm only really browsing in the category of . . . decor."

"Ah, I have a little corner there—see the red pillows? That's my minimal selection of furniture, bedding, housewares, stuff like that."

"Thanks." I paused. "How are you doing?"

"Not bad.

"I was impressed by Ben's shrine of flowers. It's lovely."

She nodded, tucking a strand of wavy blond hair behind her right ear. "I left him some roses. It felt good to do something, even a small thing."

"I agree. Did you—hear about Jack?"

Her eyes flashed over to me, surprised. "Oh—of course. You're dating the cop. Well, yes, I heard that Jack was most likely the intended victim. As you can imagine, he is not thrilled."

"He said you two have really been supporting each other."

Her brows rose again, but then she relaxed slightly and

leaned against the counter behind her. "You two really had a heart-to-heart, huh?"

"No, we just spoke briefly. This has changed him a bit."

"It has. You're very observant for someone who doesn't know him that well."

"It's just that—his face is different."

Priscilla sighed. I noticed that in the dim light of the store, her blue eyes looked almost purple. "Jack and I go way back, actually. We met just after college when we were both cast in a play in Chicago. Sparks flew, and we had—a fling. Kind of a long fling. Then we ended up going our separate ways, but every few years, we'd run across each other and start things up again." She smiled at my surprise.

"By the time we found each other in Wood Glen, we had sort of gotten tired of the whole passionate-affair thing. It was getting old. We started forming a friendship instead. And after two years, I think our friendship is pretty solid. But this thing with Ben— Well, it's bringing us closer. We're leaning on each other. It's nice to have someone to lean on." Her sad expression added dignity to her pretty face.

"I'm glad you have each other," I said. "You're perfect together."

She was amused. "Oh, so you're the matchmaking type."

"Yes, very much so."

We grinned at each other, and I told her I would go check out her furniture.

She did have a minimal selection, and I realized I'd want to look at Relics before I made any decisions. As I turned to go, I saw a wood plaque with burned-in letters that read *Books are food for the soul*. It was narrow enough to hang above a door—like the doorway of my new study. I seized it and brought it to the counter.

Priscilla wrapped it in tissue paper and tucked it into a bag, then rang me up. "You're good for business," she said, "although business has been pretty good this fall."

"That's nice to hear. I'll bet Andy composes half of your sales."

She laughed. "I told him he can't sue me for his medical bills when he needs chocolate-addiction therapy, although I might be legally seen as an enabler."

"I don't think you can be held responsible for someone else's addiction," I said.

Her eyes were on the register when she said, "And we all have them. Some of us just hide them better."

I thought about this, wondering if it was true. Did I have an addiction? I certainly loved sweets, but could I go for a few days without them? I thought I could. Was I addicted to acting? To Dash? No, I didn't think so. They were simply parts of my life that brought me great pleasure.

"There you go," said Priscilla.

"Thanks so much. Take care," I said. "I mean, really do. Watch behind you. Hopefully the police will figure this out soon."

She nodded her understanding and waved as I departed.

I decided Relics would have to wait for another day; I didn't want to be late for the castle rehearsal. I did have time to get the basket for my parents, though, and maybe something for Gen and the twins. I darted back into Portnoy's Gifts, where Andrew now stood behind the counter, reading the paper that lay flat on the glass display case.

"Good morning," I said. "I'm back for one of your lovely baskets. I accidentally consumed the first one."

Andy laughed and said, "Of course, of course. Which one did you want?"

I looked over their selection and picked one that contained two pretty red wineglasses. "This one."

"Wonderful. Let me take that to the front—you want the price tag removed?"

"Yes, please." I looked around. "Where did Millie go? I just saw her."

He rolled his eyes comically. "She obsesses over our little dog. She had to drive home and make sure all was well with Perky."

"Oh, that's sweet." I thought of Ben and his strays. That made me think of the shrine in front of Balfour Bakery and then of the inside of that establishment. "Speaking of sweet, I saw that Balfour Bakery also sells those chocolates you like."

"Oh, yes?" His face was pleasant as he peeled the price tag off of my basket.

"And it's just two doors away. That would save you traipsing all the way to Priscilla's store when you have a sweet craving."

He rang up my basket, and I handed him my credit card.

"Very practical," he said. "But Priscilla is my fellow thespian. Have to support our own clan, right?"

He winked at me, which made me feel uncomfortable. I told myself it was because I was not of the winking generation.

"Anyway, Priscilla charges slightly less than Balfour. And I get more steps in."

He pointed at the Fitbit on his wrist, and I nodded. All of this made sense, and yet I had the sense that he was improvising. But what other reason could he have had?

An image of Priscilla at practice stretching her slender arms and attracting the gaze of every man in the room. Did Andrew have a crush on Priscilla? I thought of Millie peering in the window of the diner. When I had spoken to her, she looked tempted to keep going down the next block— maybe to Light in the Glen? Had she been checking up on her husband?

My thoughts were flurrying out of control; this was a tendency of mine, my brothers often assured me. Still, I wondered if Andy, who must have been in his fifties, harbored some secret passion for Priscilla, who was perhaps thirty.

We all have addictions, she had told me. Was it really the candy to which Andrew was addicted?

On a whim, I said, "I was just in Priscilla's store, too. I didn't buy chocolate, though. Just some decor. Her store is lovely."

"It is indeed." He was putting the basket into a bag and tucking tissue around it.

"Jack was saying so, too. He was in there when I made my purchase," I lied.

Andy's head came up sharply. "Oh? What was Jack doing there?"

"Just hanging around, chatting with Priscilla. They would make a great couple, don't you think?"

He forced a smile. "Of course. That's why they're often cast together. Give me one moment; I need more tissue paper."

He moved out from behind the counter. I took out my phone and texted Dash: I have a surprise that I'm going to bring by the station. See you in ten.

I turned to see where Andy had gone—turned in time to see him flipping the Open sign to Closed.

"Calling it a day so early?" I asked brightly.

Then he turned toward me, and his face was no longer the face of Andy Portnoy, affable actor. It was gray and grim and angry. "Perhaps," he said. "I wonder, Nora, why you told me a lie just now."

Stunned, I said, "I'm sorry?"

"Jack Yardley was not in Priscilla's store. He's not even in Wood Glen."

"What?"

He took out his own phone and swiped through some screens. "Here's a text message I got from him twenty minutes ago. He's at a product expo in Chicago. He sent me a picture of this booth and asked if I was interested in any samples."

My eyes moved down to the picture, which was very obviously Jack at some big venue—McCormick Place, probably.

"Ah," I said.

"So why did you lie?"

I decided to wear Renata's queenly expression. "I wanted to see if you would be jealous."

His mouth narrowed. "What are you talking about?"

And then some of the evidence flowed into my mind: Priscilla bursting into tears at practice, and Andy coming forth to comfort her, pulling her into a hug. His face had not been sad but gratified. Happy. Possessive.

And in the picture—the one taken by Andy's own wife—he had been next to Priscilla, his eyes on her, his hand on her shoulder.

It seemed likely that he visited her store almost every day; certainly he must have disappeared often, because his wife had taken to looking for him, maybe when he was gone too long.

"Why did you think I would be jealous?"

"I just wondered. Call it a whim. No big deal, Andy." I didn't meet his eyes, and I could feel his suspicion growing.

"You suspect me of something?"

I looked past him to the door, to the people who occasionally walked past, oblivious to the tension in this room. "Like I said, I suspected you might have a crush on Priscilla. All the guys do, right?"

He seemed to be chewing something, but then I realized that his jaws were working while he processed some intense emotion. "I don't have a crush on Priscilla," he said, forcing a smile that looked sick. And he had said Priscilla's name in an almost pathetic way.

"I don't mean anything improper." I gabbled out a response without thinking. "I mean, I'm not suggesting that you see Jack as some kind of threat."

"I'm a married man."

"Listen, Andy, I don't care if you lust after Priscilla or not. I have to get going."

"I think you'll need to stay here for a while," Andy said in a toneless voice.

My stomach tightened with a sick feeling. "What are you talking about?"

"You know," he said. "You know."

And I did, then. I knew, looking at Andy's gray face, that he had meant to plunge a knife into the man he saw as his competition for a woman he loved hopelessly, and the lights had gone on to reveal that he had stabbed Ben, his adopted "son," to death.

"I see it in your eyes," he whispered.

"Andy," I said. My voice sounded like a croak. "I have to go."

I turned to grab my bag; there was a rush behind me, a flurry of sound, and then Andy's hands were wrapped around my neck. . . .

19

Perilous Paths

ANDREW WAS STRONGER than I would have thought; my hands clawed at his, but his grip tightened, and I began to choke.

"You shouldn't have lied," he said.

My thinking was growing foggy. I knew I wanted only to breathe, to breathe. But I dimly saw my brothers, energetic and physical, telling me to fight, always to fight if attacked. But how could I fight? I had no weapon; my hands pulled in vain at Andrew's desperate fingers. He dug into my windpipe and I thought irrationally that it would affect my singing voice.

I saw the boys again. Saw Jay saying, *If they attack from behind, bend* forward, *Nor. Forward, to throw off his balance. Then take advantage.*

I managed to turn my body away from the counter so that there was space before me. Nearly fainting, I threw myself forward in an attempt at a deep bow. Andrew's hands loosened, and his feet scrabbled. I spun out of his grasp; we were facing a wine rack, a display from a Michigan winery. I grabbed a bottle, swung it at his head, missing the top of his skull but catching him on the temple and eyebrow before it clattered to the floor and he lunged for me again. I dove to the side, trying to run, but he caught my hair, yanking my head back and making me lose my balance. I fell on the floor, hitting my head. I saw stars for a moment, but I heard him coming, and as he launched himself on top of me, I grabbed for whatever was next to me on the nearest shelf. Flinging my arm with all my strength, I hit him on the side of the head with the hard object in my hand. His hands loosened slightly, and I hit him again, this time in the neck. And then again in the head. His hands fell away as he tried to take the object from me. As we grappled for my weapon, he struck me a few times in the face, trying to loosen my grip. His face was bleeding, and the blood dripped onto me as we wrestled.

Knee up, said my brothers in my ear, and I jerked my knee hard into Andrew's groin.

"Aaahhhgg," he said, and tipped sideways.

I scrambled into a kneeling position and hit him again and again with my weapon, wherever I could see a vulnerable place: his temple, his throat, and back to his groin.

Finally I dropped my weapon, which turned out to be a glass snow globe that read *Welcome to Wood Glen.* Inside it was a friendly-looking deer, his antlers noble and thick as tree branches.

I pulled out my phone with shaking hands; Andy lay on the floor, very still and silent. I dialed Dash and listened to the ringing. I couldn't seem to focus on anything; in fact, my field of vision seemed to be shrinking.

"John Dashiell," said his voice.

"Dash. I'm in Portnoy's Gifts. Help me," I said, because I felt myself falling, falling, and I hoped he had heard me and that I had actually formed the words I had been thinking before I descended into blackness.

* * *

I OPENED MY eyes to see only whiteness and glare. "I can't see," I tried to say, but only a croaking sound came out.

"She's awake," someone said. "Detective Dashiell, her eyes are open."

Dash's face appeared in front of me. "Nora." He smiled, but he didn't look happy. He was clutching my hands.

"Dash," I said, "thanks for coming."

His brows went up. He told me later that he had been shocked by my formality in a moment when I should have been screaming out the name of my attacker. "How do you feel?"

I tried to gauge how severe my injuries were, blinking my eyes, flexing my fingers, trying to swallow. "Water," I said.

Moments later Dash was propping me up so that I could drink out of a water bottle in his hand. People in uniforms were moving around the room; through the sun shining in the window, I glimpsed an ambulance outside and two police cars.

"He choked me," I said.

"We can see that. Who choked you?" Dash said.

"Him." I pointed at the spot where Andy had been lying. "Ask him what he did."

Dash stroked my hair gently. "You were the only one in the store when we got here. We had to break the door down."

"Ugh. Andy. It was Andy. I—upset him, and we got into a fight, and then I realized what he had done and why. He loves Priscilla; he's obsessed with her. He thought Jack was going to take her away or something. He wanted to kill Jack because Priscilla—"

"He admitted this?"

"Sort of. Mostly he was just trying to kill me," I said.

"It looks like he nearly succeeded," Dash said grimly. "When I saw all that wine, I thought—"

"You should see the other guy," I said. "So he's gone? He escaped? I can't believe he could even walk after the number of times I hit him in the—" I pointed at my groin, and it seemed that every man in the room winced.

"We'll find him," Dash said. "But right now we have to get you checked out. These two are going to take you to the hospital for a checkup."

"Can't they just do that in the ambulance? I want to go home."

"Better safe than sorry," Dash said. "You could have a brain injury."

This silenced me, and I submitted to the ministrations of the EMTs.

Dash walked us to the ambulance and saw me tucked safely inside. "Text me when you're finished, and I'll pick you up."

"My car," I said feebly. "It's in front of Balfour. There are donuts for you and the team in there."

That seemed to make Dash angry. He touched my hand gently and said, "We'll take care of those things later. You go now and tell me when you're finished. Is it okay to kiss you?"

"Yes."

He bent to put his lips on mine; it did hurt a bit, because my bottom lip had been split open on one side.

"Ow," I said, and he looked aghast.

"I'm sorry, babe."

"I'm not."

I squeezed his hand, and I got obediently on the stretcher so that the EMTs could carry me out of Portnoy's Gifts. When the ambulance doors had closed, I stared at the white ceiling, and my eyes filled with delayed tears. I tried to wipe them away, but more flowed into my eyes.

One of the EMTs, whose tag read *Cheryl S*, leaned over me and dabbed something on my face. It was light and soothing.

"I heard you say that you nailed him in the balls," she said. "Good for you! He obviously deserved it. These are significant injuries."

The other EMT was putting a stinging substance on my various cuts.

My mind couldn't light on any one thought; I knew I was in shock. I tried to calm myself, to choose a soothing image and focus on it, but my brain went from Andy to Jack to Priscilla's store, and then it was flitting to the catacombs, and the Halloween decorations on our porch, and Elspeth and Renata knitting, and a deer with noble antlers, and Ben, laughing and excited, and his adopted father standing behind him, lifting a knife in jealousy and rage, and plunging it into the poor boy's back. At what point had Andrew realized his mistake? What level of horror had he experienced, knowing he had killed the person he loved as a son?

But I felt no pity for Andy and his vengeful anger. He had killed brutally, and to cover it up, he would have killed again. There was no remorse in him.

I thought of Millie peering in windows, and I pitied her for the love that she deserved and that her husband had not felt for her, and for the stigma that his terrible actions would place on her innocent life.

IT WAS SIX in the evening when I returned to the castle. I had avoided a concussion but was to be kept under observation for twenty-four hours. I was bandaged and drugged and put into clean clothes. The police had taken my other clothing as evidence, and the store was now being examined as a crime scene.

Dash helped me out of the car and put his strong arm around my waist. "How are you emotionally?"

"Better," I said. "But feeling kind of fragile."

"Understandable. I'm staying with you tonight, by the way."

"Bossy," I said calmly.

"Yup. Here, watch out for this step. It looks slippery."

It didn't, but I appreciated his tenderness and concern. He wanted to take care of me, so I would let him.

Connie met us at the door, and her face turned white at the sight of me. Then her expression grew furious. I had never seen Connie so angry. "Andy did that to you?"

I nodded, not wanting to talk about it. Dash had told them all so that I wouldn't have to do it.

"I could kill him," Connie said. "I could kill him with my bare hands."

I shook my head. "No, you're my sweet Connie."

She walked with Dash and me; each held one of my arms, as though they were accompanying me to my execution. They led me to the elevator and then to my room, where I was subsequently pampered in a ridiculous fashion. I was promptly tucked into bed by Connie, who then began to gently brush my hair. Dash lit a fire in my fireplace and set the Brontës on the bed to keep me company. Soon Zana appeared with a tray of food, all of it easy to chew so that I wouldn't hurt my sore mouth. I hadn't yet looked in a mirror, and I asked Connie for one.

Connie hesitated, looking at Dash, and he nodded.

"She can handle it," he said.

Connie brought my hand mirror and I looked into it; the cut on my mouth was not as shocking as my blackened right eye. The left eye looked as though it might have some lesser bruising in the morning. And my throat was encircled by black bruises.

"I have to perform onstage in less than a week," I said, my voice shaking.

Connie took the mirror away. "Elspeth works magic with the makeup brush. You know that. She'll make it look like nothing ever happened."

I nodded, and Dash fed me some of Zana's potato soup.

"Mmm," I said appreciatively. "Thanks, Zana."

"Anything else you need, hon? I'm going to be leaving soon, but I'll be happy to make you whatever your heart desires."

"No, this is lovely. Go be with your family."

She gave me a kiss on the cheek and said, "We'll talk soon."

I took another bite of soup. Dash dabbed at my mouth with a napkin, and I laughed.

"I'm not a child, Dash."

"No, but you are precious to me."

My eyes filled once again with tears, and he dabbed at them. I laughed through my tears, and Dash exchanged a glance with Connie.

"Nora, would you like me to read your book to you?" Connie asked.

"That might be nice," I said.

I lay back against my pillows. "I asked the doctor if this would affect my singing." I pointed at my throat. "He said it shouldn't have any permanent effect. I'm sort of scared, though. It felt like he was crushing my windpipe."

Anger flashed across Dash's face before he replaced it with his calm expression. "It will be fine. You'll feel like a new woman tomorrow."

I was still teary. "I love you both," I said.

They smiled at me, ready to agree with anything I said.

I turned to dash. "Have they arrested Andy?"

He ran a smoothing hand over my hair. "We'll talk about that tomorrow."

"What? Why? Is he dead or something? Did I kill him?"

Dash smiled grimly. "No, you didn't kill him." He looked at Connie, then at me. "But he remains at large. Millie swears she has no idea where he is."

AT EIGHT O'CLOCK Elspeth and Renata appeared with a bowl full of knitting equipment. "Are you up for a lesson?" they asked.

Pleased, I said yes, and they found chairs so that they could sit around my bed. The kittens showed immediate interest in the yarn, but Renata said, "Aha! We anticipated this." She took out some prerolled balls of yarn and set them on the floor for the Brontës, who spent the next forty-five minutes chasing the spheres.

Connie retrieved my bag of yarn and knitting needles. Dash was in my easy chair, texting one of his colleagues. I whispered that I didn't want him to know what I was working on, and my friends nodded their understanding. Then Elspeth positioned the needles in my hand and showed me how to loop the yarn around and around my needle. I did so, and she stood beside me, patiently giving instructions as I made my first tentative stitches.

"It feels weird," I said. "These big needles. Remember in the play when Torvald tells me that knitting is ugly?" They nodded, and suddenly I looked up. "Is the play canceled?"

Connie shook her head. "Derek told me he's going to take the role of Dr. Rank. The show must go on, despite our many challenges. Derek has some friends coming from Chicago on opening night. One's a theater critic and one is a playwright who loves Ibsen. He told them he's proud of the production, and they want to see it."

"Opening night," I said, shaking my head. "I was so excited about it. . . ."

Renata had been studying my face and my neck, and her expression was suddenly angry. "I can't believe he did that to you. The violence of it! I would like to stand before him now, this man we trusted. I would like to speak my mind to him."

"Imagine how Millie feels," Connie said.

I paused in my knitting. "Oh, no, Millie! Is she going to want to be in the play now? Will she be worried about her treatment?"

"Derek wondered that, too. He went to see her this evening and had a long talk with her. He made it clear that no one blames her since she obviously had no idea what her husband did. She's just furious. But she was touched by Derek's visit, and she said the drama group means a lot to her."

"Oh, okay."

"Keep going," Elspeth said, pointing to my knitting.

I did so, and Renata got up to make some tea on my little stove. She returned ten minutes later with tea and sliced Balfour Bars.

"Oh, at last," I said. "The dessert of legend."

The women laughed, but they watched me when I put down my knitting and took a bite. The brownie-like cake was a blend of textures and flavors: smooth, soft cake; crunchy chocolate chips; spongy marshmallow; a hint of cream cheese; a graham cracker base; and chocolate frosting on the top. I chewed and savored the sensory experience. Something like euphoria (or pure sugar) shot through my veins.

"Oh, Lord, that is almost . . . sexual."

The women laughed again, and Dash wandered over, looking interested.

Then we were all laughing, and he was being offered his own bar, and he nodded in agreement. "Yes, wow. That's intense."

By the time my visitors left, I was feeling more like myself. I had completed about three inches of what I hoped would become a scarf, and I was feeling gratitude and contentment, knowing that I had good and supportive friends.

I lay sleepily against my pillow, and Dash sat on the edge of the bed and smoothed my hair away from my eyes.

"Do you want to call your family?" he asked.

"No. Don't tell any of them, please. I'll wait until I look less horrible, and I'll break it to them gently after everything is fine."

"Hmmm."

I wasn't sure he approved of this plan, but he wasn't going to argue with me about anything.

"Do you want to walk through the passage and imagine your new room?"

I shuddered. "No, not just now. Until they start work on the renovation, I want to keep that door sealed. Bad memories. I guess I'm still feeling fragile. I'm a wimp."

He used one finger under my chin to turn my head toward him. "You are the bravest person I know. You faced Andrew down, telling him your suspicions, and then you fought him like a gladiator until he ran away. That's valor, Nora." He straightened, "Having said that . . ."

Uh-oh.

". . . I find it hard to believe that you would put yourself in such danger, so recklessly, when there are people who care about you, who want you to be safe—"

"Dash, I didn't know what I was facing when I entered the store." I touched his arm in mild entreaty. "I wasn't being a thrill seeker. I guess I was just a little too curious for my own good. But don't blame the victim."

Dash's eyes showed remorse. "I'm sorry." He paused, gently touching my cheekbone. "You're going to have quite a shiner. Your brothers will respect you even more," he joked weakly.

I laughed a little. "That's true. Take a picture," I said suddenly. "They'll want to see it."

Shrugging, Dash took out my camera and snapped a couple of pictures of me, cheerful but unsmiling.

I took back the phone and sent my brothers a joint text: Once again your instructions saved my life. But don't tell Mom and Dad. I added one of the pictures Dash had taken.

Not even a minute later, Jay texted, Is that stage makeup? No.

A moment later my phone rang. "Hello?"

It was Luke and Jay on speakerphone. "Who did that to you?" Jay asked. His voice was quiet, perhaps deceptively so.

"The guy who killed Ben. We ended up in a struggle because I figured out who he was. You don't know him."

"Is he in jail?" asked Luke. His voice, too, was quiet.

I realized suddenly that both of my brothers were furious, full of cold hate for my attacker. "No. He actually got away. I fainted, and—"

My phone was on speaker, too, for Dash's benefit, and Dash said, "But she got him good. He's definitely injured."

"Good job, Nora," said Jay.

The boys still weren't making jokes, which worried me slightly.

"Why can't we tell Mom and Dad?" Luke asked.

"You can, just not right now while he's out there and I look like this. We'll wait a few days."

"Dash, are you staying there?" asked Jay.

"Yes," Dash assured my brothers. "I am her permanent guard for the evening." And because he knew it would satisfy the twins, he said, "And I am armed."

"Are you okay to be in your play?" asked Luke with surprising sensitivity.

"I will be."

"What about—your face?" asked Jay.

"You'll never see it. The magic of makeup."

To my amazement, Jay sounded near tears. "I'm sorry this happened to you, Nor. I wish we had been there."

"You were," I said tenderly. "I heard your voices telling me to lean forward to loosen his grip on my neck. That worked. And I remembered your reminder to go for his groin, which I did repeatedly. And your reminders about vulnerable places. I punched him in the throat, the temple, wherever I could land a blow."

That pleased them. "You have learned well, grasshopper," Luke said. "But what kind of guy does that to a woman?"

Dash and I exchanged a glance. "Sadly, all sorts of guys. But then there are guys like you. Guys who help women by teaching them self-defense," I said.

"Yeah, well."

"Mom and Dad can't hear this, can they?"

Jay's voice regained some of its sarcasm. "No, they're out for their anniversary."

"Oh, right. I have a gift for them—" But I recalled, with a pang of misery that I had been forced to leave it on the counter at Portnoy's Gifts. "Oh, shoot. I don't have a gift for them."

"Whatever. We made them an anniversary PowerPoint."

Of course they had. My self-defense lessons had been PowerPoints, too, with lots of images of Bruce Lee and Jason Statham and Sigourney Weaver in *Alien*.

"I hope you were serious, for once."

"Not really. But it cracked them up," Luke said.

"Well, Nora needs her rest, and you guys probably have to study for something," Dash said.

My brothers sniggered. They were members of that annoying breed who studied very little and got A's anyway.

"If you mean, watch YouTube videos in which animals

form unlikely friendships with different animals, then yes, we will be studying," Jay said.

Luke said, "Hey, Nora—we've got homecoming in two weeks. Jay is going to the dance with Penny Langford."

"Oh, good!" I said. "She's delightful."

Jay had dated the redheaded Penny on and off for two years.

Some murmuring in the background. Then Jay said, "Luke is thinking of asking Jade, maybe." The comment was made in the offhand, casual tone of someone who was, on his brother's behalf, anxious about the response. "Do you know if she's going out with anyone?"

"I don't," I said. "But I really think she'd love to be asked. She's talking about inviting you two to a Halloween party."

"No way!" Luke yelled. "That's awesome. I'm going to hassle her on Facebook."

"Okay. Well, good night, guys."

My brothers grew serious again, but they weren't talking to me when they said, "Keep an eye out, and have that weapon handy."

I WOKE THE next morning to find Dash in the easy chair, texting again. He had slept beside me all night, his arms wrapped protectively around me. The sight of me lying in what looked, at a glance, like blood had traumatized him, and I understood that. We were being very gentle with each other.

"Hey," I said. "What's happening today?"

Dash put his phone aside and moved quickly toward me. "I need to go in to work, but Paul and Derek have volunteered for guard duty until I get back."

"In any case, I don't intend to leave the castle until Andy is caught, so I think I'm pretty safe," I said. "Besides, why would he come after me? Everyone already knows now. He was only trying to silence me yesterday because I was the only one. Now I'm assuming he's on the news."

Dash nodded. "And on the front page of the *Wood Glen Gazette*."

"Good. You make your choices," I said.

"Yes." He bent to kiss me on the cheek and give me a hug. "Derek wants you to go to his room on the second floor. He's going to do some work while you sit on the couch behind him like a pretty little princess."

I laughed. "I've had enough of the princess treatment. I'll go down there, but I'm going to ask to use his treadmill. I need exercise. That Balfour Bar was about nine hundred thousand calories."

"Okay. You do that, but keep your promise and don't leave. One way or another, I'm getting this guy today."

His eyes actually glittered when he said that—I wasn't sure whether the emotion I saw there was anger or determination or hatred. Whatever it was, it had me feeling briefly sorry for Andy Portnoy.

"See you soon," he said. He blew me a kiss from the door and disappeared into the hall.

I sighed a little love sigh. Then, summoning my courage, I got out of bed and went to the bathroom. I went through my whole morning routine before daring to look in the mirror. When I finally did, I nodded at myself. It was bad, but not as bad as I had feared. The black eye was more midnight blue. My neck was a rather shocking shade of blue-purple; the marks looked almost like a garish necklace around my throat. In one spot I could see the imprint of a finger. A momentary flashback made me sway in place and close my eyes against the encroaching memory of Andy's hands on my throat, my fear that I would die. . . .

I took some deep, slow breaths and climbed into a soothing hot shower, emerged feeling better, toweled off, put on some of my favorite perfume, and donned a soft black turtleneck with my blue jeans.

Hungry now, I made my way toward the door. I would visit Derek, but tell him I was going to run down for some food. As I reached the door, I heard a sound. I froze. And heard it again—not the raccoon sound exactly, but originating from the same corner.

Suddenly the fury of everyone else—Dash, Renata, my brothers—rose in me. The Pierce brothers were back again, despite being kicked out, despite being fired from the play, despite losing the respect of all of their castle and BC friends. They had dared to break into the castle once again. I moved to the door on trainer-clad feet, making no sound. I put my ear to the paneling of the hidden passage: more rustling. With a mighty lunge, I flung back the door and cried, "How *dare* you!"

Then my mouth dropped in amazement as did the jaw of Andy Portnoy, who squatted, dirty and exhausted-looking, in the hallway behind my door. My eyes only vaguely took in some things around him—a thin blanket, a bag of chips, a water bottle.

He stood up, and now his expression was as angry as mine. "You," he whispered. "Ruined. Everything."

"I did?" I almost screamed. "You tried to *kill* me! You killed Ben! How dare you blame me for your crimes!"

He lurched into my room. "You don't understand," he said.

"I understand." I pointed to my face. "You did this, Andy. What would Ben think of you, his father figure? Would he be proud of you beating up a woman? Trying to kill a man because you were jealous of his relationship with a woman who wasn't your wife?"

Andy had the grace to look briefly mournful, but his anger and pride returned. "I'm not going to explain myself to you. Just let me walk away, Nora, and I'll leave you alone. I just need you to walk down those stairs with me so that I know you're not calling for help, okay?"

He didn't even bother to hide the calculating look in his eyes.

"No, thanks." I started toward my door at a run, and I felt him lunging after me.

I managed to grab the knob, to open the door a crack before he tackled me. I landed on my stomach and bumped my chin on the floor. "Connie!" I yelled. "Connie! Renata!" I screamed.

I only hoped one of them was on this floor. Elspeth and Miranda were probably too far down the hall to hear me.

Andy started to drag me toward the panel in the wall. If he got me in there, I wouldn't have much of a chance, especially now that he was desperate. My feet were clutched tightly in his hands, but I tried to lunge around with my torso, hoping to loosen his grasp. The Brontës were hiding under my bed, frightened, their tails puffed huge in terror. I wished I could comfort them as he dragged me past the bed.

Then my door swung wide, and I saw feet running in— one pair of black boots, one of sturdy walking shoes. Then another pair, and another. They advanced toward us.

"Let go of her, Andy." It was Renata speaking in a cold, commanding voice.

Andy thought about it for a moment, then dropped my feet. He had decided to run, but Miranda was quick and had slipped in behind him, blocking the panel in the wall.

"Sorry," she said, "No exit."

Andy Portnoy had the wisdom to look frightened as he realized that he was facing a circle of angry women, and they were closing in.

Half an hour later my room was even fuller. We sat on the edge of my bed—Connie, Renata, Elspeth, Miranda, and I—and Dash was questioning us.

"So Nora called out for you, Connie, and you called out for the others, and then you all ran into the room to find what?"

"He was dragging Nora across the floor by her feet," Renata said angrily.

"And her chin was bleeding," Connie said, "because he knocked her down when she tried to run away."

I pointed helpfully at the bandage on my chin.

Dash observed me sternly. "And how did you end up confronting Mr. Portnoy once again?"

"I heard the noises again. I thought it was Drake or Dorian, and I felt—just—outrage. I wanted to confront them, to confront any man. So I opened the door and Andy was there, with a blanket and some food and water. Drake had bragged in town about the secret room after they got kicked out. He even mentioned to Andy where the entrance was. Andy figured that it would be a perfect hiding place until things died down."

Paul had told me this a few minutes earlier after talking to Millie.

Dash nodded, unsmiling. "So you never went to Derek's room?"

"I was just about to. I took a shower first."

"And how did Andy happen to get his injuries?"

"From fighting with me yesterday," I said.

Dash shook his head. "You told me what you did yesterday. Now he has black eyes and bruises on his neck and a bleeding chin."

"Those are Nora's injuries," Miranda said helpfully. "See?" She pointed at me.

Dash nodded. "Okay. I'll talk with you five in a minute."

He went back to my door, where Andy was about to be led away. We had bound him in some of my tights, but the police had transferred him into handcuffs. I had heard them give him his Miranda rights, a very satisfying series of words.

Derek approached the bed and went not to Connie but to me, lifting me and embracing me. "Nora, we have put you through so much."

"You haven't done anything," I said calmly into his sleeve, "except to be an ever-supportive friend and employer. I am grateful for you."

He kissed the top of my head and said, "Enough of this stress." He looked behind himself; Andy was gone now, as were several of the police officers. "From now on, this will be the best fall the castle has ever seen."

I exchanged a glance with Connie over his shoulder. Those words had sounded like Derek was on the verge of spending money again.

"It already is the best ever," I said, "because I'm with all of you."

He let me go, nodding and smiling. "I bet the piano would raise your spirits."

He was right. We moved toward the door and began to file past Dash and his colleagues, starting to move into the hall. Dash reached out a hand and grabbed my arm, still talking to a man I did not know.

"Excuse me for a minute, Bill," he said. He led me across the room, closer to my bathroom, for some privacy.

"You're not really mad at me, are you?" I said.

He touched my chin, which now sported a big Band-Aid. "No, of course not. I know what happened, and I know why. I have to go through the formal interrogation, though."

"Okay. I guess I'm pretty much like a deputy at this point."

His eyes narrowed. "You are most certainly *not* a deputy, nor do I ever want you confronting a dangerous person again. I am hoping for a future with you, Nora."

Those words had an effect more intense than the sugar in a Balfour Bar.

"Oh," I said in a small voice.

"Yes, exactly." He bent to kiss me, his lips soft, warm, exciting.

"Get rid of them," I whispered, "and we can—" I gestured to my bed, and Dash laughed.

"Later, I'm afraid. I have to go back now and file this report. It will be a while."

"Fine." I pretended to pout. "I will settle for singing show tunes with my friends."

"Like that's a sacrifice," Dash said with a smile that said he was starting to know me quite well.

20

Opening Night

ACT I HAD gone well. The stage looked amazing, with its glittering Christmas tree and its crackling "fire." Everyone had remembered lines and cues; props were in place at the proper time. Connie simply sparkled as Nora Helmer, and Jack had recovered enough of his confidence to be a very convincing Torvald.

Dash had helped with my matchmaking conspiracy, escorting Gen to the front row, where my parents and siblings sat, as well. Dash sat beside her so that he could catalog her reactions to Paul's appearance onstage and his performance overall.

Now, midway through Act II, Connie was confiding to me, as Kristine, that it was Krogstad who had lent her the money. I offered to help, and Connie as Nora asked, "How could you possibly help?"

I answered simply, "There was a time he would have done anything for me."

The audience actually gasped with this subtle little detail that changed everything. I felt a surge of energy and pleasure. How invigorating it was when a line was received well, the way the playwright (and the actor) intended.

There was one near disaster when someone took a swig of water backstage and spilled some; Derek slipped in it and almost fell. Had he broken his leg or brained himself on a prop, I would have believed the production was truly cursed. But I was determined to think it was blessed, not only because the lines were flowing well, organically, but because the theater, Derek had told us excitedly, was full to capacity.

Act III began with my dialogue with Krogstad.

"Let's talk," I said to Paul, whose anger barely concealed his terrible hurt; his eyes glittered in the stage lights as he told me that I had broken his heart. Again, I heard the audience gasp, this time with sympathy.

When I told him that I had come back for him, that I wanted to try again, to be a mother for his children, Paul began, very spontaneously, to cry. He never broke character, but wiped at his eyes and snuffled out his next lines. I heard someone in the audience sniffling away empathetic tears. I took Paul's hands, assured him I would never betray him again. Elspeth had done our makeup in such a way that when the lights grew less harsh, putting us in a slightly pink glow, we both looked younger, fresher, happier. When Paul left the stage and said, "I've never been so happy," the audience began to clap.

Then I said it was worth the try, which also received some applause, and then Torvald and Nora were back, Nora reluctantly, Torvald practically shoving her into the room. I said that I had wanted to see Nora's costume, which was a lovely black-and-red thing with subtle glitter around the hem and cuffs.

By the time Derek came in as the tragic and dying Dr. Rank, the audience was bursting with suspense. Was Nora going to kill herself? But first they had to watch another emotionally painful scene: Rank telling Nora, in a coded way, that he would die soon, and Nora whispering, "Sleep well, Dr. Rank." When he left, he turned to look at Nora (Derek looking at Connie with the obvious love he felt for her) and said, "And thanks for the light." He didn't cry, but the audience got the sense that he might do so after the door closed behind him forever.

Then came Nora and Torvald's final confrontation. I peered at the audience from the wings and saw enthralled faces; Gen was absolutely lost in the performances. Once in a while, she wiped away a tear.

When Nora left Torvald in the final scene and walked offstage, the slamming of a door was heard twenty seconds later. Then Torvald uttered his final, deluded line and the audience jumped to its feet in a spontaneous ovation. Derek sent Millie and Elspeth out for their applause; then he and Renata walked out, hand in hand; then came Paul and me. I watched Gen's face, which was, I was pleased to note, staring not at her sister, but at Paul Corby, with his distinguished but shabby suit and his graying hair. Out of the corner of my eye, I saw Paul glance down and notice her. He stiffened beside me, shocked. Then he looked around again, and we bowed a second time. And then Jack and Connie came out to thunderous applause.

We walked offstage, and Derek told us moments later, "They want us again!" This time we filed onstage in one line, hand in hand, and the applause continued.

"Bravo!" someone yelled.

I felt absolutely high, not just from the energy flow between actor and audience, but because my plan was working. Gen could not take her eyes off Paul, and Paul kept trying to pretend he wasn't staring back at her, but was stealing continual micro glances nonetheless.

When we went backstage for the final time and the audience started to file out, we stood in an excited cluster, taking apart the elements of the performance.

"I want to invite you all to Jack's Pub," Derek said (he and Jack had arranged this in advance), "and we'll go over all the elements that worked well tonight. But I am thrilled with how it went and proud of all of you! The best cast I could have hoped for!"

We clapped, and Connie said, "And we are proud of the director who stood in for a player at the last minute and did a remarkable job."

We clapped again, and I noticed that Paul's gaze had drifted to an area behind us. I turned and saw Gen, looking pretty and elegant in a red dress, standing there hesitantly in the corner.

"Dash said I was supposed to come back and say hi," she said.

Paul lunged toward her, practically knocking down poor Millie, who was righted by Derek, who slung an arm around her. Millie looked pleased and leaned on him gratefully. The actors in my circle kept talking loudly, but I tuned my ears to the conversation behind me, trying to catch bits of their dialogue.

"I didn't know you were coming tonight—"

"—last-minute decision—"

"—so amazing to see you there in the audience . . ."

"—I'm so glad I made it . . . spectacular performance—"

"—something to eat?"

"I actually didn't get a chance earlier—"

"Let's remedy that."

Nervous laughter. I turned, and they were gone.

THE TWINS WERE disappointed to go home without visiting the castle, but my parents convinced them that the cast wanted to celebrate, and there would be time enough in the coming weeks to come back for a visit when everything had settled down.

"I saw that the man who killed your castmate was arrested," my mother said. "Such a relief. Just think: if they hadn't caught him, he would have performed in front of us tonight, although I couldn't imagine anyone but that handsome Derek in the role." She gave me a significant look. "Speaking of handsome, Paul looked quite good up there. I think your sister noticed, as well."

"Yes."

My mother gave a little smile. "She disappeared almost immediately. Dad says they've gone for dinner."

"If she starts dating him, you can be utterly content. He's one of the most perfect gentlemen I've ever met and incredibly smart and talented. He and Derek have an endless well of abilities."

"Mmm." Her eyes sparkled at me. "We sat with John Dashiell. Are the two of you . . . ?"

"Yes," I said, smiling. "Very much so."

"Oh, goodness. Both of my girls are finding love at the same time."

"We'll see with Gen. But my fingers are crossed."

My family eventually said their goodbyes in the lobby and went to their B and B. My mother at least intended to watch one more performance the next day. She said the play had been "riveting."

My father had said that he needed to start reading Ibsen if "he wrote good stuff like that."

The twins had been monopolizing Dash, and he came back to me laughing.

"Those guys," he said.

"Yeah, I know. Derek's hosting everyone at Jack's Pub. Want to go?"

"If you're going," he said, slipping his hand into mine.

We went outside into the dark. The building manager was already turning out the lights. The moon was a bright crescent, reclining on dark gray clouds.

"Let's walk," he said. "We can come back for the car."

"Okay." His arm slid around my shoulders, warming me, and I asked, "So—did you like the play?"

"The play was amazing. Here's my rating. Performances: ten, especially yours and Paul's. But everyone was good. Renata was kind of heartbreaking. Set: ten. I can't believe you got the stage looking like that in a little community theater. I was expecting cardboard backdrops and minimal props. Overall impact on audience: ten. The place was electric. I heard murmurs about how the BC was so much better since Derek Corby had started directing."

"Oh, that's so good to hear. He should really get paid for what he does."

"He probably will start getting a salary, or they'll lose him to some bigger theater."

"Yeah. But I don't know if he would leave the castle." And I hoped he would never have to.

"But you, Nora Blake." He stopped and turned me toward him, near a rustling tree through which I could see the autumn moon. "You are a remarkable woman. A brilliant actress, a soulful musician and singer, a brave warrior, a good friend to your companions. Loyal and kind."

"What else?" I joked.

"I mean it," he said. "You're one in a million."

"I feel the same. I have a confession: I'm hung up on you."

He cupped my face in his hands and kissed me. "Good."

"Want to come to my sleepover tonight?" I asked lightly.

"Who's invited?"

I pretended to count on my fingers. "Right now just you."

"Then yes, I do. You can stop inviting people."

"What about Dorian?" I teased.

"Sure. If I can bring Robin."

"Touché," I said, bowing slightly.

He took my hand again, and we walked to the pub, ready to celebrate with our friends.

21

Poetic Pursuit

A WEEK LATER, we had started a busy schedule of castle performances. Derek had double-booked on some days to honor the rain checks for people who had lost their appointments because of Ben's murder. We had mastered the new script set in the library, which kept many of the same lines but dropped Dorian's part and made the family smaller. This time the father's will was said to be hidden in a tome in the library, and in fact he had told each child about a separate clue he had left there.

Elspeth had outdone herself with the library, making it look moody and mildly frightening, and bringing in a variety of lights that made some corners glow orange, some blue, some flickering white. Ultimately, we agreed that the new setting was better, as was the new script.

Paul told me, in a stolen meeting in his office, that he was pleased with the money they were taking in with the resumed castle shows. In addition he informed me, as we munched on some of Zana's pizza burgers, that Derek's critic friend had written a glowing review of the Blue Curtain production of *A Doll's House* on his blog, and that it was quoted in the Chicago papers.

"That's probably why we kept packing the seats," he said.

Indeed, every show had been performed to a full house, and even the understudies received raves for their performances. Derek's plaudits continued, even after the play's completed its run.

Paul told me that some new videos he had put on the castle website, where he regularly posted YouTube links of one or more of the castle cast singing, had been receiving significantly increased traffic since the play. "The favorites, by far, are the one of you singing 'Hallelujah,' and the duet by you and Connie. The *Toy Story* one." Connie and I had sung a very affectionate version of "You've Got a Friend in Me" for one of Derek's promotions, and it had been on our website for months.

"Twenty-four thousand likes on YouTube," he said, "and a bunch of shares."

"Well, that's good for the castle, right?"

"I hope so. People are seeing that we're distinctive, but that we also have top talent."

I nibbled at my sandwich, watching him under my lashes. "Was it fun having Gen here last weekend?"

His smile told me that he saw through me. "Let's shoot straight like Krogstad and Kristine. Yes, it was amazing to see Gen. Yes, I know you arranged it. Yes, I have very strong feelings for her. Yes, I think she has them for me, too."

I clapped, smiling.

"We've decided we'll try the long-distance thing," he said.

Gen had of course already told me this, in a breathless phone call after she was back in New York, but I had wanted to hear it verified by Paul.

"That's awesome," I said. "I guess my work here is done."

"I appreciate it, Nora. I— Your sister is very special. I'm going to do all I can to make this work."

"I couldn't have chosen a better boyfriend for her," I said. I finished my pizza burger and wiped my hands on a napkin. "What say we go to the piano and—"

Derek appeared in Paul's office doorway, his face white. "Paul, I— Oh, hi, Nora."

"What's wrong?" I said. "You look upset."

He walked to the chair next to mine and slumped down in it. "I surrender," he said. "What will be, will be."

"No luck on a grant?" Paul asked, his face grim.

"No. And I just heard from the producer. The script has changed, and the setting is now an old, abandoned prison, not a castle. So no film contract."

We sat in silence, processing this doubly bad news. Derek looked tired and defeated. I knew he did a lot behind the scenes, battling with his gargantuan energy to keep everything running smoothly, and he concealed any problems with a smile.

Paul handed his brother a piece of chocolate, and Derek smiled, but just held the little wrapper in his hand.

My eyes lighted on the framed poem on Paul's wall

"Listen," I said, standing up. "Dorian and Drake thought that poem would lead to something valuable. They believed it so much that they were willing to risk their jobs and their reputations. Let's just assume for one minute that they were right. What have you got to lose, taking some time to ponder this?"

Derek spoke in a sarcastic tone. "Phil the fantasist."

"Let's go with Nora here for a minute," Paul said. "See if it makes sense."

They both looked at me as though I had a presentation

prepared. Thinking fast, I said, "First of all, why did the Pierce brothers settle on the little library? Why not the large one? I think we have to look at the first line of the poem: 'The source of knowledge, light, and lore is just behind a certain door.'" I paused.

Paul rustled up his seat. "'Lore' and 'knowledge' suggest a room full of books, and 'light' could mean inspiration, which can also be found in books. So okay, the library might make sense. So why the small one? Could it be the word 'certain'? It's 'behind a certain door,' meaning a specific door, which implies a specific room."

Derek showed his first gleam of interest. "The big library doesn't have a door. It has an archway."

"Yes!" I said. "An archway, not a door. So they moved up to the Small Library, which has a definite door and walls of books. They were hunting through them one by one, but they had to be careful and quiet. And even then they got caught."

I turned to Derek. "We wouldn't have that restriction. What's to stop you from doing a thorough search of the whole room?"

Derek shook his head. "First of all, I don't have time to commit to a search like that. And if I hired someone to search, they'd probably have to take things apart, and I don't have the resources to pay anyone for—well, anything."

I grinned, lunged forward, and took his hand. "I know two people who would do it very thoroughly and for free."

Derek began to laugh.

A COUPLE OF days after homecoming, my brothers, wearing their beloved "Castle Security" T-shirts stood in the Small Library, covered in dust and looking frustrated.

They were both on step stools, taking the last of the books down from high shelves. I had decided to take the opportunity to catalog the books, so I was sorting them into piles on the table and floor.

"It's not looking good, Norbert," Jay said.

I sighed. "We can't give up. If there's no treasure, we have to will some to appear."

Luke was texting on his phone. He had, in fact, persuaded Jade to attend homecoming with him, and apparently they'd had a very fun time. Now they texted each other several times a day. Jay was included in most of them, but some were for Luke alone.

"Lover boy, get to work," Jay said sourly.

Luke smirked and put his phone in his pocket.

"And how are things with Penny?" I asked Jay's back.

"Fine," he murmured.

"He gave her a ring," Luke said.

"What?" I yelled.

"It was from a gumball machine," Jay joked.

"No, he spent real money on it. Penny is his redheaded goddess. They're engaged now," Luke jeered.

"Shut up," Jay said, sounding bored as he flipped through the pages of a dusty dictionary.

The two of them continued to bicker in a mild way, as they always did, and soon the shelves were empty.

"Disappointed," Jay said loudly.

"Let's think about this while we finish dusting the shelves," I said.

We dusted and sneezed for a few minutes. The wooden shelving looked lovely after I polished it with a wood cleaner. What a gorgeous study I was going to have!

We set our dusting equipment down in one corner and wiped our hands on our jeans.

"Okay, don't give up. Think about the poem. The final

phrase is 'the door they cannot see.' So we're not supposed to *see* something. We're supposed to figure out what it is despite the fact that there is no door. And it lies behind that."

Jay looked at me with suspicion, and Luke laughed. "Behind *what*?" he said.

"That's the mystery." For that, I received two sardonic smiles.

"What about this: if it's a door we cannot see, then maybe it's *behind* something, like the hidden passage! Maybe it's behind that hidden door"—I pointed to the recently revealed passage—"or under there." I pointed at the carpet.

The boys shot into action. "I'll take the carpet," Luke said.

Jay went into the hallway and examined the sliding door, the floor behind it, the ceiling, the wall. "There's nothing out here," he said. "The outside wall is brick, and none of them is loose, and the inside wall is this thin paneling. No way to hide something in it."

Luke was moving piles of books off the carpet, but that left a heavy table, which was also covered with books. "How do we do this?" he asked.

I sighed deeply. "We stack them in the hallway."

Thanks to my brothers' boundless energy, this job was accomplished within half an hour, and then the Small Library was empty and looked like a much larger room.

"Move the table to one side," Jay instructed. We did so. "Now, Nora and Luke, you tip up that side, and I'll pull out the rug."

Once this task had been accomplished, Jay joined Luke and me in studying the floor for a trapdoor. We all sighed at once.

"Here's why it doesn't make sense," Luke said. "Uncle

Philip couldn't have known if there would be a rug in this room when someone read the message. It doesn't seem as though he'd have made his clue so tentative, does it?"

"No," I said. "But you know what? That looks like vintage wallpaper. I think it might be original."

We stood in silence for a moment, and then Jay said, "Can we rip it off?"

"No!" I cried. "It's lovely."

And it was—a gentle rose color with subtle greenery and hues reminiscent of a country garden.

"What we'll do is feel along the wall, row by row, for anything that feels uneven."

"I'll take top on the south side," Luke said, grabbing his ladder.

"I'll do top north."

"You two do all the top shelves, up to the fifth shelf down. I'll start on the bottom ones from six down."

We got to work, excited again, and I realized that I had been dishonest when I told Dorian that I could not sympathize with his desire to find treasure. He had been right: everyone dreamed of it. But he and Drake had gone too far.

Sighing, I crept along on my knees, feeling along the smooth, antique paper, wondering what year it had been applied to the wall by some early-twentieth-century craftsman. What had the workers thought of the castle as they were building it? Had they talked among themselves in the long hallways while they installed the carved newel posts and ornate trim? Had they wondered at the sanity of the man who paid them to create a fantasy?

The boys adjusted their ladders to start on another section. I moved awkwardly; my knees were beginning to protest my relentless kneeling. When I got to the end of the south wall and turned to the east one, I lay fully on my stomach. I could do the bottom shelves first, then move up.

I reached into the first eastern wall shelf, rubbing my hand back and forth. I hit what seemed to be a covered outlet and almost moved on, until I realized that there wouldn't have been outlets when this room was built. And if people had put outlets in later, they would have cut a space out of the paper.

But the paper was still intact. And now that I felt it again, the diameter of that rectangular thing was much wider than that of an outlet would have been.

"Boys," I said in a weird voice.

"What?"

I had their full attention, and the silent room crackled with intensity.

"Go get Derek and Paul."

DEREK AND PAUL arrived, as did Connie, who was holding Derek's hand.

"So you found our bag of diamonds?" Derek said good-humoredly.

Paul, for reasons unknown, was taking pictures: of the books stacked in the hall, of the nearly empty Small Library, of me lying on the floor, of the twins in their matching Castle Security T-shirts.

"Not sure about that, but I may have found the 'door they cannot see.' Come and feel."

Derek squatted down and felt the wall where I pointed. "Interesting," he said.

He pulled out a pocketknife and lay down next to me. Paul snapped another picture, and Connie giggled nervously.

Carefully, Derek trimmed the paper around the mysterious rectangle. "Peel it away," he said, and I did so.

The twins were so close behind us, I could feel them breathing on my neck. I pulled gently, not wanting to rip the paper more than I had to, even if it was just a section in a place no one was ever likely to see.

When the pretty rose covering came away, we were looking at a wooden door, complete with a tiny mullioned window and a tiny glass doorknob.

"Oh, how charming!" I said. "How absolutely delightful!"

Connie bent down and began to exclaim, as well. Paul told us to move so that he could take a picture. Everyone scooched back.

"Not you, Nora. I want to get a photo of you discovering the door. Even if there's just a dead mouse back there, the door alone is good enough to put on our website and blog and Instagram. It's pretty amazing."

The others had moved back toward the library door, and when the boys started to move forward again, Derek held them back with one arm.

"Nora, you found the door, and you are the one who encouraged us to look. You get to be the one who opens it. Break it to me gently, okay?"

I felt a momentous weight on my shoulders as I turned the tiny knob and peered into the darkness behind. And that was what I saw—darkness.

"Hang on. I need illumination."

I grabbed my phone from my pocket and swiped on the light. I shone it inside. There was something there: a long tray on which were rectangles that looked like Balfour Bars or children's blocks. But then one of the rectangles gleamed in the fragile beams from my phone, and I realized what I was seeing.

"Derek," I breathed. I was on the verge of tears or a scream or a gasp of joy.

"Derek," I said again, my voice quavering now.

"What? Is it something weird?" said Derek, visibly nervous.

"Come on, Nora," said Jay, who was clearly dying of suspense.

"No, it's not weird." I turned to them. "It's wonderful."

The moment hung suspended; everyone seemed to take a deep breath at the same time.

I pulled out the tray and smiled at them. "It's gold."

22

The Door They Cannot See

HALLOWEEN WAS A crazy affair. It was only three days after Derek and Paul Corby had experienced a reversal of fortune in the form of twenty gold bars, a gift from their uncle Philip Corby. Each bar had been valued at approximately two hundred sixty thousand dollars. The story had made the news after Paul put the picture on our website and our social media. He had taken a video of the moment of discovery, with a close-up on the tiny little door. The news outlets had picked it up, and for two days straight, Derek and Paul were doing interviews: in front of the castle, in the castle hallway, in the Small Library (now filled once again with newly categorized and dusted books), even in front of the fountain behind the castle, where the gentle naiad presided over the now quiet water.

Paul had insisted that Derek let him invest some of the money so that it could keep multiplying; as the CFO, he said, it was his job to spend some of it responsibly, because he knew that Derek would use some to buy gifts and give life to his lavish visions.

"It's just like I said," Connie told me as she lay dreamily on my bed. "Derek was meant to be a king. And you helped him find his treasure!"

I nodded, happy. Then I looked at my watch. "I can't wait until the castle show is over. Gen should be getting here around five, and she said she and Paul have a great costume for the castle party."

Connie sat up and bounced on the bed. "Derek and I have one, too. Did you and Dash go for a couples costume?"

"Maybe."

"Okay, fine, keep your secrets." She grinned. "I'd better go get ready. Aren't your brothers coming out tonight?"

"Yeah, but they're going straight to Jade's party so her parents can finally meet Luke," I said. I felt nervous for him somehow. "Then they'll come back here and camp in the Small Library."

"Nice. So Dash can stay over if he wants to?"

"I suppose. The boys know—that he does sometimes. I doubt it will shock them. I doubt anything shocks them."

Connie jumped up and said, "See you in the dining room."

This was where the actors gathered before meeting the Inspectors for the revamped fall show. Then we argued in the main hall, led them down to the library, pointed them to a multitude of clues, and gave them pondering time in the great hall. Then they joined us for dinner and any accusations that people had ready (with evidence).

The winner on Halloween night was an elderly gentleman who had enjoyed the entire evening so much he said he wanted to send all his relatives to the castle. He went home with a little haunted-house trophy, and everyone left with Castle Dark T-shirts—a new addition that Paul said was relatively cheap publicity with an unfathomable reach.

After the Halloween dinner, we ran back upstairs to get ready for the castle party—the one just for us, a delayed celebration of Derek and Paul's good news.

It was chilly out, but not freezing, so Derek had made a fire in the firepit and Zana had set up a buffet table and a hot chocolate station. I donned my costume, which consisted of bell-bottoms and a midriff top, a couple of long necklaces, and some hoop earrings. I left my hair loose and straight, then ran down the back stairs to meet Dash when he texted his arrival.

He wore sunglasses and some gold chains, a half-unbuttoned shirt, a vest, and jeans. His brown hair was a bit longer (he'd been growing it since we'd decided to be Sonny and Cher).

I flung open the door and said, "You look perfect!"

"So do you. And delectable. But your tummy's going to be cold."

"I'll let everyone see my costume and then put a jacket on," I said. "I'm too practical to freeze for fashion. That mustache is outrageously sexy."

He beamed. "Yeah? I kind of liked it, too."

I kissed him. "But it's kind of prickly." I tugged him inside and up the back stairs. "I don't know what anyone else is wearing, but I want to get some good pictures."

"Speaking of good pictures," Dash said, "those pictures on your website are amazing. You're the talk of Wood Glen. The talk of the whole country if I can believe today's Twitter trends."

"Paul says our website is getting a lot more traffic, too. So things are just looking up for the Corby clan." I looked at my watch. "Could you feed the cats? I just need to put on my lipstick and grab my jacket."

"Sure."

Dash bent to play with the Brontës, then filled their bowls. They had received a Halloween present of three cloth mice, and they were nearly exhausted from playing all day.

"Okay, I'm ready," I said.

"The lipstick is nice." He was looking at my mouth; his eyes were distracted, and they flicked briefly to the bed.

I laughed. "Later. Right now I want to go to a party!"

The Bee Gees were singing "Jive Talkin'" when we came down, and we immediately spotted Derek and Connie dressed as the king and queen of hearts.

"Well, if that isn't the most perfect costume," I said. "Did Elspeth make it?"

Connie grinned. "No. I wouldn't give her a rush order like that. I ordered them online."

Derek walked up and slid his arms around Connie. He looked so natural in a crown that I laughed.

"Absolutely perfect," I said. "You must have been a royal in another life."

He grinned, and I realized he had started on the champagne; he seemed a bit tipsy.

"I'm a king in this life, too. The king of Connie's heart."

She smiled and leaned back against him.

"I'll be back," I said, "but I'm starving. I didn't eat much at the dinner because I had to answer so many questions. And then there were all those people who wanted selfies with us."

"Sure, we'll be here." Derek smiled serenely. He had deep lines around his mouth from all the smiling he'd been doing for the past several days.

Dash took my hand and we went to the buffet table, almost tripping over Hamlet on the way, who strode nobly through the crowd wearing a Shakespearean ruff and occasionally accepting surreptitious treats. Zana stood by the hors d'oeuvres in a parka, eating some food off a paper plate, stabbing cheese with her little toothpick and dancing to the music.

"You enjoy disco?" Dash asked her in an unrecognizable accent that made me laugh.

Zana smiled. "I do. Any dance music, I'm there. Try the meatballs in that pot. They're supergood."

We did, along with a pasta salad and some kind of Mexican casserole.

Zana watched me wolf down food and said, "Desserts are on the next table."

I laughed. "I'm good for now. But I will have some hot chocolate."

Dash helped me put on my jacket, and I felt much warmer, but the liquid Zana handed me warmed me even more.

"I'm hoping Dorian might come by," Zana said.

I froze. "What? He can't." I turned to Dash. "Isn't he in jail?"

Dash swallowed his food and said, "Robin's team arrested both of them earlier this week. But they were bailed out almost immediately."

"What? Who—"

"Derek," Dash said.

I stared at him, my mouth open. "Why—?"

"You know Derek. The guy can't hold a grudge. He said the Pierces ultimately did him a favor. If it hadn't been for them, you wouldn't have been so convinced there was treasure and persuaded Derek to let you search."

My mouth was still open because I was still shocked. "So they are just—walking around?"

"For now. They have a court date coming up. Derek is also paying for a lawyer."

"Unbelievable! No wonder Paul insisted that some of the money be invested. Derek just can't stop being generous."

"Wouldn't you want him to bail you out of jail?"

"Yes, but I would never be there."

"Famous last words," my boyfriend said, and kissed me.

When I pulled away, significantly less indignant, I saw my sister. She was dressed as Cupid in a pink tutu and matching top, along with white tights and ballet shoes. She held a bow and arrow, and Paul stood beside her, dressed vaguely like a mythological character with a tunic, some tights, and a garland around his hair. The shaft of an arrow stuck out of his chest, and the arrowhead protruded from his back; Cupid had shot him in the heart.

"I thought Cupid was male," Dash said, selecting some cheese.

"Nontraditional casting . . ."

Dash observed the new couple as they came toward us. "Paul is so happy, he's stupid with it," he said.

I would have told him not to be mean, except that he was right: Paul could do little more than trail after Gen and stare at her wavy titian hair, his mouth slightly open. He didn't seem to have a thought in his head other than Gen's name.

"He's smitten," I said. "The costume is apropos."

A line was forming at the buffet table and I said, "We should move away so other people can eat."

I hugged Gen and said, "You look lovely. Paul can't seem to put two thoughts together when you're around."

Gen laughed merrily, actually holding her stomach.

I leaned in. "Thanks for coming back."

She sighed. "Thanks for helping me come to my senses. But Paul's coming to me next time. The airfare is crazy."

"Maybe you can meet somewhere in the middle," I said. "Get an Airbnb or something."

Her brows rose. "That's a pretty good idea. I'm going to tell Paul." She skipped off, still clutching her bow.

I turned to find Elspeth, Renata, and Miranda dressed as *Macbeth*'s witches. They wore black cloaks, but their hats had been knitted and were three different colors, all black brims.

"You guys look great," I said. "I love the hats."

Renata looked over my shoulder. "By the pricking of

my thumbs," she intoned, "something wicked this way comes."

I swung around to see Dorian Pierce strolling through the crowd, looking handsome in a leather jacket and jeans, seemingly unworried that he might not be welcome at the party. To my surprise, he was welcome. Zana ran out to hug him and offer him food. Paul introduced him to Gen, and Derek, even tipsier now, appeared to shake his hand.

"Unbelievable," I said. "The guy is as slippery as silk."

"Speaking of silk," Dash's voice was in my ear, "are you going to wear that outfit that—"

Dorian walked up to us, fresh from his other triumphant greetings. "Hello, Nora."

"Hello, Dorian. I think you know my boyfriend, John Dashiell?"

Dash was pleased by this introduction, and Dorian held out a hand. "Yeah, I know Dashiell. How's it going?"

They chatted for a while, calling each other "man," and then Dorian looked at me. "So there was treasure after all." Not surprisingly, he smirked at me.

"Yes. You were right. And I have to admit"—I practically ground out these words, even though they were like barbed wire on my tongue—"you were right about the exhilaration of it, too."

"Right?" Dorian said affably. "I saw that little video of you lying on the floor and opening that crazy door. Your eyes were like saucers."

I laughed in spite of myself. "Yeah, it was pretty wild. Where's your brother?" I asked.

Dorian's face expressed chagrin. "He had to meet his girlfriend and—explain some things."

I stared at him. "You *are* Dorian, aren't you?"

"Yes, I'm Dorian," he said, ruffling my hair in an annoying way. "You should be able to tell by now." He said that as if I had been observing him and his brother side by side for months.

"Okay. I'm going to get a refill on hot chocolate."

"Don't go far. I want to hear more about that treasure hunt," Dorian said as though we were old friends who had been longing for coffee and a chat.

On the other hand, he sounded genuinely friendly, instead of like a guy who was hitting on me. For some reason, he was far more relaxed as a black sheep invited back to the party than he had seemed in the castle. Perhaps his secrets had weighed heavily on him, after all.

"I'll be around," I said. "Did you see the witches?"

He turned and spied Renata's getup, and sure enough he bolted toward them, clearly bent on harassing them.

Later, we sat around the bonfire and sang songs. Miranda, it turned out, was an accomplished guitarist, and she played while we sang folk favorites like "Blowin' in the Wind." I leaned against Dash, warmed by the fire in front and him on my left side.

After a half hour of singing, Connie put her head on Derek's shoulder and said, "I want Nora to sing us a love song."

"Okay," I said. "What should I sing?"

Nobody could agree on a song, despite several minutes of loud discussion.

Finally I said, "I know one. It's spooky, like a ghost story, but it's also romantic. Perfect for a Halloween date."

The group grew quiet and I asked Miranda if she could play Loreena McKennitt's version of "The Highwayman," the Alfred Noyes poem she had put to music. I told her the chords, sang her a couple of bars, and she worked out the rhythm. Then I began to tell the story of the highwayman riding across the lonely moors at midnight, longing to see the landlord's daughter, Bess, who plaited dark red love knots in her long black hair. The song was moody and chilling, and I sensed that everyone around the fire was listening to the words, caught up in the story. The betrayal of a stable boy, the courage of Bess, who warned the highwayman about the redcoats by sacrificing herself.

I sang the ending, when their ghosts reunited, and my eyes wandered away from the fire to the stars that twinkled above the castle, shining down with the knowledge of every wish that had ever been sent up into the heavens, and of some of those wishes that had been granted.

23

A Castle Reborn

B Y MID-NOVEMBER THE renovations on my room had
been completed. Now, instead of a mysterious sliding
panel and a narrow hall, I had a wide arched doorway from
which the "study" could be glimpsed. The hall now blended
into the two rooms, with a shining wood floor and a small
Persian-look carpet. The back brick wall added a surprising elegance, and the window experts Derek had hired had
managed to cut a hole into the brick and create an impressive rectangular window, which brought light into the for-
merly shadowy library. The window had a wide sill on
which the Brontës could stretch when they watched trees or
birds. It also opened so that I could occasionally let a
breeze air out the rooms. Charlotte, in particular, liked to
rest on this windowsill when she felt solitary, while Emily
had taken a strong liking to the long wooden table in the
study, where she would stretch her fluffy body to its full
length. I bought a large ceramic bowl at Relics—a beautiful blue-and-green swirl pattern glazed to a shine—and

Emily curled into it, claiming it as her own the moment it came home.

Annie, my funny little girl, liked the spot in front of the secret door, the *door we could not see*. We had left the area free of books so that the door would always be visible, but Annie took the lack of books as an invitation and climbed into the spot regularly, especially when I sat in my new easy chair (a gift from my parents, who had also bought the one in my bedroom) and read books.

The overall impression of the two-room apartment was one of elegance and charm. The designers had made it look as though they had always been meant to go together—a look they achieved by taking out part of the separating wall and creating a wide wooden arch leading from one area to the other. I loved it. Sometimes, when no one else was there, I walked back and forth between the two rooms, gazing at the space, the walls, the carpets, the windows, the books, the furniture. It was beautiful, and it was mine.

At the end of November, I threw a little housewarming party; I invited my castle friends and my remaining BC colleagues. Dorian and his brother were in the process of serving a one-year sentence, but they remained in good spirits. Derek had encouraged us to take turns visiting them; he said they had no other family, and in spite of everything, they thought of us as their relations. The prison wasn't far, so we had all pledged to visit at one point or another.

Andy was also in prison and awaiting his trial. Millie had filed for divorce, and the awning over her store now read *Millie's Gifts*.

We sat at the big table in the Small Library. I was surprised to see that Renata sat with Barbara and that they were chatting about knitting patterns. When I saw Renata slip into my bedroom, where I had set up a refreshment table, I followed her out and whispered, "I thought Barbara hated you because you're dating her ex."

Renata smiled. "I introduced her to someone new. He's smitten with her. So now we are best friends. I was hoping to win her over; she's a better knitter than I am, and her store is a pleasure to visit."

"Well done," I said, holding up my hand.

I didn't think Renata had ever slapped someone five before my brothers came into her life, but now she did it routinely.

"You know," I said as we filled our plates, "if my brothers ever get on your nerves, you can tell me. I'll tell them to tone it down. And you don't have to buy them presents and stuff."

She met my eyes with her shrewd brown ones. "Nora, I loved my parents. But they both died more than a decade ago, and my sister lives on the West Coast. No aunts or uncles that I kept in touch with since they are back in Germany. So no cousins. No one at all. My husband and I had no children, and as you know, I divorced long ago. So I have no nearby family except for all of you and any family you share with me."

I pulled her into a spontaneous hug. "If that's how you feel, they're all yours."

She giggled. "Oh, good. They do light up my life."

Priscilla and Jack came through the doorway, laughing. I noted that they were holding hands. I sidled up to Priscilla and said, "So—it's on again?"

She noted that Jack was speaking to Renata and said in a low voice, "No. Not as a fling. Jack said he didn't want to get involved again unless it was a relationship. We—kind of bonded in a different way over all this. Faced some serious realities. And—we're both really happy." She smiled. "How did your boyfriend like the green silk number?"

"He still talks about it," I said.

"Perfect. That's the entire goal with beautiful clothing." She moved closer to the table and took a plate. "Jack and I were talking, and we both feel that, despite everything, we're glad we stayed in the play. It was a great production. We couldn't believe what good press it got. We're really proud to be a part of Blue Curtain."

"Me, too," I said, "although I don't think I'll try out for another play for a while. Dash deserves some of my time, and the play didn't allow much."

"That's why you have to get him a role in the play," she said. "It worked well for Jack and me."

That was a solution I had not considered. I wondered if Dash had any acting chops. He had surprised me with a nice singing voice on Halloween night around the campfire. Maybe he had other hidden talents. . . .

We moved to the doorway, where the once dingy hall that had gone undetected behind a narrow panel was now an elegant carpeted area adding sophistication to my space. I had set up the drinks there, and I put some ice in my glass and poured some Diet Coke; my phone buzzed. I had a text from Jade.

It's official, she wrote. We're keeping them all.

Then she sent a series of photos: Jade posing with two happy-faced dogs, their tongues lolling after a walk. One was a tall animal with pointed stand-up ears and a handsome gray coat; the other was a shorter, sweet-faced dog, a beagle mix of some kind, that was half leaning on Jade.

The next picture was of Tiger sitting on her dad's stomach and looking very pleased about it. Her father was smiling with a wry expression; he was resigned to many years with Tiger.

The final picture was of the turtle, which had apparently celebrated someone's birthday, because a big bow had been pasted on his shell. His face looked both sour and endearing.

Ben would be proud, and grateful, I wrote.

Jade wrote, I hope so.

"Where did you go?" Dash asked in my ear.

His breath was warm on my neck and I shivered a little. "Stop being sexy," I whispered with a warning expression.

"Why? Will I explode?" He was grinning. He enjoyed teasing me now that our relationship was solid, and I suppose I teased him, too.

"By the way, if you help me clean up after people leave, there might be a reward in it for you."

"Sign me up."

He put his arm around me and we walked back to the big table, where Paul was saying, "Who wants to play Trivial Pursuit?"

Derek had bought several gifts with his new bank account. Zana got everything on her kitchen wish list, which included a new dishwasher and a larger microwave. Elspeth got a larger budget for the costume room, and Elspeth and Renata were given gift certificates to Skein Street. I considered my new room my present, but Derek had also given me a gift certificate to Relics, "to furnish your new space."

He bought Connie a beautiful blue winter coat—a warm wool thing that went down to her ankles and was bordered in gray faux fur, just like the Nora Helmer coat. It looked amazing on her.

The day after the party, Connie asked if I'd appear on one of her episodes of "Reading with Princess Goodbook."

"I want you to be my cousin, Duchess Goodbook, and appear in your library chair. We can sit together in your two easy chairs and read two characters from the same book."

"That sounds fun," I said. "Who watches these videos?"

"Sometimes teachers find them and show them to their classes. Other times I think kids just find them or their parents do. Some kids listen to them because no one has ever read them a story before, which I can't even fathom. Every child should have stories read to them all the time. How else can they build their imaginations?"

"Okay, I'm on board, Cousin Goodbook. Count me in anytime."

So that night Connie and I sat side by side in my study, in easy chairs that Elspeth had helped us turn into thrones. She gave us gowns and crowns from the costume room, and we were at our regal best when we read a story called "The Princess Who Needed a Castle."

Derek filmed, and we hammed it up a little, since children didn't tend to mind some overacting. Connie was the princess, and I was a wisewoman she met in the forest.

"I have no castle of my own," Connie said, her voice despairing. "I don't know why I have no castle, as I am a nice little princess."

"You have a good heart," I murmured as the wisewoman. "And when you find the castle that has always been yours, you will know it in your heart."

Eventually the princess came across a beautiful castle, and as she looked at it, the drawbridge came down. She thought that she heard a giant heart beating—the heart of the castle. She realized that it had started beating for the first time, because its princess had come home. Elated, she ran across the drawbridge and into her home.

LATER THAT NIGHT, I lay in bed, missing Dash, who had an early shift in the morning. The Brontës had deigned to sleep with me, despite their expanded options. They snuggled against me, and I recalled that they had known a precarious existence: rejected soon after their birth, caged, and then rescued by Jade, who had ridden a bicycle with my three Brontës in an open basket from which they could have fallen. It had been a perilous journey, and that was

why I had adopted them: because they were sweet and innocent, and I needed to know that they were cared for. So
they came into the castle with me, and here they had lived
ever since.

"When you find the castle that has always been yours,
you will know it . . . ," I murmured as we all drifted off to
sleep. Just before I slipped out of consciousness, I realized
that I, too, had come upon the castle unexpectedly, not
knowing that it would be my home.

But home it was.

24

A New Path

ON DECEMBER FIRST, Dash and I took a walk in the forest, on the path where I had seen my deer. We walked as quietly as we could, holding hands. I had brought an early Christmas present, provided by Derek, which Dash now hung from a heavy tree branch. It was a salt lick, a popular snack for deer and something that would lure them out for occasional viewing opportunities.

Though we were quieter than Connie and I had been, we didn't see any deer. We reached a point, after about twenty minutes, where the path forked into two new paths. I pointed to the left, and we turned onto this new path, moving softly on moss that helped to quiet our footfalls.

"I'm getting hungry," Dash whispered to me.

"Just a few more minutes— Dash!" I was still whispering, but now I pointed, as well.

He turned to look at whatever had drawn my attention. At the end of the visible part of the path stood my deer: the buck with large and noble antlers. He stood tall and strong, his antlers making him look powerful. Behind him suddenly was a rustle in the undergrowth, and a beautiful doe emerged; she nuzzled briefly against his side and then moved behind him, using his body as her protection. Behind her came two little fawns, still white spotted and gangly, but strong and curious.

We didn't say a word; we stood still. The buck seemed to be staring back at us, making eye contact. What message was he sending? I wondered. Did he sense us at all, or were we just part of the scenery? Did he know we had minds, subtle sensibilities that allowed us to romanticize him, humanize him to the point of giving him thoughts, intentions? Was there any chance that animal encounters were truly moments of grace, moments meant to guide us? Was this the future for Dash and me? Was this why we had seen the deer on a new path?

Dash quietly shifted his stance. The movement didn't frighten any of the deer, but it seemed to remind them that they wanted to be someplace else. They wandered into the trees on the other side of the path—first the doe and her babies, who were sticking close, and then, with a final significant glance at us, the buck. His antlers were the last things to disappear.

"Wow," Dash finally said. "That was kind of magical."

"Exactly." I was glad he understood.

As if by consent, we did not talk on the way back; lost in our own thoughts, we trod the moss and pine needles. The scent of fall still lingered in the air though winter was on the horizon. Once again, the castle was visible through a break in the trees. Curls of smoke rose from its central chimney, and a light shone in Zana's kitchen.

The castle that has always been yours . . .

I took Dash's hand and began to run home.

Acknowledgments

The author wishes to thank the following wonderful people: Graham Buckley, Ian Buckley, Kim Lionetti, Michelle Vega, Linda Rohaly, Linda Henson, Ferne Knauss, Gigi Pandian, Karen Kenyon, Ann O'Neill Foster, Katie Granholm, and Jenn McKinlay.

And an additional thanks to everyone who reads, reviews, and recommends my books. I appreciate all that you do.

About the Author

Veronica Bond is a pseudonym for a bestselling mystery writer who lives in Chicago with her family and a menagerie of animals. She teaches high school English, and she loves reading and writing mysteries.

Ready to find
your next great read?

Let us help.

Visit prh.com/nextread

Penguin
Random
House